PENGUIN BOOKS
Youth in China

Beverley Hooper grew up in Tasmania. She left school at sixteen, did a secretarial course and set off to see the world, working in Europe and at the Australian Embassy in Moscow. She subsequently obtained a BA from the University of Tasmania and an MA and PhD in history from the Australian National University, where she also learnt Chinese and Russian and worked as a research assistant to historian Manning Clark. She studied in Peking on a Myer Foundation scholarship in 1975–7, made research visits to China in 1979, 1982, and 1983–4, and was the Australia–China Council's 1982–3 Fellow in Australia–China Studies. She has written extensively on contemporary Chinese history and social issues and is currently a research fellow in the History Department, University of Western Australia.

Other Books

The Private Journal of James Burney
Inside Peking: A Personal Report
The End of the Western Presence in China
(forthcoming)

YOUTH IN CHINA

Beverley Hooper

PENGUIN BOOKS

Penguin Books Australia Ltd,
487 Maroondah Highway, P.O. Box 257
Ringwood, Victoria, 3134, Australia
Penguin Books Ltd,
Harmondsworth, Middlesex, England
Penguin Books,
40 West 23rd Street, New York, N.Y. 10010, U.S.A.
Penguin Books Canada Ltd,
2801 John Street, Markham, Ontario, Canada
Penguin Books (N.Z.) Ltd,
Private Bag, Takapuna, Auckland 9, New Zealand

First published by Penguin Books Australia, 1985

Copyright © Beverley Hooper 1985
Photographs © Beverley Hooper 1985

Typeset in Ballardvale Medium
by Abb-Typesetting Pty Ltd

Made and printed in Australia
by The Dominion Press-Hedges & Bell

CIP

Hooper, Beverley, 1940–
Youth in China.

Bibliography.
Includes index.
ISBN 0 14 008158 5.

1. Youth — China. 2. China — Social conditions —
1976-   . I. Title.

305.2'35'0951

Contents

v

Preface

The youth generation has been the subject of a great deal of comment and criticism throughout the world in recent years. In the West in particular, youth has become well known as a distinctive social group whose interests and behaviour do not always provoke an enthusiastic response from the older generation. Young people have also been the focus of many social problems, ranging from unemployment to crime.

It is something of a cliché to state that approximately one out of every four young people in the world lives in China and that, for this reason alone, the country's youth generation warrants a close examination. For much of the period since the 1949 communist revolution, however, little has been known in the West about China's youth. Most available information has come from two contradictory sources. The first has been young Chinese refugees in Hong Kong who have predictably presented an extremely negative view of their former lives. The second has been official Chinese news releases and publications which have praised the country's youth as enthusiastic, diligent and self-sacrificing workers for national development, or as the equally enthusiastic and highly politicized Red Guards of the Cultural Revolution of the mid-1960s, chanting Maoist slogans and waving little red books.

China's recent reopening to the outside world and its tentative moves towards social liberalization have made it possible to obtain a clearer picture of the nation's youth generation. Much of the material for this book was collected during two research trips to China in 1982 and 1983–4, set against my earlier experiences in China during 1975–7 and 1979. Owing to the co-operation of the Chinese Academy of Social Sciences and its Research Institute for Youth and Juvenile Affairs, I was able to have discussions with a large number of people involved in youth issues. These ranged from the Institute's own researchers and representatives of the Communist Youth League, the Women's Federation, and sociological and law associations, to youth newspaper editors and both administrators and young people in schools, universities, collective and private enterprises, reform schools and prisons, and marriage introduction bureaux. The discussions were supplemented by informal contacts with young people throughout the country and by access to the expanding range of academic journals and popular magazines being published in China.

My special thanks are due to the Academy and the Research Institute for Youth and Juvenile Affairs. The Academy's headquarters in Peking, and its branches in Shanghai, Canton, Harbin and Hefei, efficiently organized a lengthy schedule of discussions and visits. The Institute's director, Zhang Liqun, deputy director Li Jingxian, and other senior officials personally gave me much of their valuable time.

A large part of my research was undertaken on a fellowship from the Australia–China Council and I wish to thank the Council for its generous support, including the financing of my 1982 research trip to China, and for encouraging me to write this book. While the book would have been impossible without the assistance of both the Council and the Chinese Academy of Social Sciences, the views expressed are my own.

I am also grateful to the Contemporary China Centre at the Australian National University and the School of Human Communication at Murdoch University for providing an atmosphere conducive to research and writing. Professor Wang Gungwu, Stephen FitzGerald and Tim Wright were generous with ideas and practical advice at various stages of the project, while a number of Australians who have recently lived and studied in China provided a lively arena for discussion. My major debt, though, is to the numerous young people throughout China who were prepared, sometimes unwittingly, to share with a foreigner their attitudes, aspirations and problems.

Beverley Hooper
December 1984

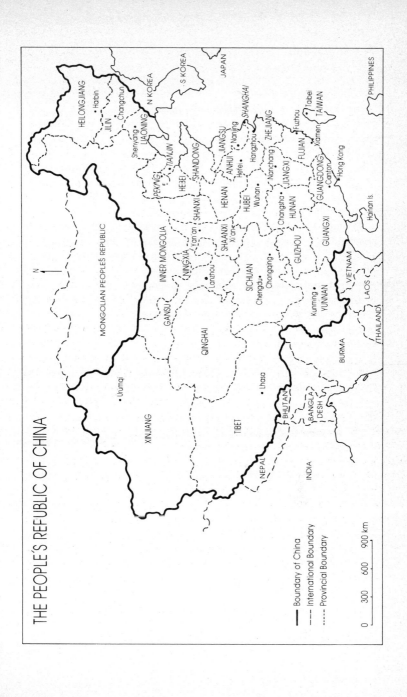

THE PEOPLE'S REPUBLIC OF CHINA

——— Boundary of China
– – – International Boundary
········ Provincial Boundary

0   300   600   900 km

Author's Note

The real names of Chinese people are used in the case of formal interviews and magazine and newspaper sources. The names of people with whom I had private conversations have been changed in order to preserve their anonymity.

The *pinyin* system, officially used in China and now generally accepted internationally, is used for transliterating Chinese words, including the names of people and places. Exceptions are Peking and Canton which I have retained because of their familiarity.

The basic unit of Chinese currency is the *yuan*. In late 1984, one yuan was equivalent to approximately 50 cents Australian, 40 cents American and 30 p. in British currency.

CHAPTER ONE

Chinese Youth in the 1980s

'On the whole China's young people are enthusiastic about socialism and working hard for modernization,' said Zhu Shanqing during our discussion of youth affairs in Peking. One of China's top youth officials, Mr Zhu is Vice-Chairman of the All-China Youth Federation and Director of the Communist Youth League's International Department.

'Of course we have a few problems,' he acknowledged when I mentioned recent reports in Chinese newspapers and youth magazines. 'Young people's education and employment, for instance, and youth crime. Also some young people do not have a correct attitude towards socialism. But we're gradually overcoming the problems through our new programmes and ideological education.'

In a Canton restaurant – at the other end of China – I repeated Mr Zhu's comments to 20-year-old Li Hongwen, an airlines employee who had recently been assigned to Canton from his home city of Peking.

'Don't believe what officials tell you about young people,' retorted Li. 'They're all members of the older generation and they don't understand today's youth. They just tell us what they think is good for us. We're not even allowed to have our own organizations. There's only the Youth League and that's run by the Communist Party.' He went on. 'Young people in China are tired of politics and ideological education. What we want is a better life. But what's the use of working hard for modernization? China is so far behind the industrialized countries. And life here is very boring. No wonder a lot of young people are fed up. No wonder some of us would leave China if we had the opportunity.'

Was this just one disillusioned young man's personal opinion or a typical voice of contemporary Chinese youth?

'When we're talking about the youth generation, we're talking about almost one-quarter of China's population,' commented a Youth League official in Shanghai. Although the expression 'youth' or 'young people' is often used as loosely in China as it is in most countries, the Chinese government goes along generally with international classifications in using it to refer to people aged between 14 and 25. (The 15–24 age group is the classification used by the United Nations.) According to China's 1982 census, the number of people falling into this age group was 243 million – roughly the equivalent of the entire population of the United States or the Soviet Union and greatly exceeded only by India.

The large proportion of youth in China's total population is similar to that in many developing countries – including Thailand, Malaysia and the Philippines – which have had population explosions because of declining infant mortality. In some industrialized countries of Western Europe, in contrast, the youth group constitutes little more than one-eighth of the population.

Despite the commonly used statistical classification, 'youth' is not really a precise age group but a distinct phase of life covering the transition from dependent childhood to independent and responsible adulthood. In the words of psychiatry professor Kenneth Keniston, 'They have not settled ... questions of relationship to the existing society, questions of vocation, questions of social role and life-style.'[1] Youth is generally the most dynamic and potentially changing period of life as the individual undergoes the process of emerging self-identity and independence, completes basic education, joins the workforce or embarks first on higher education, develops contacts with the opposite sex and possibly gets married and has children. But it is also a time of relative social and political powerlessness. As young people assert their personal identity within both their own family and society at large, they frequently come into conflict with the older generation.

China's leadership is keenly aware of the significance of the youth generation. The revival of the social sciences since the late 1970s, set against official concern at the level of youth unemployment, crime and political disaffection, has led to the development of 'youth studies' in China. In December 1980 the Research Institute for Youth and Juvenile Affairs was established within the Chinese Academy of Social Sciences to carry out research on youth and to advise the government on youth issues. 'We regard youth studies as an inter-disciplinary approach to youth,' the Institute's director, Zhang Liqun, told me in Peking. 'We utilize the expertise of a wide range of researchers – physiologists, psychologists, sociologists, educators and lawyers. It is important that we find out all we can about the current youth generation in China.'

No single feature makes China's youth distinctive in the international context.

'They're not really so different from young Chinese in many countries of the world,' commented a colleague who had spent lengthy periods in both Taiwan and the People's Republic. In terms of family and inter-personal relationships, in particular, young people in China have a lot in common with their brothers and sisters not just in Taiwan, which regards itself as the true preserver of China's Confucian tradition, but even in Hong Kong and Singapore.

When it comes to the outside controls on their everyday lives, though, China's youth often seems more akin to young people in Russia and Eastern Europe. The Chinese Communists, like other communist governments, have always stressed the importance of young people as the 'vanguard of the future', the successors to the revolution who will eventually bring about a true communist society. 'You young people, full of vigour and vitality, are in the bloom of life, like the sun at eight or nine in the morning,' Mao Zedong had proclaimed in 1957. 'Our hope is placed on you.'[2]

Like other communist governments, the Chinese authorities see themselves as youth's moral guardians and attempt to mould young people in accordance with communist ideals. They have a view on everything from how youth should approach their studies to what they should wear, what contacts (if any) they should have with the opposite sex and when they should get married. Many sources of influence on youth in the

West – from education and youth groups to the media and even family and peer values – are subject to heavy official involvement in China.

'No, I really think that China's youth should be compared with young people in developing countries like India and Indonesia,' remarked another colleague. In terms of living standards, urban–rural differences and the gap between aspirations and opportunities, China's youth does seem to have more in common with young people in developing nations than in more advanced communist societies such as the Soviet Union. China's annual GNP per capita of $260 puts the country in equal 98th place out of 124 countries: on a par with Pakistan and Zaire and lower even than the majority of African nations.

China's young people are mobilized not just for political purposes but also for participation in the nation's development programme, a policy common to developing countries whatever their political system. At the UNESCO Conference on Asian Youth at Katmandu in 1978, for example, delegates from countries ranging from the Philippines to India and North Vietnam endorsed youth's role in development as a major official policy. Such a policy calls for the active role of government in training youth in technical and associated fields, and usually includes sending young people to developed countries for further education.

Since the inauguration of the dramatic drive for modernization following Mao's death in 1976, China's new leadership has put increasing stress on the role of youth in development. In the words of senior Party official Hu Qili, 'Youth is of key importance in realizing China's four modernizations* ... Whether China's modernization succeeds will depend largely on young people.'[3]

It is the combination of these three basic features and pressures – the legacy of the Confucian past, the communist political system and its implications, and the low level of economic development – that distinguishes China's youth from young people in other countries. There has been a lengthy debate in the West about which of the three features has most characterized China since the 1949 communist revolution. In

---

* The four modernizations: the modernization of industry, agriculture, science and technology, and defence.

particular, writers have constantly argued about whether contemporary China has been 'more Chinese' or 'more communist'. The point is not really to take sides in the debate but to see how the factors have interacted and even reinforced one another.

In recent years, the relative significance of the various features has shifted. The paramount stress on development since Mao's death has involved a backsliding from communist ideals and the resurgence of traditional Chinese social patterns, especially in the countryside. The lives of China's current youth generation, described in this book, clearly reflect this changed pattern.

Young people in general tend to be more vulnerable than other age groups to current political, social and economic trends. China's youth are in the forefront of the impact of the fairly dramatic changes that have recently occurred in their country.

Perhaps the best expression to describe Chinese society since the early 1980s is that used by Roger Garside in the title of his book *Coming Alive: China after Mao*. As Garside sees it, China had been a 'nation half alive' from the mid-1960s to the mid-1970s.[4] In 1966 Chairman Mao Zedong – seventy-two years old and probably already suffering from Parkinson's disease – had launched the so-called Cultural Revolution to renew revolutionary fervour in China and to eradicate bureaucratism and personal materialism. In the name of revolutionary purity, China was cut off from its own traditions and even from the culture of the 1950s and early 1960s.

Living in China in the mid-1970s, just before Mao's death, reminded one constantly of Orwell's *1984*. There was one acceptable way of thinking – officially known as the 'correct socialist line' as revealed in glorious Mao Zedong Thought. Almost one billion people were confined in ideological straitjackets and all creative and individual expression was stifled. Even showing an interest in one's personal appearance or listening to a foreign radio broadcast could lead to official denunciation and subjection to a 'struggle and criticism' session. China was indeed a 'nation half alive' or, to put it another way, a 'nation half dead'.

Although some Western writers regard present-day China as

a severely repressive society, the general atmosphere is one of relative liberalization and diversity compared with the Cultural Revolution decade. The overwhelming stress on ideology and class struggle has given way to an emphasis on modernizing the nation and China overall has begun to 'come alive' economically, socially and culturally.

The former entirely state-controlled economy and employment market have been replaced by a three-part economic structure: state, collective and private. A substantial collective sector now produces over 20 per cent of gross output value for industry. In the countryside, the rigid commune structure has largely been supplanted by the production responsibility system, under which individual peasant households farm an area of land, handing over a quota of their produce to the state but retaining the rest or selling it for personal profit. The burgeoning private markets – for everything from meat and vegetables to clothing and furniture – have changed the face of both rural and urban China.

Since the late 1970s there has been an official emphasis on the production of consumer goods, both in the bid to encourage people to work hard for modernization and its rewards, and to demonstrate the efficiency of the new leadership. After the cult of austerity of much of the Mao era, the general environment can be described almost as one of rampant consumerism. Most Chinese people have little time for admonitions from idealistic Westerners, or even from their own government, that money and possessions are not everything. With dramatically rising expectations, the old list of consumer desirables – a radio, bicycle and sewing machine – has been superseded. 'These days people have their eyes set on colour television, a washing machine and a refrigerator,' remarked a Peking school-teacher. 'Also modern bedroom and lounge furniture.'

The Communist Party's earlier attempts to create an egalitarian society have been largely abandoned, also in the interests of modernization. A renewed emphasis on professionalism and expertise, including the re-establishment of key schools and universities, is promoting elitism all along the line. Intellectuals and professionals are being wooed by the authorities with higher salaries and improved housing.

Social and cultural life in China is far more relaxed than it was during the Cultural Revolution decade and probably also

Enterprising rural dwellers living on the outskirts of large towns and cities profit from selling produce on the private market (Canton)

The new consumerism: a billboard in a bicycle park in Peking

during the 1950s and early 1960s. Traditional Chinese art and opera have been revived, providing a veritable feast compared with the 1970s. The expanding film industry and television network are similarly diverse. Nearly 300 publishing companies produce books on both traditional Chinese and contemporary literature and a wealth of other subjects.

The range of magazines, which disappeared almost completely during the Cultural Revolution, gives an indication of the varying interests of the Chinese people. One of the most popular is the Shanghai monthly *Culture and Life*, a publication that has something for everyone: sections on famous local people (usually actors, musicians and sporting stars), current events, Shanghai's history, sport, art, health, food and fashion. There is also a section called 'Opening a Window on the World' which features stories on everything from daily life in India and Spain to the sights of Paris and the latest American architecture.

Indeed one of the most dramatic developments in post-Mao China has been the country's reopening to the West after thirty years of virtual isolation. China's so-called Westernization has tended to be exaggerated and trivialized in the foreign press; some writers suggest that all every Chinese person really wants is a frisbee and a Coca-Cola. At the same time, the renewed presence of Western culture, as well as foreign tourists and businessmen, is already having a considerable impact inside China.

But in spite of the general liberalization and increasing diversity of life, China remains a highly controlled society by Western standards. Strict censorship is imposed on all information and culture. People have little or no choice of where they live or work; it is impossible simply to move from one part of the country to another or just from a small town to a nearby city. Even the personal lives of individuals – sex, marriage and having children – are subject to a level of official interference that many Westerners would regard as intolerable.

A great deal of personal energy is expended on circumventing these controls, even though they are ostensibly exerted in the people's interests with the aim of creating an ideal communal socialist society. The use of private 'connections' and the 'backdoor' is rife at all levels, to obtain everything from urban transfers to overseas trips.

8

Other cracks have also appeared in the socialist system. China's earlier claims to have solved all social problems have been shattered by recent revelations. In 1982 an estimated 14 million people were without jobs. Corruption exists at the highest levels and the government's attempts to eradicate the problem in the early 1980s only demonstrated its pervasiveness. By 1983 some 192 000 cases of official corruption, ranging from the embezzlement of public funds to the illegal importation and sale of consumer goods, had been exposed. In late 1983 the level of general crime, including murder, rape and robbery, prompted the government to launch a drastic campaign during which some 6000 criminals were reportedly executed.

It is in this environment that China's young people are currently growing to maturity and facing the most decisive changes in their lives.

CHAPTER TWO

Self and Society

'Young people from the West seem so independent and strong-minded. They have their own opinions about everything,' remarked a young school-teacher in Peking. 'Young people in China are a bit different, I think.'

To many Westerners, Chinese in their teens and even early twenties often appear rather immature, even adolescent, in their general attitudes and behaviour, closely tied to their families and lacking independence of thought or action. This is hardly surprising. China's youth live in a society in which individualism and personal independence have always been dirty words, whether within the authoritarian Confucian family network or in a communist society which stresses the subordination of the individual to the interests of the nation as a whole.

But a relative lack of independence also means that China's youth are partially cushioned from the identity crises and the need to make personal decisions faced by young people in the rough-and-tumble of individualistic Western society. 'Our youth generation does not really seem to go through the psychological traumas that young people do in many countries,' a Chinese youth researcher confirmed in Peking. 'Yes, I think it's got a lot to do with the nature of Chinese society.'

This does not mean that young Chinese become adults without some problems of developing self-awareness. Even the Chinese authorities have recently begun assessing the psychological characteristics of their youth generation, after over thirty years of ridiculing all psychology as irrelevant to a communist society in which personal behaviour is purely a product of one's environment. The publication in 1982 of *Youth*

Psychology, written by researchers at the Psychology Research Institute of the Chinese Academy of Social Sciences, was the first work on the subject since the establishment of the People's Republic. While hardly free of the obligatory ideological and moral overtones – youth psychology must be studied 'from a Marxist-Leninist standpoint' – the book revealed that young Chinese go through the customary process of emerging personal identity, vulnerability to peer pressure, and sexual awareness.

More down to earth are the comments of young people themselves, both personally and in letters to the correspondence columns of youth magazines and to special booklets designed to answer their queries. Like teenagers all over the world, young Chinese are intensely concerned about their changing appearance, especially about seeming at all different from the norm. 'I'm too fat. What can I do about it?' 'How can I get rid of the pimples on my face?' 'I'm only 1.56 metres tall (5'1½"). Won't I grow any taller?'[1]

Books such as *Wishing You Health and Beauty* not only answer these questions but provide information on everything from diet, skin and health care to what to do about bad breath, body odour and sweaty hands. They also take the opportunity to put young people on the right path so far as their personal habits are concerned.

'Most of the young men in my workshop smoke,' wrote a young man from Shandong province, 'They say that smoking is quite good for you . . . it even improves your memory. But some people say that smoking is a way of committing suicide. Is smoking really harmful?'[2]

Yes it is, was the response, explaining the connection between smoking and lung cancer and warning that even non-smokers are affected by cigarette smoke. While this warning hardly seems unusual, it is only recently that the Chinese authorities have begun cautioning people against smoking. In 1979, in contrast, a huge billboard in the centre of the city of Xi'an highlighted an American finding about a connection between eating meat and cancer – a warning that was hardly relevant given the tiny quantities of meat consumed by most Chinese.

Much of the male population, including members of the top leadership, smoke heavily but the major target to date of the limited anti-smoking drive has been young men. With the exception of a few older women – once the educated, urban, 'modern young women' of the 1930s and 1940s – smoking is an almost exclusively male habit. While young men see smoking as a symbol of adulthood and sophistication, there is no similar image for young women. 'It's just not the custom for women to smoke in China,' a female university student told me when another foreign student offered her a cigarette.

The authorities have even stronger ideas when it comes to young people's burgeoning sexuality. Chinese society is extremely restrained in its discussion of sexual matters and only recently have youth magazines and booklets even broached the subject at all.

'I have a masturbation habit,' one young man wrote to an advice booklet. 'Some people say it's harmful. Is it?'

It certainly is, was the gist of the lengthy response which reflected the authorities' distinctly Victorian attitudes towards sexuality. Not only might it make the young man feel tired, run-down and even dizzy, it might also affect his work or study. And it could well lead to problems of impotence or premature ejaculation after marriage.

How could he and others overcome this undesirable habit? He should not wear tight-fitting clothes, especially tight underpants, explained the editor. He should get out of bed as soon as he woke up in the morning. Before going to bed he should have half an hour's physical exercise and be careful not to smoke or drink – not even tea or coffee. He should make sure his bed was not too soft, his bedclothes too hot or heavy, and should not sleep on his stomach.

And for those young men already severely afflicted with the habit? 'Before going to bed have a cold wash all over or rinse your scrotum in cold water for two to three minutes' was the editor's advice.[3]

In terms of their changing physiology, young women seem more concerned with menstruation pain and discomfort. This is a widespread problem in China, probably because of the fairly poor diet and low energy level set against women's continued participation in quite heavy physical labour. Period pain, together with a lack of commercial sanitary napkins – far less tampons – makes menstruation loom large in young women's lives.

13

'Wang Ping can't play basketball today. She's got her period.' 'Xiao Li doesn't feel like going shopping today because it's that time of the month.' These were frequent comments made by my fellow-students at Peking University in the mid-1970s.

Booklets advise young women that they can, and should, carry on most of their normal activities, subject to a number of precautions. To Western ears these sound rather outdated and only emphasize the disruption to young Chinese women's lives caused by their capacity for child-bearing. 'Keep warm,' is the usual message. 'Don't sit on anything cold. Don't use cold water to wash yourself . . . Don't go swimming . . . Tell your supervisor that you've got your period if you do heavy work, or if your work involves standing in water in a paddy field.'[4]

'Today's youth are rather different from Chinese youth of the 1950s or 1960s – even the 1970s,' one of China's top youth researchers told me. 'Young people in the 1950s were generally idealistic, keen to contribute to the success of new China. Youth in the 1960s and early 1970s were caught up in the drama of the Cultural Revolution. Whether they liked it or not, they were highly politicized. But today's youth seem more concerned with personal matters.'

His comment was confirmed by Wang Dao, a Shanghai student. 'Young people these days want better clothes, lots of personal possessions – the good life. They're basically interested in one thing – themselves.'

'What about serving the people?' I asked, citing a favourite communist expression and the government's renewed urgings to youth to emulate Lei Feng, the model young soldier who had denied all personal aspirations and worked only for the common good.

Wang grinned. 'That unbelievable character! There aren't too many young people in China who want to be like Lei Feng.'

China's youth are in the vanguard of the new materialism, keen to acquire the latest products – both locally produced and imported – as they come on the market. Smart clothes, a digital watch, calculator and camera have all become part of the fashionable young person's wardrobe. A major status symbol is a large stereo radio-cassette recorder costing 600 to 700 yuan: around nine months' average urban wage. The ultimate acquisition, still fairly rare, is a small motor-bike which sells for about 2000 yuan.

Despite the increasing range of consumer goods, young people are not always satisfied with their availability or their ability to purchase them. In the words of the *People's Daily*: 'Some young people have luxurious hopes incompatible with the present level of economic development.'[5] But while they complain about the rising level of personal acquisitiveness, the authorities must themselves bear a large part of the responsibility. Huge billboards and television commercials advertise everything from colour television sets and cassette recorders to face cream and egg and lemon shampoo.

The growing availability of consumer goods and clothing, set against a lessening of the rigid official controls on people's everyday lives, is creating a distinctive youth ethos in China. This still cannot be compared with the youth culture of the West which became full-blown with the rebellious generation of the 1960s and has since been encouraged and exploited by capitalist entrepreneurs. Many aspects of Western youth culture, from clothing to pop music, have become virtually internationalized and even China is no longer completely immune. But strict censorship means that China's youth ethos is still largely home-grown.

'A stroll down any Peking street this past scorching summer has been enough to show how things have changed,' commented a Chinese magazine in early 1982. 'There were skirts, even some rather short skirts, particularly on young women, shirtwaist dresses with belts, shoes with mid-high heels, bell-bottom trousers and close-fitting shirts; and everywhere a rainbow of light and bright colours.'[6]

In China, as in most countries, young people are in the forefront of fashion. While older Chinese tend to cling to the drab attire of earlier years, though now using better quality fabrics, young men and women have taken full advantage of the government's slightly liberalized attitude to what is considered appropriate attire. The first-time visitor to China might still be struck by the relative uniformity of the clothing scene but there have been dramatic changes from the ubiquitous baggy blue and grey crumpled cotton trousers and jackets of the Cultural Revolution period.

As always, it is Shanghai that leads the way in fashion. Even in the early 1970s, when any interest in personal appearance was denounced as bourgeois and decadent, young Shanghainese wore trousers that were just that bit more form-fitting than those of their brothers and sisters in Peking. And young women in Shanghai were the first to appear in cotton jackets with polka dots or traditional Chinese fastenings.

Nowadays it is the glossy Shanghai edition of *Fashion*, fast becoming the Chinese equivalent of *Vogue*, that introduces young men and women to the latest trends. Stylish young men in the city deck themselves out in figure-hugging trousers and imitation leather jackets, or even Western-style suits; young women in well-fitting skirts, high heels or boots, and nylon stockings.

'There's been a new craze recently,' one young woman in Shanghai told me in late 1983. 'Perfumed stockings. The advertisements say they will retain their perfume through ten or more washes.'

There is a strong sense of what is considered suitable clothing for people in their teens and twenties, as opposed to other age groups. 'But you wouldn't wear that if you were over twenty-five, maybe thirty,' commented Wang Mei, a smartly dressed young Shanghai woman in her early twenties when I pointed to a colourful outfit in a fashion magazine.

Even the large stores on Nanjing Road in Shanghai and Wangfujing in Peking give little indication of the latest styles favoured by young people. In spite of the occasional well-publicized fashion exhibition, off-the-peg clothes still tend to be poorly cut and unimaginative. The popularity of home dressmaking is apparent from the lively market for sewing machines (old-fashioned treadle types), clothing patterns and a wide range of natural and synthetic fabrics. But the most stylish young people, women and men alike, take their fabric to a local tailor.

'The old tailors are the most popular,' Wang Mei told me. 'They learnt their trade before liberation and they can make virtually anything just from looking at a photograph.'

Shanghai hairstyles also set the tone for the rest of China, at least in urban centres. Along with skirts, waved hair has been a curious barometer of ideological intensity ever since the communist revolution. Banned as bourgeois and decadent during the Cultural Revolution – in 1976 my roommate at Peking University criticized even my naturally curly hair as a bourgeois affectation – cold waves and perms were one of the

The Shanghai fashion magazine *Shizhuang* (*Fashion*)

first signs of personal liberalization in the late 1970s. While older women are not averse to having their hair waved, it is young people, both female and male, who most regularly frequent the hairdressing salons whose windows feature photographs of the latest styles available for both sexes.

'At first everyone was obsessed with having curly hair – it was such a novelty,' remarked Wang Mei. 'But it's more fashionable now to have fairly short well-styled hair – or even to let your hair grow long and free.'

For young women there is also a growing range of cosmetics. 'Chinese girls are putting on a pretty face,' one newspaper headline declared in late 1982. 'Urban residents are demanding such cosmetics as lipstick, face powder, hair-dye, toilet water, perfume, and various kinds of creams and balms that may help to preserve the skin.'[7] Total cosmetic sales for the previous year had amounted to nearly 410 million yuan, it reported. Per capita expenditure had, in fact, been highest not in Shanghai but in Peking, at over four times the national average. A substantial part of this was probably taken up with face creams and hair conditioners to help combat the savage dryness of the Peking winter.

Young people's enthusiasm for smart but generally conservative clothing, along with carefully arranged hairstyles, is similar to that in many other developing countries – and in the West in the 1940s and 1950s. These are outward symbols of the new material prosperity and almost bourgeois respectability emerging in China. Like Akaky in Gogol's moving story 'The Overcoat', young Chinese will scrimp and save for months – perhaps even years – for a smart woollen overcoat.

The availability of reasonable quality clothing is too novel for most young people to embrace Western youth's preference, at least in their leisure time, for casual or scruffy clothes. Even denim jeans, adopted in the West as a symbol of independence and protest, are regarded in China as symbols of the growing material prosperity. There is little interest in the patched or faded variety.

Chinese university students, doing their best to look smart within their financial limitations, are sometimes puzzled by the crumpled jeans or baggy corduroy trousers worn by some foreign students – male and female. 'They have lots of things like cassette recorders and expensive cameras. And most of their parents seem to earn a lot of money,' remarked one Peking student. 'Their clothes just don't seem to match their obvious prosperity. Some of them even buy old-fashioned Chinese clothes like cotton trousers and jackets. And cloth shoes!'

Chinese students who go overseas are often surprised to discover that their earlier images of Western affluence are not always reflected in people's clothing. 'Some young people wear patched jeans even when they go out on the street,' a student in New York wrote in a letter home. 'My Shanghai jacket is much smarter than what a lot of young people wear here.'[8]

The young woman in the postal section of Shanghai's Peace Hotel gave an approving nod as she looked through the calendars and books I was sending back to Australia. 'Everyone's buying a copy of that film star calendar,' she told me. 'My favourites are Zhang Yu – I think she's the one for February – and Gong Xue. I've seen nearly all their films. Have you bought the individual posters of them as well? Of course most young women are crazy about Li Lianjie. He's the only man in the calendar.'

Like youth in the West, China's young people are beginning to have their own youth heroes and role models: not officially created revolutionary models like Lei Feng but TV and film stars, popular singers and top sportsmen and women. The star system, a feature of individualistic Western culture and normally suppressed in communist countries, is making itself felt in China. Young people often know more about their favourite stars than they do about the nation's top political figures and widely publicized official heroes.

As the martial music and revolutionary operas of the Cultural Revolution period fade into the background, China's youth is developing a wide range of popular cultural interests. There is a growing market, for instance, for the records and cassette tapes produced by Chinese recording studios. (Much of contemporary Western and Hong Kong music is still banned in China.) Local singers like Su Xiaoming sing an array of traditional and modern Chinese popular songs and the occasional foreign song of 1930s or 1940s vintage. The smiling figures on the record jackets and cassette covers are invariably young, glamorous and smartly dressed, with little to distinguish them from their Hong Kong and Taiwanese brothers and sisters.

The songs too are strongly reminiscent of their overseas

A new role model and calendar celebrity: Gong Xue, winner of the 'Golden Rooster' and 'Hundred Flowers' awards for the best actress of 1983

Chinese equivalents, lilting and rhythmic but without the soft sexy overtones. Unlike many Western pop songs, they are not about personal problems or social protest but beautiful scenery, bright moonlight and happy young people: 'The First Morning of Spring', 'The Young Girl Walking along the Seashore', and 'The Happy Little Girl'. The occasional hint of a love song is likely to be sung in a foreign language, like Su's rendition of the Japanese song: 'I and you: loving each other, the two of us are together . . . We'll never be separated. In this world life is so beautiful.'

In large department stores and tiny shops alike, it is young people who cluster around the music counters, gazing longingly at the stereo cassette recorders and asking sales assistants to play the latest recordings.

Young people are also in the majority at TV counters, comparing the reputation and quality of the various local and foreign brands on offer. With 43cm (17″) colour sets costing about 1000 yuan – around a year's average wage – and a Toshiba 53cm (21″) Blackstripe set selling for over 2000 yuan, the purchase of colour television is often one item to which both young people and their parents are prepared to contribute.

'Most people still have black and white TV, but colour is a status symbol as well as being better,' commented a young man in Shanghai's No. 1 department store. 'Of course we argue with our parents about which channel to watch, even with colour TV.'

What did he think of the programmes overall?

'Not so good,' he replied, 'even though many people are completely besotted with TV. The sports programmes are best, especially soccer. And other competitions, like when the Chinese women's volley-ball team won the world championship in 1982. That was really exciting.'

I knew what he meant. At the hotel where I was staying in Harbin, even the lift service had come to a halt as young hotel workers crowded round the communal TV set or sneaked off to unoccupied rooms to watch the match in comfort on sets provided for foreign guests.

Another young man at the TV counter had strong views on the local programmes. 'They don't show nearly enough sport,' he told me. 'There's too much stuff like Chinese opera. Older people like it but we get bored. Occasionally there's something a bit different. The world magicians' championship was on a few nights ago.'

As their enthusiasm for film star calendars suggests, young people are also the country's most avid film watchers, whether on television or at the cinema. They have responded eagerly to the upsurge in the Chinese film industry since the late 1970s: new films based on historical events such as the burning of the Summer Palace by foreign troops in the mid-nineteenth century, on famous plays like Lao She's *Rickshaw Boy*, and even on contemporary social issues. The 1982 film *Neighbours*, for example, created widespread interest with its frank depiction of the overcrowded housing conditions endured by urban residents and its exposure of the special privileges enjoyed by many officials. But in this film, like others, the ideological overtones of socialist realism persist and the goodies invariably win out over the baddies. On this occasion it is an honest official who predictably puts everything to rights.

'There's still too much politics in most films,' remarked a young woman standing in a cinema queue in Hefei. 'It used to be Chiang Kai-shek or counter-revolutionaries. Now it's often the wicked Gang of Four. Or at least the inevitable victory of the correct socialist line. You always know what's going to happen in the end.'

'Even so, films are far better than they used to be,' said her companion.

As well as being keen readers of the latest film and television magazines, young people are the major market for popular magazines of all kinds. While the more affluent flash around the latest copy of *Shanghai Pictorial* or *Culture and Life*, others flock to the second-hand magazine stores where back copies sell at one-third to one-half of their regular price. The popularity of various magazines is apparent from the length of time they stay on the shelves. There are usually ample supplies of *People's Education* and *Chinese Youth*, the official youth magazine published by the Communist Youth League. But film, TV and sports magazines disappear almost as soon as they are put on the shelves, becoming tattier with each reappearance.

'It's almost impossible to find a copy of *Popular Cinema* or *New Sports*,' remarked a young man riffling through the piles of magazines at a second-hand store in Shanghai, expressing surprise at my own interest in finding back copies of *Chinese Youth* and *Chinese Women*.

A distinctive youth literature is also emerging in China, with magazines such as *Youth Literature* and *Sprouts* giving young writers and poets the opportunity to publish works of particular interest to young people. But like other literature, they invariably have strong ideological overtones. After a short breath of fresh air with the so-called new realism literature of 1979–80, the classic prescription for Chinese communist culture has been largely reinstated. As Mao had expressed it at Yan'an in 1942: 'Literature and art are subordinate to politics ... Revolutionary literature and art are part of the whole revolutionary cause.'[9]

Some young people are unimpressed. 'The newspapers keep saying that literature must be socialist, not bourgeois and decadent,' commented one Shanghai student, 'But I can't really see what's bourgeois about writing about life as it really is, instead of how it's supposed to be.'

'Still, it's just as well there's more for us to read these days – and there's TV,' said his friend. 'Because life otherwise is pretty boring.'

One of the most frequent complaints made by young Chinese is the lack of social activities. Occasionally there is the chance to attend a Chinese opera or play, a gymnastics display or an international sports competition. But most tickets are distributed through work units – the *danwei* which controls so many aspects of individuals' lives – and all too often the more junior employees miss out. Public restaurants hardly fit into the category of social recreation. Usually concrete-floored and smoke-filled, they tend to be overcrowded to the point where patrons gulp down their meal conscious of the next customer standing behind their chair. And they generally close at around 7 in the evening.

The youth entertainment and social scene familiar in the West is almost completely lacking in China: no pop concerts, bars or discos and little concept of private parties. Most Western-style social activity is denounced as bourgeois and decadent, with young people being encouraged to concentrate on improving themselves, not to waste time being frivolous.

But the lack of social facilities has been perturbing even the authorities, worried about the level of youth crime and the problems experienced by young men and women in meeting prospective spouses. 'We need more healthy recreational activities for young people,' confirmed a Youth League official. 'Some youth centres have been established recently, even in the countryside. If they're well off they have colour television and music; if they're poor maybe just table tennis.'

Young people are not always impressed by the authorities' rather puritanical concept of 'healthy recreational activities'. 'We don't want to play table tennis all the time,' commented one young man. 'We want to dance and have some fun.'

Dancing is one social pastime that the authorities cannot quite seem to make up their minds about – not Western-style disco or flash dancing, which are regarded as completely beyond the pale, but simply old-fashioned ballroom dancing. The official attitude towards dancing has been another of those odd barometers of ideological intensity in post-1949 China. (Ironically both Mao and Zhou Enlai had the reputation for being keen dancers at the Communists' Yan'an base in the 1940s.) It was tolerated during the period of the Sino–Soviet Alliance in the 1950s, mainly because the Russians still permitted it in their own country, frowned upon after the Sino–Soviet split, and banned completely during the Cultural Revolution.

Following Mao's death, dancing became a veritable symbol of the new liberalization. Universities and even factories organized Saturday evening dances where young men and women sedately practised the steps they had learnt from their parents or grandparents: the waltz, foxtrot and tango. Even the lack of a dance floor was no deterrent. From Harbin in the north-east to Kunming in the south-west, young people danced happily in public parks to scratchy recordings of 'Old Black Joe' or 'Auld Lang Syne' and to the occasional livelier Western tape recorded from the Voice of America.

But after the initial tolerance, dancing has again become ideologically suspect. Even foreign students in China are periodically banned from holding dance parties, regardless of whether or not there are any Chinese present.

Perhaps it is partly evening social activities that the authorities are trying to control. Even the major cities virtually close down after 7 or 8 in the evening. People are expected to be in bed by 10 o'clock or soon after, so they can be up at 6 in the morning. In China everything tends to happen an hour or two earlier than it does in the West. The rush hour is around 7 a.m.; classes at Peking University start at 7.30, even in mid-winter when it is barely light.

'It's healthy for people to get up early and go to bed early,' one of my teachers at the university had explained to me in 1977. 'I know young people in the West like to go out and enjoy themselves late in the evening, but we think that sort of behaviour is bourgeois and decadent.'

With a six-day working and studying week, leisure and social activities are left mainly to Saturday evening and Sunday. While married people, especially women, tend to spend Sunday catching up with housework and shopping, many teenagers take the opportunity to go out to *wanr* – a favourite Chinese expression meaning 'to enjoy oneself'. 'That basically means going to the park,' commented a youthful factory worker. 'It's about the only place there is to go.'

Although they are often extremely crowded, especially in warm weather, Chinese parks provide the great escape from congested living conditions. It is in the parks that young and old alike meet their friends, play cards, and go boating in summer and skating in winter. As loudspeakers keep reminding them, the parks now belong to the masses: the notorious Empress Dowager's Summer Palace on the north-west outskirts of Peking, Beihai Park in the centre of the city with its seventeenth-century white *dagoba*, the People's Park in Shanghai which was once the foreigners' racecourse. With their traditional Chinese-style buildings, pavilions and lotus-covered lakes, the spacious parks present a graphic contrast to most people's everyday living and working conditions.

'But I've been to all the parks – again and again,' complained a Peking teenager when I commented that Chinese people were lucky to have so many historical and charming places to visit. 'And they shut at about 5 o'clock anyway.'

For a few young people – the sons and daughters of high-ranking Party and Army officials – the social scene is rather more exciting. They share with their parents the perks of belonging to an elite in a society in which position, not money,

25

Popular Sunday outing: boating on Beihai Lake in Peking (*dagoba* in background)

is God. Official privileges and family connections give them access to entertainment normally beyond the reach of ordinary young people, tickets not just to public performances of all kinds but also to 'private' drama or film screenings whose audiences are restricted to the select few.

Not for these young people the grubby crowded sections of public restaurants. While their unconnected fellow-youth wrestle for table space, they scamper upstairs to the carpeted or tiled section reserved for the privileged – and foreigners. Here the waitresses wear clean aprons, the tables are covered with cloths, and the beer is served out of glass tumblers instead of cracked porcelain bowls.

In one of Xiamen's best-known restaurants I watched a group of smartly dressed young men and women scarcely out of their teens walk straight through the main dining hall and have a word with an attendant. They then proceeded to a comfortable reception lounge where they reclined with hot hand-towels, cups of tea and top-brand cigarettes before being served dinner in a spacious tiled dining-room. In the superior surroundings even the table manners were different: no spitting on the floor and no peanut shells or chicken bones dropped onto the floor to be mopped up periodically.

For some privileged young people there is even the chance of a night life. If they are particularly lucky they might get to frequent the bar of a hotel normally restricted to foreigners or overseas Chinese. While the rest of the city goes to sleep, they dance to the strains of 'Cherry Pink and Apple Blossom White' and 'In the Mood' played by a Western-style band. For others the stylish thing to do is drink coffee and eat ice-cream in the musak-filled coffee shop of a hotel like the White Swan in Canton.

'You really have to have connections to get in there,' a youthful taxi driver outside the hotel told me. 'Any ordinary Chinese person is turned back at the entrance.'

But even privileged youth sometimes fall foul of the frequent political campaigns against bourgeois decadence. During the 'campaign against spiritual pollution' in late 1983, for example, the bar at the Peace Hotel in Shanghai – the celebrated Cathay of the 1930s – had a Chinese-language sign at the entrance: 'Foreigners and overseas Chinese only. Please co-operate.'

For some, exclusion from public places only means more

private parties. These are held in their high-ranking parents' relatively spacious apartments or perhaps at a special retreat for the privileged few, like the villas in the hills outside Canton. Here the 'in set' dance to recorded Western music, eat delicacies from the special shops for top officials, and sometimes get up to high jinks that would make Mao turn in his grave – if he had one. But even the offspring of the highest ranking are not always immune from censure when the political heat is on.

If the social life of privileged Chinese youth presents a striking contrast to that of the bulk of their urban brothers and sisters, it is completely beyond the imagination of most young people in the countryside. Rural life in many areas is much the same as it has been for a thousand years or more – a routine existence of ploughing, planting and harvesting. But even young rural dwellers are becoming aware of another world beyond the village and the wheat or paddy field. News from the outside comes from the occasional villager who goes to a senior high school in a larger town, from radio and increasingly from television.

The 80 per cent of China's young people who live outside the major cities and towns are becoming increasingly restive and vocal about their lot. 'Life here is just so boring,' one young man in Henan province wrote to *Youth Letterbox*. 'There's hardly ever a film. There is just no entertainment. There's nothing to do but wander round the village. What can be done about it?'[10] 'My friends tell me not to think about it – this *is* life in the countryside,' wrote a young woman. 'It's simply a matter of eating and sleeping, getting married, establishing a household, having children. Is this really how I must pass my life?'[11]

Expressions of discontent with rural life have increased despite a substantial rise in the general standard of living. Although the average per capita income is still only just over half that in urban areas, it has more than doubled in the past five years. Enterprising rural dwellers living on the outskirts of large towns and cities, in particular, are benefiting from the relaxed agricultural policy and making substantial profits from the sale of their products on the private market.

While young peasants in the poorer areas of China still dream of a time when they no longer have to fetch water from the river on shoulder poles, others are beginning to have expectations

Life for rural youth: carting human fertilizer for the vegetables that are not very different from those of their urban brothers and sisters. In late 1983 a local Party official in Jiangxi province informed the Party's Central Committee of the current wishes expressed by peasants in one county. 'They want a richer and more varied cultural life,' he wrote. 'Some peasants say that black and white TV sets are not good enough. They now want colour ones ... They want to buy high quality ready-made clothes. They want good quality sweets and pastries.'[12]

The Party official did not include the heartfelt desire of many a young rural dweller to leave the countryside for the city. A provincial capital with its big stores, sealed roads and cinemas seems glamorous to most villagers; a city like Shanghai is positively utopian. 'I've heard of someone who went to Shanghai once,' a young woman told me in 1979 in the south-west province of Yunnan. 'He said they have tall, tall buildings and lights that change colour.'

The starry-eyed perception of China's largest city has not changed much over the years. When young peasants in the People's Liberation Army reached Shanghai in mid-1949, they were quite overcome. As the Filipino Consul-General described it at the time: 'They wandered around like shy little country boys, open-eyed, obviously bewildered by the ornate and magnificent buildings of the city.'[13]

Escape to the cities, always a magnet in developing countries, is virtually out of the question in China. Controls on urban residence are so tight that several million couples live apart because one of the partners does not have an urban residence permit. Some of these people married during the Cultural Revolution when around 17 million educated youth were sent to rural areas. Even most of those who were married preferred to return to the cities, leaving their spouses in the countryside and sometimes obtaining a divorce, when the policy changed in the late 1970s.

Joining the Army used to be seen as a means of leaving the countryside and even as the possible pathway to an urban job. But harsh conditions and the high casualties of the 1979 confrontation with Vietnam, set against rising rural incomes, have made army service less attractive. And with the authorities facing a continuing youth employment problem in the cities, the chance of an eventual urban job has become fairly remote.

Most young rural dwellers have little choice but to accept their lot, assured by the government that things will improve as the economy develops. As it points out, rising incomes have already made life in rural areas more varied and interesting, especially in the more prosperous regions. But not interesting enough, according to many. In mid-1983 a Youth League activist in Shandong province told *Chinese Youth* that the young people in his village were complaining bitterly about their lack of social life. 'They want something more to do in the evening than just go to sleep,' he declared.[14]

Between the Generations

'I am finding it increasingly difficult to understand my son Gu Cheng's poetry,' wrote Chinese poet Gu Gong of his 23-year-old son in a 1980 essay entitled 'The Two Generations'. He went on to quote another writer's reflection on the younger generation. 'Nowadays parents everywhere are saying that they do not understand their own children. Yes, there appears to be a gap between us and young people.'[1]

In the central Chinese city of Hefei I talked with 20-year-old process worker Wu Lihua. 'Our parents simply don't seem to understand us any more,' Wu complained. 'Everyone is talking about a generation gap in China.'

The generation gap is hardly unique to China or to contemporary society. It is probably as old as human history. 'They are passionate, irascible, and apt to be carried away by their impulses,' wrote Aristotle of youth some 2300 years ago. 'They regard themselves as omniscient and are positive in their assertions . . . they carry everything too far.'[2]

It is these characteristics that invariably bring youth into conflict with the older generation, confident that their age and wider experience of life have given them greater wisdom and authority.

In traditional China, though, there were few opportunities for open conflict between the generations. The tightly structured Confucian family system prescribed absolute obedience to the father, enshrined in the concept of filial piety. Even the most important decisions about young people's lives were made by the head of the household. 'I think we can say that I've fulfilled my duties as a father,' a typical patriarch tells his

19-year-old son, Juexin, in Ba Jin's famous novel *Family.* 'I've raised you to manhood and found you a wife . . . I've found you a position in the West Sichuan Mercantile Corporation. You start tomorrow.'[3]

Although young people occasionally protested against supreme patriarchal authority, especially on the question of arranged marriages, compliance rather than rebellion was the order of the day.

As in other countries, China's generation gap has been most marked during periods of rapid social change when young people have been the first to respond to fresh ideas. In the early twentieth century the Confucian family system came under assault from ideas of individualism and personal independence emanating chiefly from the West. The resulting conflict between the generations was perhaps no more graphically portrayed than by Ba Jin: 'Ma, times have changed. It's more than twenty years since you were my age. Something new comes into the world every day,' argues Juexin's cousin Jin.[4] Strongly influenced by Ibsen's *Doll's House*, Jin and her female friends insist on being educated and even cutting their hair short in the style of the 'modern woman'. And Juexin's younger brother simply rejects parental authority and abandons his family for an independent city life.

Tensions between the generations took a fresh turn following the communist revolution. While not attempting to destroy the family as such, the new government wanted to replace absolute allegiance to the family, a threat to its own authority, with allegiance to the Communist Party. Regarding youth as the most progressive force in society, it encouraged young people to criticize the traditional 'feudal' family system and throw off supreme parental authority. This reached a climax during the Cultural Revolution when many young people, members of the militant Red Guards, publicly denounced even their own parents as remnants of the old feudal order.

The post-Mao era has seen a twist in the government's attitudes. Instead of urging youth to reject family authority, it tends to support parental criticism of the youth generation and even urges young people to return to the 'fine traditions governing Chinese families for thousands of years'.[5] At the same time, it officially dismisses the widespread talk of a generation gap. 'We should not speak of a generation gap in China,' a

Communist Youth League official told me solemnly in Peking. 'What we are talking about are merely a few prejudices and misunderstandings between the generations.'

But the frequency and vehemence of official assertions that there is no real generation gap in China, accompanied by attempts to play down the problem with political double-talk, only draw public attention to the issue.

Many of the parents of today's youth were themselves members of the youth generation of the 1950s, the only decade of general optimism and real enthusiasm about creating a 'new China' to replace the old class-ridden, poverty-stricken society. The enthusiasm has since declined – shattered by contradictory political campaigns, personal repression, hesitant economic development and the emergence of new classes – but the lives of today's forty- and fifty-year-olds have been inextricably bound up with China's post-revolutionary history. Although many have become cynical about the revolution, they cannot simply dismiss politics the way that many of their children do. Young people nowadays seem just too uninvolved, too wrapped up in their own interests.

Following the screening of *Youth Everlasting*, a film about 'progressive youth' in the 1950s based on a novel by Wang Meng, a correspondent wrote nostalgically to the *China Daily*: 'We see the happy days of the 1950s when people helped each other.' The film, he thought optimistically, should have a 'profound educative effect on the present younger generation'.[6]

Another parent commented to me: 'Many young people don't accept there are other things in life apart from their own personal interests. They're too selfish and they complain too much about China's backwardness. Instead of comparing China with what it was like before liberation, they contrast it with Japan and the West. They don't appreciate how much better things are now than they were in the old society.'

But the appeal to youth to think of the old days is little more effective than reminders to the Western youth generation of the 1950s or 1960s about their parents' sufferings in the world depression. 'We're tired of hearing about the old society,' retorted one Shanghai youth. 'What we're interested in is now.'

Like Western parents of the 1950s, today's Chinese parents

For sale

want their children to have the things they lacked. But they also criticize them when they become obsessed with acquiring material possessions. 'All they think of these days is buying cassette recorders, cameras, and the latest fashions,' grumbled a Peking parent. 'They spend most of their time hanging around stores and reading magazines.'

As some young people point out, such criticism tends to be somewhat misplaced. The choice of products might be different but many older people are little less acquisitive than their offspring. After years of material deprivation, they too are now clamouring to buy the latest consumer goods as they come on the market. Some are succumbing to the recently introduced temptation: buying the more expensive goods on hire purchase.

For all the tensions over different attitudes, the greatest area of generational conflict in China continues to be that of parental authority. Like their counterparts all over the world, Chinese parents criticize their teenage children for lacking respect for their elders and consideration for other members of the family, playing music too loudly and being late for meals. These tensions are multiplied in China because of continuing parental expectations of complete youth obedience and also because of the tiny space within which family members generally have to co-exist. Many of the conflicts in Liu Xinwu's revealing short story 'Overpass', for example, occur as a result of three generations – up to eight people – sharing one partitioned room of only 16 square metres (19 square yards) in Peking. '"What a dog den!" he muttered angrily. To call it a dog den was, of course, wrong – a human den would be far more appropriate. Indeed, the word "den" gave the only accurate description of the cramped nature of his family's living space.'[7]

In response to criticism, young people allege that their parents are too strict and will not allow them to express their growing sense of personal independence. When it suits them, they even use the familiar political rhetoric to support their arguments. 'My parents have old-fashioned feudal attitudes,' declared one 19-year-old Shanghai youth. 'They still think they should have supreme authority over me.'

Youth's main reaction against parental authority is not to break away from the family, as many teenagers do in the West, but to assert some independence within the family circle.

37

Economic independence is regarded as vital. In a survey of workers in a collective enterprise in Tianjin, over 60 per cent of those questioned said their major objective in getting a job was to avoid dependence on their parents.[8] But a new wage in the family sometimes only results in quarrels over how the money should be spent; in traditional China individual incomes were usually handed over to the 'family purse' and distributed according to need. 'These days many young people want the independence to buy whatever they fancy,' grumbled one parent. 'Even more. Some of them think they are entitled to keep all their money for themselves. They don't even want to contribute to household expenses like food, let alone furniture or household appliances.'

For all the signs of generational conflict, the Chinese family continues to be a fairly tight-knit unit with young people tending to be more subject to parental authority and influence than they are in the West. This is partly because they normally continue to live with their parents until, and even after, they get married, a result not just of accommodation shortages but of traditional practice. Indeed the sense of family identity is still strong in China, just as it is among Chinese people throughout the world. Most young Chinese want to live and work in the same city or town as other members of the family and express surprise that some Westerners voluntarily move to another country to live and work, making no effort to take their parents with them.

The acceptance of parental authority also derives from the importance of family influence and connections in obtaining a good job or even getting to university. As in traditional times, most parents will do all in their power to advance the interests of their offspring, regardless of tensions within the family. In the words of one Shanghai parent: 'The family still comes first in China, despite all the talk of a generation gap.'

Young people have difficulties and conflicts not only with their parents. One of the major rifts is that with their immediate elders in their late twenties and early thirties: the 'lost generation' of the Cultural Revolution. This group was the first generation to grow up under socialism and subsequently either participated in the Cultural Revolution or was severely affected by it.

The gap between today's youth and the lost generation is particularly strong in intellectual and professional families. Having missed out on obtaining a higher education because of their wrong class background, the members of the lost generation are now largely unskilled or semi-skilled workers while their parents, and possibly older or younger siblings, are professionals and intellectuals. In a society that still draws rigid social lines between mental and manual labour, those of the lost generation feel their position very keenly. 'There's simply no hope for the members of my generation,' a 29-year-old process worker told me in Canton. 'My father is a university professor. I didn't have a proper education because of that fact. Now I'm stuck.'

Not surprisingly, this group does not always see eye-to-eye with today's youth who at least have the opportunity for higher education and professional advancement, partly *because* of their intellectual background. The older group regard their younger siblings or relatives with envy; the younger men and women sometimes treat their comparatively uneducated elders with much the same contempt they have for all people doing mundane jobs and especially manual labour. 'I know it's not his fault,' said a recent Peking science graduate of his elder brother. 'But he even looks and sounds like a worker. He's so ignorant – and he says he hasn't got the time or the energy to do anything about it.'

There is just as great a gap between the current youth generation and those few people of the lost generation who did manage to get a limited tertiary training during the latter part of the Cultural Revolution, the 'worker, peasant, soldier' students educated in the early and mid-1970s. China's present crop of young intellectuals regard these people as professionally incompetent and see them as a threat to their own career advancement. The 'worker, peasant, soldier' graduates think the new generation is cocky and ambitious, over-confident of its role in the forefront of China's modernization drive and favoured by the current leadership.

The two groups came into direct conflict at tertiary institutions in the years immediately following the reorganization of the university system in 1977. At Peking University, for example, some of the newly enrolled younger students, entering university through the revived national examinations and mostly coming straight from school, pasted up wall posters criticizing the 'worker, peasant, soldier' students, for their low academic standards. In retaliation, some of the 'worker, peasant, soldier' students pasted up wall posters declaring 'We have practical experience of life which is essential to becoming effective professional workers.' The new students, they maintained, were naive, arrogant and knew nothing at all of the realities of life.

China's young people sometimes also partially blame their immediate elders, whatever their background or education, for the chaos and disruption of the Cultural Revolution in which they were active participants. Like some of the current Chinese leadership, they also suspect this group of continuing to be sympathetic towards Maoist ideas of revolution and class struggle instead of believing in the pre-eminence of economic progress.

The gaps between today's youth and other age groups in Chinese society – whether their parents or immediate elders – are only part of the complex web of age relationships in China. The nation has a multiple generation gap, brought about largely by the dramatic political changes over the past thirty-five years and focussed on the communist revolution of the late 1940s and the Cultural Revolution of the mid-1960s.

'People's perceptions and attitudes are very much tied up with their personal experiences,' commented a Shanghai grandparent. 'Even people born a decade apart sometimes seem to be a world apart. Politics has played havoc with family and personal relationships in China.'

CHAPTER FOUR

The Rungs of the Ladder

'I'm seventeen, my friends tell me I'm very pretty, and I want to be a film star. How do I go about it?' wrote a hopeful village girl from Hunan province to the advice column of a youth magazine in Peking.[1]

Young people everywhere have their fantasy aspirations. In China they're to be a famous film or TV star, a singer like Su Xiaoming whose recordings sell millions of cassettes each year, or even a top gymnast or table tennis player.

But like youth elsewhere, China's young people also have more realistic hopes. 'The main aspiration of most Chinese these days is to get a good job,' said Lin Huitang, a 16-year-old Shanghai youth in his final year of high school. 'A job that's interesting and preferably well paid. And one that has high social status and prospects of perks like travel and access to foreign goods.'

If China's youth have similar aspirations to young people in many countries, whether capitalist or socialist, these aspirations are not easy to fulfil. Despite improving living standards in the countryside, most young peasants are still involved mainly in routine manual labour. Even in urban areas interesting, well-paid and prestigious jobs are at a premium because of China's low level of development, a general lack of economic diversification, and a largely state-controlled employment market.

The major, even the only, pathway to achieving high personal aspirations is seen as being through tertiary education. 'It's really the only way to get ahead in China,' said Lin. 'Getting into university or an institute is the big dividing line – between having the chance of a good job and its accompaniments, and probably being doomed to a boring job for life, maybe after a lengthy period of unemployment.'

But obtaining a higher education in China is no simple matter. Although the post-Mao leadership has gradually been expanding the number of tertiary institutions and students – total enrolment has doubled since 1976 and is expected to redouble by 1989 – only a tiny proportion of young Chinese have access to higher education. About 350 000 new students are currently admitted each year: under 5 per cent of the 6 to 7 million young people graduating from senior high school and only around 1.2 per cent of young people in the relevant age group. In contrast, approximately 35 per cent of all young people in the United States, and over 20 per cent of those in Australia and the Soviet Union, receive a tertiary education.

Competition to gain access to higher education in China is ferocious and fraught with personal tension, beginning as early as primary school. By far the easiest path to tertiary level is first to pass the examination to get into one of China's 6000 key high schools (about 5 per cent of the total). Denounced as elitist during the Cultural Revolution, key schools were revived in the late 1970s as part of the new leadership's emphasis on producing highly qualified people able to cope with the demands of China's modernization. These schools receive the lion's share of the limited educational resources, especially teaching expertise. Although staff–student rations are reasonable in China, overall teaching standards are low. According to the report of a national conference on primary and high school education held in November 1983: 'Many schools have more non-teachers than teachers able to stand before the blackboard.'[2]

Key schools are also the best equipped. 'We're very proud of our language and science laboratories,' said the headmaster of Peking's No. 8 High School, one of the city's best-known, whose superior facilities present a striking contrast to those at most regular high schools, even in urban areas.

While less than 5 per cent of senior high school graduates overall make it to the tertiary level, key schools often have a success rate of 70–80 per cent. Approximately 75 per cent of students at Peking's No. 8 High School pass the university entrance examination at their first attempt. Virtually all

Already on the road to success: thirteen-year-olds at Peking's No. 8 High School,
a top key school

students at Harbin's No. 1 High School eventually go on to higher education, the school's headmaster told me. His key school, like most others, has a special revision class for students who don't pass the exam at their first try. 'They nearly all get through the second time around,' he commented.

Even many regular high schools have what they describe as 'fast classes' for the brightest students who receive the bulk of the best teachers' time and energy. In addition, the quest for high university entrance rates, which might entitle a regular high school to be reclassified as a key institution, led in the late 1970s to the practice of severely restricting the number of students permitted to take the university examination. 'There were eighty students in our final year but only twenty-three were allowed to sit the exam,' a young man from Changchun complained to a youth magazine. Thirteen had passed, he said, giving the school a success rate of almost 60 per cent.[3]

Students who have already been cast aside often show little further interest in their studies and tend to present substantial discipline problems. Despite official admonitions that they should complete their education, they are sometimes urged by heavily burdened teachers to leave school before the end of their courses.

'They're not learning anything and they're just creating a nuisance,' commented one overwrought teacher. 'They're only wasting our time.' When they do leave school, these young people, along with those who subsequently fail the university entrance examination, discover that their academically oriented education has given them none of the vocational skills necessary to obtain even a moderately satisfying job.

In the effort to make education more relevant to the country's needs and defuse the intense competition to go on to university, the Chinese authorities have revived vocational schools as an alternative for students after they complete three years' junior high school. These schools provide semi-professional and technical training in areas such as accountancy, electrical trades, building, catering and cookery. They were an important part of the educational system in the 1950s and early 1960s but were denounced during the Cultural Revolution for creating a two-tier elitist educational system. While the eventual plan is to have approximately equal numbers of each type of institution, progress has been slow in converting senior high schools into vocational schools.

Despite their practicality, the vocational schools tend to be regarded as second-best in the educational stakes. Past attempts by the Communists to break down the distinction between mental and manual labour in China had a limited impact and the Confucian intellectual tradition remains strong: scholars at the top of the ladder and little respect for people who work with their hands. This is only being reinforced by the government's present emphasis on the need for professional experts for the nation's modernization.

In the current tight higher educational environment, some parents with a worker's background consider that the vocational schools at least offer their children the opportunity to gain technical skills and a reasonable job. Most professionals and intellectuals, in contrast, equate their children's inability to gain entry to senior high school with failure. In the words of one middle-ranking bureaucrat: 'What hope is there for your children if they can't even complete a proper high school education?'

But for many young people, especially in the countryside, proceeding beyond junior high school at all is a substantial achievement. Even universal primary education is still a fair way off: only about 65 per cent of all children in China complete primary school. Some youngsters in the countryside never go to school at all; others have no more than two or three years' basic education.

The recent changes in the rural economy might only be aggravating the situation. A survey of primary school dropouts in the countryside near Suzhou in east China found that increasing numbers of parents were keeping their children at home, either to do domestic chores while their mothers worked in the fields or to help with the growing and selling of produce.[4] This development gives little hope for eradicating illiteracy which, according to the 1982 census, stood at some 238 million people: 31.9 per cent of all people over twelve years old.

Of those boys and girls who complete primary school and go on to junior high school, only about 40 per cent subsequently make it to the senior high level. 'If you live in the countryside it's unlikely that you'll ever get to senior high school, let alone to university, no matter how clever you are,' said one student at a top language institute. This alert and articulate young man had himself managed to break out of the rural syndrome, but only after moving from a small-town high school to one in a larger town where he'd spent a further two years and eventually passed the university entrance examination – at his third attempt. He'd been fortunate, he told me, to have relatives who were prepared to encourage and support him, as well as a few vital contacts along the way. 'But there must be thousands of potentially great scientists and writers in the countryside who spend their whole lives growing rice and never even learn to read or write,' he added.

Those young people who have so far managed to stay on the academic track face tremendous pressures in their final years of schooling. They do little but study, both at school and in their free time, urged on not just by personal ambition but also by their elders. One pressure comes from teachers, keen to improve their school's university entrance statistics. In the quest for high entrance rates, 'teachers mercilessly crammed students with huge quantities of facts and loaded them with homework,' admitted an official book on the educational system.[5]

'Even so, parents are generally far more merciless than we are when it comes to putting pressures on students,' one high school teacher told me indignantly. 'They never let up on their kids.'

The pressures have been causing both physical and psychological problems among would-be examination candidates. Lack of sleep, set against the general subsistence level diet of many Chinese, has made students particularly vulnerable to colds, flu and even hepatitis which has reached alarming proportions in some schools in the Canton area.

Eye-strain and poor eyesight, especially extreme short-sightedness, are constant problems. The intense study of often poorly reproduced material is not helped by the dim lighting characteristic of Chinese classrooms and living accommodation. High electricity costs and power shortages – and in China one generally has to hand in a used light bulb to purchase a new one – illustrate China's present modernization dilemma. Students are being trained to participate in China's modernization but improved educational facilities and student achievement depend to a large extent on modernization.

After a period of almost sole emphasis on academic studies, most senior high schools now have compulsory physical education classes and sporting activities. Special attention is paid to vision problems, particularly eye-strain. Even the lower classes in high schools have regular breaks for eye exercises. At Peking's No. 8 High School, for example, I watched a group of thirteen-year-olds go through their ten-minute, twice-daily, eye and neck exercise routine.

Perhaps even more widespread are psychological problems, especially a high level of anxiety, as personal tensions and teachers' urgings are supplemented by parental pressures, threats and even bribes.

'It's for my son to take to university,' said a solidly built middle-aged man travelling in the same railway compartment when I admired his pale blue imitation leather suitcase. The case had cost 35 yuan, he told me: the equivalent of around two weeks' wages for the average urban worker. When I asked which university his son attended, he replied: 'Oh, he won't be going to university for almost another year. That's if he passes the exam, of course. I don't really know whether he's got much chance. But we can hope – and encourage him to work hard.'

Some teenagers wilt under the constant parental pressure, expressing their anxiety in anonymous letters to the advice columns of youth magazines. 'Ever since I started senior high school my mother has made me study all the time,' wrote a female student from Henan province. 'She won't let me read anything but my school books. When my friends come around on Sunday to see me she tells them to go away. Even at Spring Festival I was made to stay at home and study while the rest of the family went to see films and visit relatives. If I don't pass the university entrance exam, I simply won't bo ablc to face my family.'[6]

Others sound even more desperate. 'My parents keep saying that if I don't pass the exam they'll throw me out of the house,' wrote a young man from Jiangxi province. 'What would I do then? Where would I go? Will life still be worth living?' He was not alone in his predicament, he said. Many of his friends were having similar experiences with their parents. 'They're all anxious and worried.'[7]

The effects of parental pressure have aroused the concern of senior officials, including the Minister for Education, and prompted media warnings to parents not to expect too much of their offspring. 'Failure to get to university does not mean that a person is not clever or is not a conscientious student,' declared the official youth magazine *Chinese Youth*, reminding ambitious parents that only a tiny proportion of high school students are able to go to university. 'Parents must have realistic expectations of their children . . . They should not make them feel too terrified to face their families if they fail the exam.'[8]

The big test comes each July when the three-day national university entrance examinations are held. By this stage even more would-be candidates have fallen by the wayside, victims of a preliminary screening process that now makes the national exam more manageable. Some 5.7 million people sat the examinations when they were revived in 1977; in 1983 preliminary screening reduced the number of candidates to 1.67 million, of whom some 360 000 were successful.

So for more than three out of four final candidates, the 1983 examinations only brought bitter disappointment. 'My world just collapsed,' said one distressed student. 'All those hopes. All that hard work and effort. All for nothing.'

Each year some young people are completely shattered by their failure, especially if their parents had anticipated success.

'My dear mother and father, this is the last letter I'll ever write to you,' wrote one young girl in an apparent suicide note published in *Chinese Youth*. 'I've failed the examination and I know that if I come home I'll be cursed and scolded. You said that death would be less of a burden to bear. Tears flow down my face . . . death is the only road left for me. If you feel at all sad seek out my body, burn it and put the ashes back into the soil so I can at least make some contribution after my death. If you're not sad then don't bother about me . . . let me be fed to the fishes.'[9]

Whether this young girl had carried out her intention to kill herself was not mentioned in the magazine. But each year there are several suicides by young people who simply cannot bear the burden of failure.

There are also those who, after the initial disappointment, scurry back to their books and begin studying for the next year's examinations. As well as special revision classes in key high schools, it's possible to attend daytime or evening classes in a variety of examined subjects. Some hopefuls simply stay at home with their books and pursue their own study programmes.

But many face further disappointment the next year, and maybe even the next. 'I've failed the exam three times,' a 19-year-old grumbled to me in Harbin. 'Apart from eating and sleeping all I do is study. What's wrong with me? Am I simply stupid?'

Although the maximum university entrance age is normally twenty-five (twenty-three for some foreign language institutes), most would-be tertiary students give up after their second or third attempt. A few keep persevering, often pushed on by status-conscious parents. One young man complained to a Peking newspaper that his mother refused to let him take up an ordinary job, even though he'd failed the exam three times. 'I'm a teacher,' she'd told him. 'How can a teacher's child not go to university? Maybe you don't feel embarrassed but I do. You must keep studying until you're admitted or you're past the age limit.'

But the young man had had enough. 'I'm already twenty-one and I feel ashamed of still being supported by my parents,' he protested. He had reached the stage where he was prepared to take any job, he said, even that of a sanitation worker (one of the most despised jobs in China, sanitation work is a euphemism for street-sweeping and nightsoil collection).[10]

The survivors of the university entrance examinations are eligible for enrolment in one of China's 700-odd tertiary institutions: ranging from prestigious key national universities like Peking University, Shanghai's Fudan University and the top language and technology institutes, through to provincial universities and lower-status teachers' universities and colleges.

'It's a tricky business working out where to apply for,' explained an English literature student at Harbin's Teachers' University. 'I put Peking University as my first choice, just in case. But of course they always have huge numbers of applicants. I put this teachers' university as my second choice to be fairly sure of getting in somewhere. I'd rather have gone to the main university in Harbin but if I'd put it as my second choice

Peking University, one of the most prestigious tertiary institutions

and missed out, the quota at this university might already have been filled by the time they considered my application.'

The selection of specialization is also something of a gamble. The most favoured fields of study, and the departments with the most pressures on them, are the areas in the forefront of China's modernization: science and technology, computer studies and engineering. With China expanding its contacts with the outside world, English language studies also rate high in popularity, especially at top centres like Peking's and Shanghai's foreign language institutes.

Some areas of study, like some universities, are acknowledged to be easier to get into than others. In 1982, for example, around 18 per cent of all Peking applicants to study English were successful, compared with only 12 per cent of those applying to study science. 'I really wanted to do science but my results weren't good enough and I didn't get into university at all,' one young woman told me in Peking. 'So the next year I took the exam I applied for English, and got in. Of course the fact that my mother's an English teacher and could coach me was also a great help.'

With places in tertiary institutions being so keenly sought, it's hardly surprising that university enrolment has been a major area of abuse and corruption in post-Mao China. Official warning notices issued each year on 'preventing unhealthy practices in higher education enrolment' reveal interference with the system all along the line. The 1981 notice, for example, complained that examiners, educational officials and university administrators had tampered with students' examination results, not just those of their own and their relatives' offspring but in response to approaches and bribes from influential people.[11] The 1983 warning notice sternly reprimanded both sides. Parents should not 'make use of personal relationships to advance their children's education, get in by the backdoor, or otherwise act improperly,' it stipulated. Officials at all levels must not 'break enrolment regulations or rashly interfere with enrolment work'.[12]

In addition to blatant corruption, there is scope for more subtle fiddling with the system because of the supplementary criteria for student enrolment. These were added when doubts arose about the do-or-die nature of the annual examination and because of the lingering feeling that academic prowess was not the only desirable quality for the country's future decision-makers, even in times of supreme pragmatism. Universities now take into account not just students' examination results but also their school records, sporting ability, physical health and moral conduct. In official parlance, the single-minded academic emphasis has been replaced by considerations of students' 'all-round intellectual, physical and moral development'. While examination marks are paramount, say university administrators, other factors are also considered, especially in borderline cases.

In practice, top sportsmen and women have been admitted to university even when their examination results were well below par. In Hebei province in 1981, for example, applicants were officially entitled to preferential treatment if they'd been in the first five places in individual sporting competitions – or the first three in team contests – in either regional or city competitions over the previous three years. As a result, eighty-seven young people gained special entry to tertiary institutions: to key universities if they had achieved at least the minimum entrance level and to ordinary universities even without the number of points normally required for admission.[13]

At the other extreme, Chinese universities have little time for students in poor physical condition or for those with permanent disabilities. In spite of a satisfactory performance in the entrance examination – a substantial achievement in itself – students have been knocked back following the requisite medical examination because of kidney or liver diseases, blindness in one eye or even severe myopia, and for being crippled or suffering the aftermath of polio.

But hospitals and doctors have proved every bit as corruptible as education officials and university administrators. While students with obvious physical defects can do little to hide them, those with less visible problems sometimes manage to obtain the necessary medical clearance through the usual practice of family connections and bribery. In 1983 the government officially warned hospitals and doctors that they must make their comments and conclusions 'in a serious and responsible manner ... and sign their names when conducting physical examinations.'[14]

Even more open to subjective interpretation is the question of a student's so-called moral development. Correct socialist attitudes and behaviour, which were major criteria for university enrolment in the early 1970s when the educational emphasis was more on 'redness' than 'expertise', are again being taken into account. A background of activism in the Communist Youth League, which recruits young people from the age of fourteen, is considered a definite asset. As one high school student put it: 'If you want to go to university you'd be foolish not to join the Youth League.'

Students even with high examination marks are excluded from university if they're discovered to have committed what are officially described as 'serious mistakes in political thinking and moral cultivation'. This would normally rule out an applicant who had been in reform school, let alone anyone who had already attempted to rock the political boat by openly expressing dissatisfaction with socialism or the Communist Party. 'These are not the sort of people we want as tomorrow's leaders,' confirmed one top university administrator.

Even at the high school level, the path of obedience and conformity is the only sensible one for young people with any aspirations to get ahead in China.

CHAPTER FIVE

The New Elite

'You don't have to come from a professional or intellectual background to get to a key school or to university,' a student at Anhui University told me. 'But you don't really stand too much of a chance otherwise.'

China's current educational system is proving to be a highly elitist one. Students at key high schools and at university, especially the top universities, come overwhelmingly from privileged urban backgrounds. For example, some 80 per cent of the parents of students at Peking's No. 8 High School and Harbin's No. 1 High School are senior Party or Army officials, professionals or intellectuals. A similar proportion applies to Peking University, according to one of its administrators. Foreign students at other top universities in China confirm the overwhelming predominance of students from privileged backgrounds.

In addition to the continuing importance of high-level connections and influence in university enrolment, a privileged background gives young Chinese the same advantages it does in other countries: a general environment of intellectual stimulation and the greater likelihood of a quiet spot to study, not easy to come by given China's overcrowded living conditions. Parents are more likely to be able to help children with their studies or even to be prepared to hire private tutors to coach them for the university entrance examination. If a student fails the exam at first try, better-off families are also more able and willing to support their children financially while they revise for a second or third attempt.

Having enrolled students from the privileged sectors of society, the university system produces a further elite. In 1981

China revived the awarding of degrees which, as in imperial times, bestow social prestige and pave the way to career advancement. Even more prestigious are higher degrees. In mid-1983 China awarded eighteen PhD degrees, the first ever to be granted in the People's Republic. Some 15 000 students had already received Masters degrees under the revamped educational system. But the most prestigious higher degrees, particularly in scientific fields, are those from prominent Western universities, just as they were in pre-communist China. A new crop of Chinese PhD graduates, mostly the sons of high officials, already share with their scholarly predecessors of the 1930s and 1940s the prestige of a PhD from such universities as Harvard, Yale, Oxford and Cambridge.

Before receiving even their basic degrees, Chinese students face four or more years' intensive study with regular examinations and few social or personal diversions. According to a university administrator in Harbin: 'Tertiary education in China has one basic purpose – to produce the professional experts necessary for China's modernization. We expect students to devote themselves single-mindedly to their studies.' While Chinese students are undoubtedly serious about their studies, it is not always for this official reason.

The current elitism and intensity of higher education is a far cry from the so-called educational revolution of the Cultural Revolution period. Following the reopening of the universities in the early 1970s, students were enrolled without formal entrance examinations. In theory these 'worker, peasant, soldier' students were selected chiefly because of their sound class background and correct political outlook; in practice the lack of formal entrance requirements often resulted in officials exercising favouritism and pulling strings for relatives and friends.

Once at university, students found themselves virtually free from examinations which were denounced for promoting competitiveness and a quest for personal gain. If exams were held at all, they tended to be based on co-operation among students. Degrees were abolished on the grounds that they were elitist and characteristic of bourgeois individualism.

Entering university with a limited educational background, students subsequently spent much of their time at political meetings and participating in mass rallies against Confucius

University education during the Cultural Revolution
The author and another Australian student as factory workers at Peking's
No. 2 Machinery Factory in 1976

and alleged 'capitalist roaders'. They also spent lengthy periods, up to two to three months a year, back in the factory or down on the commune so that, as China's new breed of intellectuals, they would not become divorced from the masses. What formal education they received was either extremely basic and practical, as in the case of science and technology, or loaded with ideological jargon, as in the case of humanities subjects such as history and philosophy. There was no room even for theoretical science, let alone fanciful social science subjects like sociology or psychology.

Maoist ideology and learning from experience were the order of the day. One history lecturer at Peking University in early 1976 actually apologized whenever he suggested that students should read a volume of more than about a hundred pages. 'We shouldn't read too many books,' he liked to remind Chinese and foreign students alike, quoting Mao's famous anti-intellectual adage.

Even China's Minister for Education, Zhou Rongxin, complained that academic standards were undergoing a steep decline. Denounced by the radical leadership for having a bourgeois elitist attitude to education, Zhou apparently died of a heart attack in April 1976 after a lengthy criticism session, not knowing that his views would be officially endorsed following Mao's death later in the year.

Now ridiculed for their low level of professional expertise, the university students of the Cultural Revolution period are only too aware that they will probably soon be bypassed by a new generation of well-trained graduates. 'We're simply missing out,' complained one of my former classmates at Peking University. 'Perhaps it wouldn't be so bad if we hadn't been told that we were in the vanguard of the educational revolution and China's hope for the future.'

Significantly, the average age of China's first group of PhD graduates in 1983 was thirty-eight; they had mostly been undergraduate students *before* the Cultural Revolution.

With a renewed emphasis on academic achievement, a Chinese university campus in the 1980s is rather different from what it was in the early and mid-1970s. It's also a far cry from most Western universities. Highly structured and disciplined, life at a Chinese university is rather similar to that at a strict Western boarding-school, with administrators and teachers taking responsibility not just for students' education but also for their personal behaviour.

The high level of discipline is made possible by the fact that the overwhelming majority of students live on campus, usually a wall-enclosed compound which has gate-keepers on duty during the day and is locked at night. Within the compound there are not just lecture rooms, libraries and student accommodation, but housing for staff and their families and even small factories and workshops. Many campuses seem more like busy self-contained villages, complete with retired grandmothers or grandfathers looking after babies and toddlers while their parents work, and children going to and from the university's own kindergarten and school.

University students might be China's new elite but their living quarters are both spartan and crowded. This comes as no great surprise to students even from intellectual and professional backgrounds but is probably something of a shock to the sons and daughters of high Party officials whose privileges usually extend to superior housing. At Peking University, for example, as many as seven students share a room of around 12 square metres (about 14½ square yards). A typical room has four double-decker bunks placed against two walls (there is often a free bunk piled high with students' belongings) and tiny desks along the other walls.

Large enamel bowls, used for washing one's body, hair and clothing – either with cold water or with hot water from the ubiquitous thermos flask – are sometimes stacked on a wooden stand. A smaller enamel bowl and chopsticks accompany the student to the canteen for meals. Even if bowls are provided students generally prefer to take their own; the prevalence of tuberculosis and hepatitis deters them from using poorly washed communal eating utensils.

In common with many a Chinese canteen, whether for students, professionals or workers, the frequent talk during mealtimes is not politics or current affairs but the day's food. Despite the apparent variety of produce in the markets, students usually have to make do with a bowl of cereal (rice in the south, sometimes noodles or steamed dumplings in the north) and a few vegetables, occasionally supplemented by tiny portions of meat. If this is similar to the food endured by most of the population – fish, meat and other delicacies are expensive and are eaten in any quantity only on special occasions – its mass production makes it as unappetising as student meals in many a university dining hall all over the world.

'But it wouldn't be so bad if it was nutritious and if we got enough to eat,' grumbled one student. 'I'm always hungry well before the next meal, even though virtually all my monthly stipend of 19 yuan goes on food.'

One survey of students who graduated in 1981 from seven industrial universities, mostly engineering institutions, revealed that some of them were in worse physical shape than when they'd commenced their studies. A greater proportion suffered nervous problems and chronic illnesses than newly enrolled students. The report blamed a combination of over-work and poor nutrition which was claimed to be at a lower level than in the mid-1960s, immediately before the Cultural Revolution.[1]

Many foreign students in China, keen to mix as freely as possible with their Chinese fellow-students, are deterred from eating in student canteens because of the poor food. 'I really tried,' said one English student at Peking University. 'But I simply got too rundown and kept catching colds and flu.'

The Chinese authorities invariably provide special eating facilities for foreign students where the food is reasonably nutritious, if not always appetising. Chinese students are not permitted – and could not afford – to share the foreigners' eating facilities but a few sometimes have the opportunity to share their superior living conditions: only two or three people to a room and access to hot water for showers and washing clothes for a couple of hours every day or every second day. 'It's the space and the hot water,' one Peking student told me. 'The temptation's too much for some people, even though they'd normally prefer to live with other Chinese students. Foreigners don't usually like to sleep after lunch and they stay up too late at night, especially French students. And we have to be particularly well-behaved and watch what we say if we live with a foreigner.'

Despite their cramped living conditions and frugal diet, Chinese students have to cope with a demanding study programme. The day normally begins at around 6 a.m., usually with the first bell of the day. Bells on many campuses tell

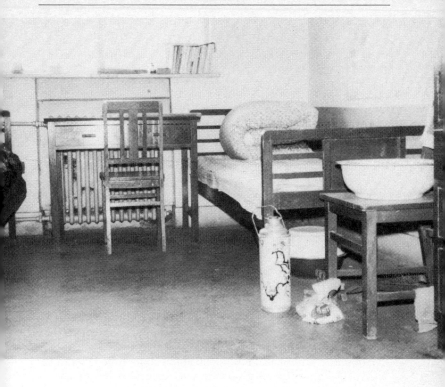

Spartan but superior: sharing a room with a foreign student has its attractions

students when to get up, when to have breakfast, when to go to class – right through to the 10 p.m. bell telling them it's time for bed. Some institutions still have regular loudspeaker broadcasts throughout the campus, beginning their ideological exhortations as early as 6.30 a.m. and continuing intermittently during lecture and meal breaks.

Classes are normally held six days a week, with none on Sunday. Attendance is compulsory and absentees lay themselves open to questioning and criticism. 'If you miss a class you'd better have a medical certificate and be in bed when a teacher comes around to the dormitory in the evening to check up on you,' commented one student at Peking University. 'Otherwise you might be reported to the administration.'

The classes themselves tend to be formal with little opportunity for general discussion. Even tutorials in the humanities often consist of series of prepared speeches with little interaction, an atmosphere hardly conducive to lively academic debate. In contrast to the anti-elitism of the Cultural Revolution period, when students were prompted to question and even criticize their teachers, the old Confucian tradition of respect for teachers has been thoroughly reinstated. 'But we decided not to make students stand up for lecturers when they enter the classroom,' one university academic told me.

Another Chinese academic who spent some time teaching at an Australian university said he was surprised by the casual attitude of his students towards class attendance, arriving late or sometimes not at all, and towards submitting written work on time. 'And they don't seem to have much respect for teachers,' he commented. 'They question teachers and argue with them quite openly, even in front of other students. This is very different from China, although I think perhaps our system is too rigid.'

For the unwary foreign academic in China the different practices can have disastrous results. An American lecturer at a prominent language institute was appalled when one student finally admitted half-way through the semester that virtually no one in the class had understood her somewhat rapid-fire, fragmented lectures on American literature.

'But why didn't someone say something earlier?' she protested. 'I always ask whether anyone has any questions.'

'You're a teacher and we didn't want to be impolite,' replied the student.

Much of the time not taken up with classes is spent studying either in the crowded dormitory or, if there's a seat available, in the university library. Some Chinese university libraries are theoretically on a par with the best in the world, at least in terms of their holdings. The Peking University library, for example, is one of China's largest with over 3 million volumes. But the amount of material available to students varies dramatically according to the current state of official censorship. Libraries normally have 'closed stacks': students are not permitted to peruse what is on the shelves but have to fill in request slips using information from the card catalogue. During the latter part of the Cultural Revolution the card catalogue at the Peking University library was minuscule, giving no indication of the library's huge holdings.

While students are expected to concentrate almost exclusively on their studies, some institutions have reintroduced a token amount of physical labour, usually no more than an hour or so a week. 'Many of our students come from privileged backgrounds and there's a danger they'll become too elitist and not be prepared to dirty their hands,' stated one university administrator. 'Anyway, they usually do general cleaning on the campus so it saves us paying extra people to do the work,' he added with a grin.

There has also been a revived emphasis in universities, as in high schools, on students' all-round fitness, both physical and mental. The report on the deterioration of student health complained about the effects of overwork: a general lack of physical fitness, including more eyesight problems, as well as tension and anxiety.[2] Regular participation in sporting activities is not just encouraged but is now compulsory on most campuses. In the late afternoon, basketball and volley-ball courts, football fields and table tennis rooms are all crowded. In warm weather, shuttlecocks fly through the air around student dormitories even as it gets dark.

Regular sporting contests are held both within and between universities, with star sportsmen and athletic no-hopers alike being urged, even cajoled, into participating. 'It's getting fit that's important, not winning,' declared one lecturer, uttering a revised version of the old Maoist slogan 'friendship first, competition second'.

Apart from sport, Chinese tertiary institutions lack the variety of extracurricular activities to which most Western students are accustomed. 'It's plain boring,' complained one frustrated American student. 'There's really nowhere on campus you can get together for a chat and a cup of tea – far less any Chinese equivalent of a coffee shop or bar. It's just studying, eating and sleeping. Mostly studying.'

University officials justify the lack of opportunities for socializing on the familiar grounds that students are at university to study, not to waste time enjoying themselves. As they point out, students do have the opportunity to participate in what are described as 'cultural activities': the occasional organized visit to a gymnastics display or a local opera. Most universities also have regular film screenings, especially on Saturday evenings when studying is over for the week. These are often held out of doors with students taking their own chairs and turning the sportsground into an instant cinema.

The popularity of the brief diversions from studying, eating and sleeping is apparent from the large numbers of people who roll up to the film screenings. Rugged up in padded jackets and gloves – even Canton can be chilly in late December – it was near impossible to find a place to deposit a small chair on the sportsground of the Canton Foreign Language Institute. Despite the biting wind, few students left before the end of the film, a dated and hardly gripping Japanese production about a bear-hunter.

Even more striking to anyone from a Western university is the lack of campus clubs and societies. There are virtually no hobby, drama or debating clubs, far less societies for such things as nuclear disarmament, women's rights or environmental protection. There is one political club, if that's what it can be called: the Communist Youth League. The youth wing of the Communist Party, the League spreads the current political message in schools, universities, factories and other work-places. Despite a high level of political cynicism among university students most students join the League – if they have not already done so at high school – to demonstrate their outward political compliance.

If life on campus seems to offer little excitement, there are few opportunities to go off campus. 'We don't really encourage students to leave the university during the week,' one university administrator told me. 'They don't have much time to spare.'

Perhaps it's no accident that many universities are sited a considerable distance from the city centre. The hub of Peking's tertiary institutions, including Peking and Qinghua Universities, is located not far from the Summer Palace on the northwest outskirts of the city, an hour and a half by bicycle or two bus changes from the centre. The pattern is repeated in many cities throughout China. While Canton's Foreign Language Institute is only about twenty minutes' bus ride from the city, the last bus arrives at the Institute at around 6.30 p.m.

Only Sunday presents the opportunity for some variety in the daily routine. Those students whose families live in the city where they study usually go home after class on Saturday. Others join the crowds to visit a local park, go shopping for soap, toothpaste or a new magazine, or perhaps just browse in the bookshops or do some window-shopping and look at the latest fashions.

Some stay on campus, avoiding the overcrowded buses and store queues. They play badminton, grab the opportunity to read a book unconnected with their studies, and catch up with washing both their clothes and their hair. By Sunday afternoon most dormitory washrooms or balconies are dripping with wet clothes. By Sunday evening other students have returned to the campus to organize themselves for a further week of studies, and then a further week: a routine that is broken only by the annual two-month summer vacation and the two-week winter one.

Even during their leisure time Chinese students face controls on their appearance and behaviour. Most institutions have fairly strict dress regulations even though students are, in any case, usually conservatively attired by Western standards. 'We expect students to look neat and tidy,' said an administrator at Anhui University in Hefei. 'We don't allow young men to wear bell-bottom trousers or grow their hair too long. And female students must not wear short skirts or have long unruly hair.'

In many universities young men are not permitted to grow moustaches, far less beards. 'These are bourgeois affectations and look untidy,' the administrator told me.

Students' personal relationships are also subject to official scrutiny, though not to the extent that they were a few years ago when even foreign students seen spending too much time together were formally criticized by university administrators or teachers.

'But we don't encourage the formation of relationships,' said an administrator at Harbin's teachers university. Students are, of course, expected to be thinking about their studies, not about love and romance. Those young people who do establish relationships often try to keep them quiet. 'It's amazing,' commented one former student, 'how just a few months before graduation young men and women start producing boyfriends and girlfriends and even agitating to get jobs in the same city.'

If the official attitude towards personal relationships is more relaxed than it was during the Cultural Revolution period, the marriage of undergraduates is strictly vetoed. In addition to the oft-repeated argument that students should be concentrating on their studies, not on personal matters, there is the practical problem of campus accommodation. When married students have attended university, as they did during the Cultural Revolution and in the first couple of years after the reorganization of the examination system, they normally lived in single-sex dormitories and went home only on Sunday.

'We don't have sufficient accommodation for married student couples to share a room,' said the Harbin administrator. 'They might find having to live in separate dormitories during the week rather difficult! Anyway, they'd be distracted from their studies.'

A further reason for not permitting undergraduate students to marry is that it would severely complicate the assignment process following their graduation because of pressures to assign couples to the same city or town. The separation of married couples is a volatile issue in China, creating considerable heartbreak and hostility.

Travelling by train from Peking to Shanghai, I talked to a young woman who was sobbing her heart out. Married only a few months, she had just been transferred to Shanghai while her husband had to remain in Peking, probably for the conceivable future. 'What's the point of being married if you can only see your husband for two weeks a year,' she spluttered.

In practice, the marriage veto on undergraduate students is not as harsh as it ostensibly seems. No one in China, especially in the cities, is supposed to get married before their mid-twenties because of the late marriage policy. The overwhelming majority of students enter university at seventeen or eighteen so, when they graduate four years later, marriage is still some way in the future. But with the maximum university entrance age set at twenty-five, there are always a few students in their mid-twenties. For young women, in particular, the decision to go to university at this age is not always an easy one. 'I had to think about it seriously, even though I was so excited about passing the entrance exam – at my fourth try,' said Zhang Huilu, an attractive 26-year-old student of English literature in Harbin. 'I'll be almost twenty-eight when I graduate. Most people in China marry in their mid-twenties and it's often difficult for a woman of twenty-eight to find a husband.'

Chinese university administrators are often surprised to hear of the lack of rules and rather free-wheeling atmosphere on most Western university campuses.

'You allow your students to have children – and even bring them onto the campus?' exclaimed one administrator. 'It can't be a very orderly environment.'

'But how do you discipline your students?' asked another administrator. 'We *need* to have rules to make sure that students study hard and behave properly.'

The Chinese concept of proper behaviour is undoubtedly a rather strict one. Most Chinese students appear striking compliant and obedient, even passive, in the face of regulations that horrify not just many Western students in China but some of those from other socialist and developing countries.

Appearances can sometimes be deceptive. Over the past few years Chinese universities have experienced a number of discipline problems, some serious even by Western standards, which partly reflect the general upsurge of unruly behaviour and youth crime.

Probably the major infringement has been theft, despite the habit of keeping bicycles and even cupboards and doors securely locked. The wave of consumerism has meant increased temptations on campus: digital watches, radio-cassette recorders, fashionable clothing, and even the extra food that more affluent students buy to compensate for their poor diet.

'We tend to have an occasional rash of thefts,' one university administrator told me. 'We warn foreign students in particular to keep all their things under lock and key. Otherwise the temptation is sometimes too great.'

The other major problem is physical violence. 'Fighting breaks out every now and again – among male students, not female,' said the same administrator. The major causes are short tempers brought about by intensive study and the frustration of living cheek by jowl with six or seven other people, not all of whom always want to study or go to sleep at the same time.

Serious differences even over fairly minor incidents have occasionally led to students being wounded, usually by stabbing. In 1981, for example, one otherwise promising student was expelled from Peking University for allegedly stabbing a fellow student 'without cause' (the wound must have been a fairly minor one as he was apparently not charged for the offence).[3]

Apart from severe infringements of discipline, there is also the occasional student who, having made it to university, decides to relax and coast along without over-exerting himself or herself. Another young man at Peking University who'd won a national mathematics contest at high school found after he commenced university that he preferred playing cards and chess to studying. Unlike most other disobedient students, he simply ignored his teachers' constant admonitions to attend class and twice failed his first year examinations.[4]

Discipline infringers are usually expelled, not just on account of their misbehaviour but also because they're regarded as divisive elements in an otherwise smoothly operating system. 'We just can't afford to have this sort of person living and studying with other young people,' one university administrator told me.

Few other Chinese students leave university once they have taken up their studies. Unlike Western countries, China doesn't have a dropout problem with students deciding they're tired of studying or they want to experience the real world. Tertiary education in China is too difficult to obtain, there's no second chance later in life, and it is seen as the only avenue to getting what most people want in life: a good job.

The second major hurdle, after actually getting into university, is obtaining that good job. University students are a favoured group compared not just with other young Chinese but even with fellow-graduates in many countries of the world: there is still basically no graduate unemployment in China. At the same time, Chinese graduates are not free to select their own jobs, or even their place of residence, but are assigned work in accordance with national needs.

As the final semester gets under way, there's only one question on everyone's mind: 'Where will I be assigned?' Rumours abound about various ministries needing or not needing a lot of graduates this year, about there being a shortage of secondary school-teachers in a particular region, and about whether or not the number of postgraduate students is going to be increased. The main topic of conversation in the student canteen switches temporarily from the day's food, or lack of it, to the question of jobs.

The preferences are well known. 'Nearly everyone wants to work in Peking or Shanghai, or at least in their home city or town where their family is,' said a final year science student at Peking University. 'The best jobs are those in the big central organizations. For example, scientists and engineers want to work in research institutes, not in factories or mines. There's a popular saying "a big unit in a big city".'

There was little hesitation when I asked a group of final year English language students in Canton where they'd like to be assigned. 'The diplomatic service, or foreign trade, or some other organization dealing with foreigners. There's more chance of advancement and also the opportunity to go overseas.'

'What about teaching?' I asked some other language students.

'Some of us would like to stay on at the Institute to teach or preferably do a postgraduate degree,' one student ventured. 'But none of us want to be school-teachers. Chances are you'll be stuck in the same school for life. The pay's low. And there's still the shadow of the Cultural Revolution when teachers were treated very badly by their students. It probably won't happen again, but who knows?'

Even for university graduates there's frequently a wide gap

between aspirations and opportunities. As in most countries, the big cities are best endowed with professional people, whether engineers, doctors or administrators. China currently has a great need for graduates to work outside the major urban centres and especially in the more remote provinces. This is part of the overall plan to modernize agriculture and develop heavy industry, including mining. With key high schools being concentrated in urban areas in the major provinces, few students have so far been enrolled from rural and border areas – and few urbanites want to go there.

'Most students' greatest fear is that they'll be sent somewhere like Tibet or Xinjiang,' another final year student told me. 'Officials are starting to stay that you have to stay there only a few years, then you can get a transfer. But up to now, once a person's assigned it's usually been for life. What guarantee is there you'll ever get back?'

With tertiary study being seen as one of the few avenues of escape from rural life, the government's current plan to enrol more students from areas where graduates are particularly needed seems unlikely to solve the problem. 'We former rural residents are particularly afraid we'll be sent back to the countryside,' commented one graduate. 'Many city people have only heard about the poor living conditions and boredom of life in small towns. But we've experienced them first hand. Who'd ever want to go back?'

The plum assignments usually go to graduates who have studied in the key universities and institutes and have already climbed a number of rungs of the elitist ladder. 'All my graduating class received good assignments in Peking,' said Zhang Ziyang, a recent graduate of the city's prestigious Foreign Language Institute who'd been assigned to the foreign relations section of the Academy of Social Sciences. 'My girl-friend's already got a job teaching English at the Institute. I expect she'll go to the States soon for graduate study.'

Many students are satisfied to hear that they have got a job, virtually any reasonable job, in a major urban centre. Not all are so lucky. 'Our major problem this year was a young man we assigned to Gansu province in the north-west,' said an adminis-trator of Anhui University in central China. 'His girlfriend lives here in Hefei and he wanted to get married. Maybe she could have transferred to Gansu – moving away from the major centres isn't usually too much of a problem – but she didn't want to go there either. It took us three months to persuade the young man to accept his assignment.'

'Persuade' is something of a euphemism. If graduates don't turn up at their assigned job within three months, they can be stripped of their university degrees and not be eligible for state employment for five years.

Shanghai graduates are usually the most intransigent. Living in China's largest and most sophisticated city, young Shanghainese think even of Peking as little more than a provincial backwater.

'Quite a few graduates simply refuse outright to leave Shanghai,' said one final year university student in the city, showing me a newspaper article complaining about the number of graduates who were dilly-dallying in taking up assignments. 'Some university graduates in Shanghai would rather get casual jobs than go out in the sticks.' In early 1984, six Shanghai graduates had their qualifications revoked for refusing to accept their official assignments. This was a warning, stated the *People's Daily*, to more than ninety other Shanghai graduates who had been assigned in the second half of 1983 but had so far failed to register at their designated workplaces.[5]

A few graduates simply disappear after receiving an undesirable assignment. Ren Zhenhua, a graduate of the Chengdu Geology College in Sichuan province, received the dreaded call to go to Tibet, though it was at least to a geological college in Lhasa, the capital. Reporting a month overdue, he decided that the job and the place were not what he wanted and simply went back to his home town in Sichuan. After being tracked down by the local Communist Party branch and receiving 'ideological education', he was ordered back to Lhasa. But he never turned up there. Even though the young man was qualified in a technological area considered vital to China's modernization, the authorities refused to budge and took away his graduate qualifications.[6]

'Obey your assignment made by the state. Go where your motherland needs you,' urges the Chinese media, publicizing cases such as that of Ren and accusing defaulters of ignoring organizational discipline and being unwilling to work in tough conditions.[7]

The media also holds up as models those graduates who apparently happily accept their provincial assignments and go off full of enthusiasm and determination to make their personal contribution to China's modernization. One Peking graduate had not only obeyed instructions to go to Tibet, reported a radio broadcast, but had ridden his bicycle there – a distance of around 4000 kilometres (2500 miles) – as an example to his fellow graduates. Other students were said to have volunteered, even before the end of their courses, to go wherever they were needed, whether it was Shanghai, Tibet or Xinjiang.

And a technology graduate wrote an article for the magazine *Chinese Women* proclaiming that she was actually knocking back the opportunity to do a postgraduate degree which would assure her of a prestigious job in a central scientific research organization. Even though her family and friends thought she was crazy, she intended taking up a job in a factory in Gansu's capital, Lanzhou, because of the dire shortage there of trained personnel. Lanzhou is hardly considered a desirable assignment by most Peking graduates, let alone someone with an excellent record from the nation's top technological institution, Qinghua University.[8]

Despite media pressure, few graduates are prepared to forego a prestigious job and comfortable lifestyle in the interests of making a greater contribution to China's modernization. Youthful idealism has undergone a drastic decline since the 1950s and early 1960s when some young people did respond enthusiastically to official calls for personal sacrifice in order to build a modernized China. The political turnaround after the Cultural Revolution and the present level of official privilege and corruption have made young people cynical of media rhetoric. 'Why should we listen to officials telling us to go off and face hardships when most of them continue to sit here in Peking enjoying all their perks,' commented one recent graduate.

Any suggestions of idealism are usually quickly squashed by parents, keen to see their offspring established in privileged urban jobs. After their own sufferings in the Cultural Revolution, intellectuals and professionals in particular have little time for official exhortations about self-sacrifice.

Indeed the authorities see parents as a major stumbling block in carrying out the assignment process. As the final year class of 1983 was about to graduate, the Minister for Education sent an open letter to parents of graduating students throughout China entitled 'Let your children go wherever the motherland needs them most to put their abilities to good use.' The letter urged parents not to oppose the assignment of their children to distant or difficult jobs. 'If we really love our children,' it maintained, 'we should let them go among the masses of the people and into the practice of production.'[9]

Chinese students do not regard a good assignment merely as a matter of luck. 'Of course we work hard at university,' said one second year languages student when I mentioned that Chinese students often seemed to be rather more conscientious than their Western counterparts. 'We need good grades to get a good assignment. The pace really intensifies in third and fourth year.'

In addition to the battle for good grades, it is well known that it's essential not to rock the political boat during one's time at university. Despite their general cynicism about socialism, university students were conspicuously absent from the Democracy Movement in 1978–9. Unlike the activist members of the 'lost generation', they no doubt considered they had too much at stake. As anticipated, harsh assignments were handed out to those students who protested over an alleged rigged election at Hunan Teachers' College in Changsha in 1980 and to Peking University students who published some unofficial literature a year later.

University administrators do not deny that they take students' political attitudes into account when they allocate assignments. 'We look at their all-round performance,' said one administrator. 'Just as we do when we enrol students in the first place.'

There is a further way of getting a good assignment, just as there is of getting into university in the first place: through having the right connections. When the first students enrolled under the new examination system graduated in 1981, there was widespread corruption in allocating jobs. 'It didn't really matter how good your examination results were,' confirmed a Shanghai graduate. 'The student in our class who got the best assignment was a long way from the top of the class. His father just happened to be a high official at the university.'

Although leading Party officials had never been completely immune from exerting their influence in obtaining special consideration for their own offspring, especially in the awarding of overseas scholarships, the extent of malpractice that year threatened to undermine confidence in the entire university system. The Central Government put the matter in the hands of special discipline inspection committees, then conducting an onslaught against official corruption over a wide front, which issued detailed circulars prohibiting interference in graduate assignment.

Individual institutions also released their own assignment regulations. Those issued by Nanjing University, one of the most prestigious universities, gave some idea of the range of malpractice. 'All graduates must be treated equally ... the children of leading cadres and of the masses, as well as the children of university staff members. Personnel responsible for assigning jobs to graduates are not allowed to promise rewards, give warnings, pass on informal notes or disclose information regarding the assignment of students. They are strictly forbidden to accept gifts and bribes.'[10]

Practical steps taken to prevent malpractice have included the inspection of assignment records by Party discipline committees and assignment following consultation among a number of university administrators.

'We practise the system of assignment by collective discussion,' said an administrator at Anhui University in Hefei. 'We're always on the lookout for any signs of favouritism. For example, I would question a mediocre student being assigned to a top government ministry.'

If one avenue to obtaining preferential assignments has been partially closed, another may well have been opened, reflecting the general conflict between maintaining centralized labour control and modernizing the country. In 1983 a pilot scheme was introduced at four key universities – in Peking, Shanghai, Xi'an and Tianjin – for the assignment of graduates through direct contact between universities and organizations requiring more staff. Instead of placing their request for new employees with the Labour Ministry, which subsequently approached the Education Ministry, employers were to be permitted to contact the four universities and even individual students direct. This procedure had been vehemently denounced as a 'backdoor' activity when it was undertaken informally during 1982.

The adoption of the scheme followed regular complaints about the misemployment of many graduates. One survey revealed that about one-third of 1981's graduates of Shanghai's Communications University and of social sciences at Tianjin's Nankai University had been assigned jobs unrelated to their field of specialization. There were computer science graduates employed as printing workers, refrigeration technology graduates working in hotels and cigarette factories, and social science graduates working as truck drivers. According to the survey report, it was extremely difficult for graduates to obtain a transfer once they had been assigned to a job, regardless of whether it was relevant to their training.[11] 'It's really most distressing,' one former student wrote to Shanghai's Communications University. 'When I was at university I studied hard night and day. I didn't expect to discover immediately after I'd taken up the post that the job was not suited to my special training. I've reported the situation many times, but the problem remains unsolved.'[12]

Needless to say the pilot scheme has been welcomed by students, both those who mistrust the unwieldy bureaucratic network and those who have family connections in favoured organizations. 'The authorities are fighting a losing battle against the use of connections in university assignment,' a Peking graduate told me. 'A strongly centralized system simply doesn't work. Family connections and influence have always been an important way of getting things done in China. It's just unfortunate for those people who don't have any.'

From school to university to a good assignment: the pathway to success is fraught with competition and personal drama for young people in China and abounds with elitism and opportunities for the exercise of privilege and influence. The stakes are high. As one 16-year-old high school student put it: 'It's a period of only four or five years. But it determines the rest of our lives.'

The boredom of unskilled work: senior high school graduates as shop assistants

CHAPTER SIX

'Waiting for Employment'

'We don't need only university graduates for our nation's modernization,' proclaimed the official youth magazine, *Chinese Youth*. 'Even young people who fail to qualify for university and participate directly in socialist construction have a bright future.'[1]

Wang Biwei, a 17-year-old waitress in a Harbin hotel restaurant, was not convinced by such words of attempted reassurance. 'What's sweeping floors and dishing out dumplings doing for China's modernization?' she asked. 'I'll probably be stuck here for ever, just because I didn't pass the university entrance exam.'

One of the most striking features of personal encounters in China is the large number of well-educated young people, mostly senior high school graduates, whom one meets doing unskilled or semi-skilled work in hotels, stores and factories. Intelligent, alert and highly articulate, they are victims of the lack of diversification of China's economy and represent a huge pool of disillusionment in a country that is supposed to hold so much promise for young people.

Along with less well-educated teenagers, many show little interest in their work. A national survey on youth employment undertaken by the Youth Research Institute in 1981–2 reported a general laxity of labour discipline among young people, poor quality work, rising factory accidents and falling labour productivity. 'Some young people view their jobs merely as positions to earn money,' the survey concluded.[2] This finding is only confirmed by the comments of many individual young workers. As one female sales assistant put it: 'The job's boring.

All most of us think about during the day is getting off work and going out to enjoy ourselves.'

For those young people who have been to vocational schools, rather than regular senior high schools, the prospects of a reasonably satisfying job are somewhat brighter. But despite government control of both education and employment, manpower planning continues to be woefully inadequate and there is not always a correlation between the skills being taught and those needed in the workforce. Some of the 1981 graduates of Hangzhou's vocational schools, for example, found that the areas in which they had obtained their qualifications – including mechanical drawing, accountancy and electromechanics – did not even correspond to the job recruitment categories of government departments, factories and other organizations. As a result, they were treated in the same fashion as other candidates for jobs and had to take the standard recruitment tests.

'Often the Education Ministry and the schools have no idea which specialized subjects need to be offered and developed,' declared the *People's Daily* in an article on the situation in Hangzhou, delivering a strong attack on continuing bureaucratic ineptitude and complacency in the educational system.[3]

The general mismatch between employment opportunities and education in both regular and vocational schools was at the crux of the Youth Research Institute's report on youth employment. 'The lack of co-ordination between secondary education and the requirements for economic development has become more serious than ever,' it complained, adding that it was unlikely that the contradiction would be speedily resolved.[4]

Although some young people see little way out of their predicament and concentrate on making the most of their time away from work, others have a driving ambition to improve their lot as they serve out dumplings, clean machinery or serve shop customers. Encouraged by the government's constant admonitions to educate themselves further through 'self-study', they spend much of their spare time, sometimes even their working hours, absorbed in textbooks.

Once they take up full-time employment most teenagers have given up the idea of getting into regular universities. But there's a growing variety of alternative higher education available. Some of the most industrious young people attend the so-called spare-time universities: a gruelling four or five evenings a week for classes alone for a period of five years or more, on top of their six-day working week. Others do correspondence courses, offered by some seventy universities, or enrol in the radio and television universities which now have twice as many students as the regular universities.

While the range of alternative institutions is impressive, their status is lower than that of universities and the completion of a course is no guarantee of finding satisfying employment. When the first intake of students at the Central Radio and Television University graduated in 1982, they mostly had the choice of going to border regions or, in the words of the authorities, 'finding their own jobs'.[5] Despite China's proclaimed need for more professional experts, that need is limited in the major urban areas where most young people want to live, as even regular university graduates quickly find out. It is also skewed in terms of demands for certain skills, such as agricultural and mining technology which are themselves non-urban occupations.

Other young people, both senior and junior high school graduates, attend spare-time classes in everything from technical subjects to foreign languages. The study of English, officially considered vital for China's modernization, became a virtual obsession when China reopened its doors to the West in the late 1970s. 'I have to work most evenings,' a young hotel employee in Hefei told me. 'So I go to class at 7 a.m., four mornings a week.'

The media publishes success stories of young people who have bettered themselves by attending classes or by studying at home by themselves: the ordinary factory worker who eventually became an engineer and the high school graduate who studied solar energy by himself for seven years and built a high-temperature furnace.

'A survey of 400 famous scientists has found that 54 per cent of them did not go to university but succeeded through self-study,' declared a somewhat unrealistic article urging young people not to be deterred by a lack of opportunity for formal higher education.[6]

In reality, the familiar bugbear of bureaucratic inflexibility often makes it difficult for young people to change their jobs, even within the same organization. There are frequent complaints in youth newspapers and magazines that, in spite of lengthy periods of private study, no one seems to want to know about added qualifications and skills.

When it comes to everyday work, there are jobs and jobs, even if many of them are considered boring. Although young people in the countryside are absorbed fairly easily into the rural workforce, those in cities and towns face a competitive selection process just to obtain unskilled or semi-skilled employment. The system of labour allocation is less rigid than that for university graduates, with young people not so much being assigned particular jobs as applying for them through their local labour bureau or neighbourhood committee, the basic unit of urban administration in China. Most recruiting organizations, including banks, factories and hotels, have their own entrance tests.

According to an official of the Yan'an Road Central neighbourhood committee in Shanghai, some of the most popular jobs are those in hotels, stores and other organizations catering especially for foreign visitors. Since China reopened its doors to the West, these have been a burgeoning source of employment for recent school-leavers. 'They have a spacious and even luxurious environment compared with most Chinese establishments,' he said. 'In addition, they often provide smart clothing and good meals. And the work tends to be fairly light.'

'So far as ordinary jobs go it's not bad at all,' smiled Wang Hanli, a handsome bright-eyed senior high school graduate working in Harbin's International Hotel. Wang's main job is to do what elderly women on each floor of many Russian and other European hotels do: hand out room keys and keep an eye on guests' comings and goings. While many young people in these jobs idle the day away reading popular magazines and even listening to music through headphones, Wang spends much of his time concentrating on his English language textbooks. 'I have plenty of time to study,' he told me, adding hopefully: 'Perhaps when my English is good enough I'll be able to get a job looking after foreign visitors.'

Other jobs in the service sector, whether in regular hotels, stores or restaurants, are seen in a rather different light, lacking both the pleasant environment and the perks of foreigners' establishments. They are not generally as popular as clerical work, still a major employer in China's pre-computer administrative network. (Cautious bank tellers often check their adding machine calculations on an abacus.)

Factory jobs generally tend to be farther down the popularity ladder, despite the financial attraction of bonus incentives. The reason is not just the nature of the work but the social stigma attached to 'blue collar' (in China blue denim overalls) jobs by young people who have completed a high school education, particularly if their family background is a professional one. Among the least popular of all jobs, according to the neighbourhood committee official in Shanghai, are not surprisingly the dirty noisy jobs in heavy industry, the crux of China's modernization.

'We have trouble getting young people to settle for these jobs,' he said. 'Young women in particular – they don't want to get dirty. Some school-leavers, especially those with better-off parents, simply refuse to apply for tough factory jobs and hang around for ages hoping that something better will turn up.'

Even some young people with dirty noisy factory jobs think they are comparatively well off compared with their fellow youth who don't have jobs at all and who face an even wider gap between their aspirations and opportunities.

'We don't have unemployed youth in China the way you do in capitalist countries,' a senior Communist Youth League official told me solemnly in Peking. 'We have awaiting employment youth,' he added predictably, using the expression familiar to readers of Chinese newspapers and academic journals. In theory at least, 'awaiting employment' is an accurate description because it is basically only school-leavers who currently lack jobs.

The problem, whatever one calls it, is not a new one for China. Finding jobs for young urban people has been particularly difficult since the 1960s when, because of the increasing birthrate in the post-1949 years, the number of school-leavers began outstripping the demand for new workers. During the Cultural Revolution decade the problem was overcome by sending many urban school-leavers to the countryside where, along with rural youth, they could more readily be absorbed into the labour force. The programme, usually somewhat

Well-educated young woman as factory worker

romantically translated into English as the 'rustication of youth', not only alleviated potential urban unemployment but fitted in with Mao's basic policy of attempting to break down social differences in China – between urban and rural areas, and between mental and manual labour.

The major feature of the programme was its unpopularity. School-leavers, especially in major urban centres like Shanghai and Peking, wanted to do anything but be rusticated: living in primitive rural conditions, probably without running water, having to do tough manual labour usually without the assistance of mechanized farm equipment, and being isolated from the attractions of big city life. The peasantry were equally unreceptive, regarding the intruders as soft city slickers who were ignorant of thousands of years of farming wisdom and unused to back-breaking agricultural labour.

China's post-Mao leadership eventually brought a halt to the rustication policy and promised those educated youth who had been sent to rural areas – some 17 million in all – that they would be able to return to their former homes. The official plan for their gradual reabsorption into urban life was upset by their impatience to get away from the countryside. Some had already returned illegally, living with their families without proper registration. In 1979, thousands of young people who had visited Shanghai to spend Chinese New Year with their relatives refused outright to go back to distant provinces such as Xinjiang and Yunnan. Following a series of meetings and rallies, on 5 February they marched to the Shanghai Railway Station and simply lay down on the tracks, disrupting rail transport in and out of Shanghai for some twelve hours.

The ending of the rustication policy created a huge employment problem, with work having to be found both for the returnees and for each new crop of urban school-leavers. Because of the relatively advanced age of rusticated youth – some were in their mid or late twenties – they often received preference in employment, arousing the anger of fresh school-leavers who had been told that they were in the forefront of China's modernization. When 25 000 demobilized soldiers were also given preferential employment in Shanghai in early 1982, over 500 young people staged a sit-down demonstration in one of the city's main government buildings. Twenty were arrested before the demonstrators were dispersed.

Although the youth employment situation improved some-what in the early 1980s, the problem has been a continuing one as 5 to 6 million fresh school-leavers come on to the urban employment market each year. In a confidential report to high Party officials written in March 1982, Party Secretary Hu Yaobang put the total number of young people 'awaiting employment' at 14 million.[7]

Youth employment 'is a social problem on which the eyes of the whole country are fixed,' wrote the Communist Youth League secretary of Gansu province at around the same time. 'The number, the degree of influence and the extent of involvement have all reached the point where they can no longer be avoided or overlooked. How this problem is going to be solved directly concerns the immediate interests of thou-sands of households, the growth of a whole generation of youths, and the stability and unity of the whole society.'[8]

A few newspaper articles have recently claimed that the problem has now largely been overcome but private and some official sources, as well as special advice books for young people, reveal a rather different picture.

'When people leave school it's often a matter of waiting one or two years, sometimes even three years, for a job,' claimed one recent Shanghai school-leaver. And in Peking it was not until March 1983 that the backlog of young people who had left school in mid-1981 and earlier had been cleared.[9] On a national level, a report issued by the Labour Ministry stated that by September 1982 some twenty-four out of China's twenty-nine provinces had found jobs for almost all young people who had been seeking work since *before* 1980. The remaining five prov-inces expected to achieve this target only in 1985, it admitted.[10]

Young people without jobs in China are sometimes even worse off than their Western counterparts. With no unemploy-ment benefits, they are completely dependent on their families. Many Chinese parents have little sympathy for their unem-ployed offspring, sometimes blaming them for their predica-ment, and Chinese society as a whole shares with many coun-tries the tendency to regard unemployed people as second-class citizens. As one disgruntled young man in Shanghai com-plained: 'I'm generally looked down on wherever I go, just because I can't get work.'

Like unemployed youth all over the world, young Chinese without jobs often develop feelings of personal worthlessness and hopelessness about life in general. One desperate young man in the northern city of Taiyuan put his feelings in a letter to his local Communist Youth League: 'I've spent springs and autumns depending on my old parents for a living. Youth is dying. Time is flying. Years pass away just like the spring waters down the river.'[11]

Some young people express resentment when their fellow-youth jump the employment queue. In addition to the continuing problem of 'backdoor' entry into employment through parental connections, there is the officially endorsed 'substitution system' whereby enterprises provide a job for the son or daughter of an employee who retires. Because of the youth employment problem, parents of pre-retirement age (sixty for men, fifty-five for women) have recently been encouraged by their employers to make way for the younger person.

The practice of keeping jobs in the family – not necessarily the same job but employment in the same enterprise – often means the employment of school-leavers with few or no skills ahead of better qualified young people, especially graduates of vocational schools. According to the Youth Research Institute's 1981–2 report on youth employment, the practice has the effect of inhibiting some youngsters from studying hard even while they are still at school. 'Competing to be a good student is considered a waste of time . . . many high school students think that what counts is good parents.'[12]

The government's constant reassurances to young people that they are not unemployed, simply 'awaiting employment', only create further antagonism. This was graphically illustrated in a letter sent by seven young Wuhan residents to a Peking newspaper. 'It is a matter of rejoicing,' they wrote sarcastically, 'that the beautiful description "young people awaiting employment" serves to cover up the ugly side of our lives just as the fashionable dresses of Paris beautify the wearers. We cannot help appreciating this charming name. We recommend that the creator should be given an award.'

On a deadly serious note they added: 'For living people, there is no greater suffering than that of living as parasites on society.'[13]

The Chinese authorities have been making sustained efforts to overcome the youth employment problem. This has not been easy because of their efforts to rationalize the economy by closing down inefficient enterprises and cutting the number of employees in the unwieldy bureaucracy. The past few years have seen less and less room for new workers in the state economic sector, the conventional employer in a socialist economy. In 1980 it absorbed some 40 per cent of all new workers, in 1981 just under 30 per cent and in 1982 barely 20 per cent.

Youth unemployment has been attacked by finding and creating jobs outside the planned economy in accordance with the new three-part economic structure: state, collective and private. Denounced as bourgeois and individualistic during periods of ideological extremism, most notably in the Cultural Revolution, the non-state sectors were revived in 1978. The basic rationale for this apparently non-socialist economic policy has been the need to boost production and improve services by encouraging individual enterprise and initiative, as well as providing the much-needed jobs.

Besides urging young people to establish collectives and private enterprises, the authorities have been helping to provide youth with some of the practical skills necessary for success. Labour service companies, set up on a district or neighbourhood basis, offer courses in subjects ranging from accounting and tailoring to electrical appliance repair and cookery.

The government has also permitted the setting up of private training schools. Staffed mainly by retired people and others who lack regular jobs – they often ran such institutions before they were banned in the mid-1960s – these schools charge students about 1 jiao (5 cents or 3 p.) an hour for tuition. Peking alone has over fifty training schools, including tailoring, photography, typing, foreign languages and hairdressing. The Peace School of Tailoring, for example, guarantees students that they will learn to cut out and make forty different styles of clothing during their three-month course; if the guarantee is not fulfilled students are entitled to stay on at the school tuition-free. Graduates of these schools have been in the forefront of new participants in collective and private enterprises.

By 1983 the collective sector employed some 28 million people, of whom 17 million were officially described as 'young people'. Often organized semi-officially by the labour service companies, collectives can borrow money from the government at about 5 per cent interest in order to get themselves established and are generally exempt from taxation for the first three years. Profits are distributed according to the amount of work done by individual members. Wages vary: some are below or barely on a par with those in the state sector, others are considerably higher.

A growing range of collectives provide services and produce goods that have always been difficult to obtain or in short supply. Food and drink come near the top of the list. One of the most successful and widely publicized collectives has been the Qianmen Tea and Pastries Cooperative, set up by thirteen unemployed young people in 1979 to sell tea, pastries and ice cream in one of Peking's busiest shopping districts. By 1982 the co-operative had nine retail outlets, a wholesale department and a monthly turnover of 1.4 million yuan. Its 236 workers earned an above-average salary of 60–70 yuan a month. On a smaller scale are many collectively run restaurants and cafes. One group of enterprising young people set up the Twilight Cafe on the north-west outskirts of Peking, not far from the Peking Language Institute.

The manufacture of clothing and knitwear is another favourite collective activity as people clamour for more style and variety in their dress. The demand for household furniture has spawned collectives producing everything from basic chairs and vinyl-covered two-seater settees – a current vogue throughout China – to top-of-the-market double bed, wardrobe and dressing table ensembles.

And there are gimmicks and toys. In Shanghai I met a group of ten young women in their late teens, all senior high school graduates, who had formed a collective to make colourful dolls. With Western features, blonde hair and wearing lots of bright blue and pink lace and tulle, the dolls sold for the rather high price of 8 yuan. The young women earned 80–90 yuan each a month, almost twice what they would receive in an unskilled state job. 'The dolls are quite expensive but they're in great demand by newly-weds to decorate their bedrooms,' one of the young women told me.

Private enterprises are still in their infancy, with a total official participation of around 2 million. (The actual numbers are probably much larger because, as the press complains, many people simply engage in business without an official licence.) These enterprises are normally self-financed, giving the usual advantages to young people from more affluent families. Some are run as family ventures and are permitted to employ a few apprentices in addition to family members.

Along with collectives, private enterprises have changed the face of Chinese cities and towns. Over half of all private entrepreneurs are engaged in what is described as 'commerce': basically buying and selling everything from clothing and shoes to pot plants and goldfish, usually in a street or private market area specially set aside for the purpose. Food stalls sell noodles, dumplings, beancurd and a variety of quick-fry specialities. Like their counterparts throughout Asia, they provoke some concern from the authorities because of hygiene problems, especially the disposal of waste, although they often appear much cleaner and more orderly than the state-run cafes.

Probably the greatest scope exists for repair services for the growing range of consumer goods: watches, electric fans and rice cookers, as well as television sets, washing machines and refrigerators. China's rising standard of living is also symbolized by the virtual army of shoe repairers who provide a while-you-wait service as they sit on tiny stools behind an array of artificial leather soles and heels.

Other private entrepreneurs have more substantial investments. In Harbin's private market I chatted with 20-year-old Chen Gaoli who owns a large book kiosk, more like a small bookstore, which he had built with capital provided by his parents. Taking advantage of young people's obsession with learning English, Chen had stocked his store with dictionaries, English language textbooks and language cassettes. But his chief money-maker, he told me, was his Remington portable typewriter, bought for him on the private market in Canton at the inflated price of 400 yuan.

'A lot of young people in Harbin want to study overseas so they ask me to translate and type letters for them to foreign universities, especially in America,' said Chen. He had learnt English by going to evening classes and listening to the Voice of America and Radio Australia. If his translations would hardly

宏业外文资料综合服务部

Chen Gaoli with his parents outside his private bookstore

impress most Western university administrators, his young clients – paying 1 yuan a page for his services – were not to know this.

Chen told me his average monthly profit was an immense 300 yuan, four or five times what he would earn in a factory.

'Two years ago I was waiting for work. Now I'm a very rich young man,' he said proudly. 'I've got a Sony stereo cassette recorder – it cost 700 yuan. And I've just bought this,' he added, pointing to the shiny motor-bike, the latest Shanghai model, standing in the corner of the store. 'It cost over 2000 yuan but I'm the envy of almost every young man in Harbin.'

'What do the authorities think of your wealth?' I asked. 'Don't they disapprove?'

'Not at all,' replied Chen, pulling down a scrapbook of newspaper and magazine cuttings. He had already had his photograph and stories about his initiative and enterprise in a number of local papers and even in the national youth magazine *Chinese Youth*. 'What's more, I've been invited to the next Youth League Congress in Peking, as an example of how young people can help overcome the employment problem.'

Despite the substantial profits being made by some young people in collectives and private enterprises, there is still reluctance on the part of many, as there was in the early 1960s, to do this type of work. The non-state sectors are seen as lacking security, medical and retirement benefits, and even social respectability.

'Some people think that only working in a state enterprise is real employment,' reported a Party secretary in Heilongjiang province. 'They think that working in collectively run enterprises is semi-employment and engaging in private household occupations is no employment at all.'[14] And, according to one despondent 'awaiting employment' young man in Hefei, 'most Chinese girls want boyfriends and potential husbands with real jobs.'

As past experience has shown, non-state jobs are also extremely vulnerable to changes in the political wind. The existence or otherwise of any form of private economic activity has been yet another barometer of ideological intensity ever since the establishment of the People's Republic.

Even less popular are the temporary jobs, which tend to distort official employment statistics. For 1.5 yuan a day, about half a basic factory wage, unemployed young people can some-times pick up a few weeks' work in factories and other enter-prises during particularly busy periods. In a bid to keep their unemployed youth out of mischief and to provide additional local services, some neighbourhoods organize youth service teams to do everything from delivering coal to shopping, household maintenance, washing, cleaning and looking after children for busy professional couples and elderly or incapaci-tated people. 'I know there's a big need for this sort of thing,' commented one Shanghai teenager. 'But people often can't afford to pay much. And you'd hardly call it a substitute for a real job.'

The authorities are doing their best to promote confidence in the collective and private sectors as genuine alternatives to state employment. 'Every job that benefits the country and the people is to be respected,' declared Party Secretary Hu Yaobang in August 1983 at a conference commending pace-setters in the non-state sectors.[15] The media publicizes individual success stories such as the Qianmen Tea and Pastries Co-operative and the young bookseller in Harbin, stressing that many of these young entrepreneurs are earning even more than they would be if they had state jobs.

Such publicity can sometimes be a trifle too effective, reflect-ing the basic dilemma of having private economic activity within a society attempting to inculcate communal socialist values. It only increases the characteristics of individualism and pursuit of private gain, not to mention outright capitalist tendencies, that the media already complains about. Checks of business licences which control the level of private econ-omic activity usually reveal a substantial number of illegal operators. In one crackdown in 1983, over 2500 unlicensed retailers were discovered in Shanghai. In the Chongwen district of central Peking alone, 279 individual retailers were found to be unlicensed. Of these, 115 already had regular employment and were attempting to make a bit of money on the side, often by taking unlawful absences from their jobs.

A more problematic issue is that of moonlighting: indulging in private enterprise activities either on one's day off or outside working hours. In Jiang Zilong's short story 'All the Colours of the Rainbow', two young male factory workers create a great deal of disputation when they make and sell pancakes outside the factory gates as their fellow-workers arrive for work each morning.

Other ambitious private entrepreneurs include high school students who, not expecting to pass the university entrance examination, drop out before graduation to try their hand at business of one kind or another. As the press complains, the practice extends to students in more junior classes who play truant from school for the same purpose.

'Aren't you still at school?' I asked a youthful-looking thirteen- or fourteen-year-old selling second-hand magazines in the early afternoon in the coastal city of Xiamen.

'Oh yes, some of the time,' he replied cheekily.

Other young people venture beyond legal or quasi-legal enterprises into making a 'fast buck'. As one young man touting tickets outside a Shanghai theatre put it: 'Everyone's making money one way or another.' A favourite activity is to buy up goods that are in short supply – from nylon stockings to leather boots and saucepans – and resell them at inflated prices. With unemployed young people generally having no money of their own, such speculative activities often have the backing of parents or relatives.

So too do the provision of private services. 'My dad's a driver for a factory and it's his day off,' said a young man who runs a profitable enterprise, on just one day a week, operating a private taxi service for frustrated queuers at Peking Railway Station. 'The car's not a problem,' he explained. 'The petrol's a bit difficult to get hold of, but you can get almost anything you want in Peking through the backdoor.'

Despite the convenience, I said I thought 8 yuan for a taxi ride that normally cost 3 yuan was a bit excessive.

'I'd usually charge about 5 yuan – but foreigners don't normally know the difference,' he said grinning.

The success of some youthful entrepreneurs, who flaunt their new-found wealth in huge radio-cassette recorders, motor-bikes and fashionable clothing, is only provoking resentment from those unemployed young people who lack entrepreneurial talents or access to private capital.

As a young man outside Chen's book kiosk in Harbin put it: 'It's all right for some. But where would I get that sort of capital? My parents don't earn much money and they have to support both me and my brother because neither of us have jobs.'

So while the authorities are assuaging the discontent of some of the potentially most disaffected sections of urban youth, they do so only by fomenting further discontent on the part of those who are still missing out.

CHAPTER SEVEN

From Feminism to Femininity?

'We need to utilize the talents and abilities of all young people if China's modernization programme is to be successful,' declared a Communist Youth League official in Shanghai. 'Females as well as males.' In theory, it seemed that the present generation of young Chinese women might move even closer to equality with men as the nation's drive for modernization got under way in the late 1970s. Perhaps, as Mao had promised, women would finally 'hold up half the sky'.

Few people would disagree, of course, that the position of young women in China was already very different from what it had been in traditional times. While feminist historians point to the lack of rights enjoyed by Western women in earlier decades and centuries, the status of women in Confucian China was even lower, probably comparable only to that of women in Muslim countries.

'How sad it is to be a woman! Nothing on earth is held so cheap,' Chinese poet Fu Xuan had written in the third century BC. 'No one is glad when a girl is born. By her the family sets no store.'[1]

As she grew up, the Chinese girl quickly became aware of the reality of the Confucian precept 'males are honourable, females are inferior'. The life of a female was governed by the three obediences: first to her father, then to her husband, then – if her husband died – to her eldest son. Her major role in the patri-archal system was to produce sons to perpetuate the male line.

The woman's social role was non-existent. The ideal situation, not always adhered to in poor peasant families, was her seclusion indoors where she attended purely to domestic matters. 'We were not allowed, my sister and I, on the street after we were thirteen,' recalled a woman raised in a modest family in Shandong province in the late nineteenth century.[2] This lack of social participation was reinforced by many a popular expression: 'A woman without talent is virtuous'; 'an educated woman is bound to cause trouble'; 'women should not meddle in politics'.

Of course the lives of women in traditional China varied considerably over the period of more than 2000 years, and also according to their geographical location and social class. Some women eventually exerted considerable power within their own families, although it was often at the expense of another woman – their daughter-in-law. And one should not forget that China produced a few all-powerful women: the notorious Empress Wu in the seventh century and the almost equally notorious Dowager Empress in the late nineteenth century. Overall though, women were not only outsiders in the patriarchal family system but had little opportunity to venture beyond that system.

'Women never go anywhere to speak of, and live the existence of a frog in a well,' a foreign missionary observed in the late nineteenth century.[3]

The altered status of Chinese women today cannot be attributed solely to the Communists, as they themselves like to maintain. Changes in the early twentieth century were initiated by Western missionaries and general ideas of female emancipation coming from the West. Ibsen's Nora was an inspiration and model for many 'modern young women' of the era: upper-class urban women who insisted on being educated and who became China's first female teachers, doctors and even bankers.

But it was only with the advent of communist power that ideas of male–female equality spread among other classes and also to rural areas. One of the Communists' first actions after establishing a national government in 1949 was to renounce the old Confucian ideas and officially guarantee women equality with men in all spheres of life, including the socio-economic and domestic spheres. The basic road to equality was to be through their participation in the workforce in accordance with Engels' theory that 'the emancipation of women will only be possible when women can take part in production on a large social scale.'[4] Once this happened, it was assumed that changes in other areas of life, including the family, would occur naturally.

By the end of the Mao era, the official attack on Confucian attitudes, together with increased female participation in education and the workforce, had brought about dramatic changes in women's lives. But 2000 years of tradition could not be wiped out in a single generation. Although the Chinese media in the mid-1970s made much of China's women engineers, doctors, train drivers and powerline workers, women still had a long way to go, both in achieving socio-economic equality and on the domestic front. 'The unfinished liberation of Chinese women' was how one Western writer described the progress of women in China up to 1980.[5]

Despite continuing official guarantees of male–female equality and the declared need to utilize all available talent for modernization, young women are still missing out on playing anywhere near an equal role in Chinese life. Indeed the situation of Chinese women bears striking resemblances not just to that of their Western sisters but also to young women in other socialist countries such as the Soviet Union. This gives some credence to the feminist argument that sexism is older than political systems and that socialist revolution is not a sufficient condition for female liberation.

In China, as in many countries, young women come off second best both in obtaining the education vital for full participation in society and in securing either professional or unskilled employment. 'At the present time males are about three times as likely as females to get a higher education,' a Women's Federation official complained to me in Peking. In 1982 the female proportion of all tertiary students was 26.2 per cent, hardly striking compared with the 1951 figure of 19.8 per cent. If the number of young Chinese obtaining a teritary education is fairly low overall, therefore, the number of females is minuscule: about three in a thousand.

'Young women are playing even less of a role in the top universities and in the subjects of vital importance to modernization,' the Women's Federation official added. While females represent up to 50 per cent of students at some of the low-status teachers' colleges, they form only 16.5 per cent of students at

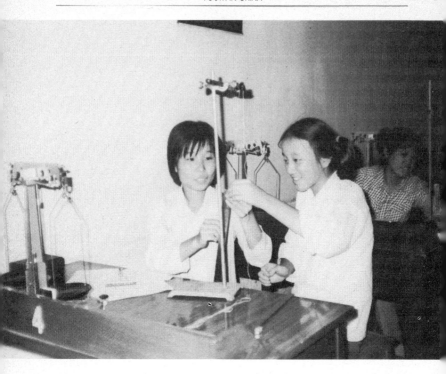

Female high school students studying science: the odds are against them proceeding much further with their studies

the nation's top technological institution, Qinghua University in Peking.

The differences seem to be even greater at the graduate level. In late 1982, the prestigious China University for Science and Technology, the training ground for the Chinese Academy of Sciences, sent seventy-two students to the United States to do PhD degrees. I asked one of the university's administrators how many were female. 'Three', he replied. And China's first group of eighteen PhD graduates, who received their degrees in May 1983, included only one woman.

These discrepancies are likely to perpetuate, rather than alter, the minor participation of women in the top echelons of science and technology. As veteran woman sociologist Lei Jieqiong has pointed out, women comprise some 38 per cent of all 'scientific workers' in China but hold only 2 per cent of the top scientific research positions.[6]

Male–female educational differences do not begin at university. They go all the way up the educational ladder, with discrepancies expanding at each rung. In 1982, girls represented 43.7 per cent of all primary school students in China (a rather low proportion in itself) and 39.7 per cent of high school students. Within high school, girls tend to be clustered at the lower levels. In Hunan province in 1979, for example, they comprised 41 per cent of students completing junior high but only 33.8 per cent of those finishing senior high.

Even more striking are male–female differentials in literacy figures. According to the 1982 census, over 70 per cent of China's 238 million illiterates were women: almost one out of every two women in China. In the 14–25 age group, some 15 per cent of females were illiterate, compared with less than 5 per cent of males.

'And young women are not just missing out on education. They're also missing out on jobs,' stated the Women's Federation official. 'Somewhere between 60 and 70 per cent of all young people awaiting employment in China are female.'

In theory, employers are not permitted to discriminate on sex grounds. But according to a Peking Labour Bureau spokesman: 'Most of our employment work seems to be to crack down on job discrimination against young women and getting enterprises to accept the women we send them.'[7]

While a lack of employment opportunities for young women

is only to be expected in the light of their lower educational standards, many lose out regardless of qualifications. In some cases the level of discrimination is measurable. For example, one Guangdong bank testing applicants for clerical jobs reportedly required women to have thirty more points in the test than men. And according to an indignant article in the national magazine *Chinese Women*, some organizations prefer male graduates who have barely scraped through a university course to female graduates with the equivalent of A grades.[8] This is common knowledge even among students still at university. 'Some of the top students all the way through our course have been female,' remarked a final year social sciences student in Shanghai. 'But we all know the men will tend to get the best jobs.'

'There are many reasons why females aren't getting equal treatment in education and employment,' commented one tertiary-educated young woman. 'Not least the continuing belief that women are inferior to men – mentally and socially. Or at least that they're not as important as men.'

The persistence of the traditional concept of female inferiority is reflected in the image young women have of themselves. 'Girls often don't consider themselves to be as intelligent as boys,' a Women's Federation official said in Harbin. 'They tend to apply for the lower prestige tertiary institutions, even though their exam marks may be sufficient for admission to a top university. On the other hand, boys tend to be confident – even over-confident – of their abilities.'

Girls also sometimes find their opportunities for education curtailed by their family. In rural areas, where traditional ideas remain strongest, boys still receive family preference in obtaining education. A survey undertaken in the countryside outside Suzhou in east China revealed that 72 per cent of primary school dropouts over a six-month period were female.[9]

One correspondent to a women's magazine complained about coming across a number of young girls herding cows in the Anhui countryside. He asked one ten-year-old whether she'd had any schooling.

'I went for six months but then I became a cowherd,' she replied. 'My elder and younger brothers are still at school.'

'Why don't you go to school too?' he asked.

'Because my dad said it's OK for me to work as I'm a girl.'[10]

Even in urban areas, girls who are preparing for the university entrance examination tend to miss out when it comes to hiring private tutors or freedom from helping with household chores. As one 16-year-old Shanghai girl complained: 'When my brother was sitting for the exam everyone made concessions for him. All he had to do was study. The family's whole focus that year was on getting him into university. But no one cares about me now it's my turn.'

Girls sometimes also face official or semi-official discrimination in high school and university enrolment. According to a Women's Federation official: 'College administrators have a tendency to accept men rather than women, even if their marks are the same or even lower.'

The discrimination is officially justified on the grounds that girls might well do better in high school or even university entrance examinations, but that in the long term the balance may change. 'Boys mature later than girls,' explained the headmaster of Peking's No. 8 High School. 'So they might be behind girls in the entrance exam. But they often catch up and even surpass girls during their early teens.'

Some university administrators argue a similar case even for students in their late teens or early twenties. In the words of an administrator at the Shanghai Metallurgical College: 'Girls tend to do quite well initially, but they fall behind in second or third year.'

What seems to be virtually absent from these perceptions of male–female differences is the whole question of social expectations and female motivation.

Even if girls are not considered intellectually inferior to males, they are usually thought to be endowed with different mental capabilities. As an official of the Yan'an Road Central neighbourhood committee in Shanghai expressed it: 'Young men have superior technical and practical skills; young women are more verbally skilled and better at fine detailed work and looking after people.'

Once again, both educators and employers take little heed of the influence of sex-role stereotyping from early childhood. Despite the ostensible stress on male–female equality, children's picture books feature young men as scientists and aeroplane pilots; young women as assistants to men and in 'caring' positions in lower level teaching and welfare work.

In China, as in the West, sex stereotyping results in the sharp sexual division of labour, seriously diminishing the avenues open to young women and partly accounting for their higher level of unemployment. Where jobs are available, young women tend to be channeled into unskilled or semi-skilled clerical work and light industry, especially textiles and handicrafts. While women form 36 per cent of the urban workforce, they represent over 80 per cent of all commercial and textile workers.

'Of course the government insists on equal pay for equal work,' remarked a female process worker. 'But typical women's jobs are less well paid than the skilled or heavy jobs usually done by men.'

Young women also miss out on jobs because of their allegedly distinctive female personalities, a concept accepted not only by the general population but by officials and social scientists. 'Males are logical, assertive and out-going; females are imaginative and passive,' commented a recent book written by researchers at the Academy of Social Sciences.[11]

Personality stereotyping means that even young women trained in areas in which they are supposed to have superior capabilities, such as foreign languages, sometimes lose out to men in obtaining employment. While the 1982 women graduates of Peking's prestigious Foreign Language Institute had superior examination results overall to their male fellow-students, many employing units were reportedly unwilling to give them jobs. Men, they alleged, were better suited psychologically to dealing with foreign visitors and delegations.[12]

This argument is used not just for jobs dealing with foreigners but for a wide range of occupations involving professional contacts and negotiations. According to a fairly senior bureaucrat in Peking: 'Women are simply not suited to some jobs, regardless of their abilities.'

Although young Chinese men do often appear to be assertive and confident and young women shy and diffident, Chinese spokesmen once again seem to be ignoring the vital question of social conditioning. Traditional male and female personality stereotypes are taught and reinforced right from the toddler and early childhood stage.

'Little boys like to go outside and run around and play football. Little girls like to stay indoors and help their mothers,' one Peking mother of two told me. Did she ever encourage her little girl to play outside, or her little boy to stay inside and help her? I asked. 'Oh no, they wouldn't want to do that,' she replied. 'It's not part of their nature.'

A further important reason for discriminating against young women in employment, and even in higher education, is the concept of their distinctive biological and domestic role as future mothers and housewives. This argument has long been familiar to women attempting to enter the workforce in the West, whether as unskilled workers or academics. As one neighbourhood official in Shanghai explained: 'It's hard to persuade employers to accept young women when they know that, once they get married, they will also have heavy household responsibilities. And they may need leave from work to care for a sick child.'

The government's policies on maternity leave (56 days in urban areas) and the provision of child-care facilities have increased rather than diminished employer hostility. 'Most organizations and factories prefer to employ young men if they have the choice,' confirmed a Communist Youth League official. 'Then they won't have future obligations to provide maternity leave and child care.'

Reinforcing female stereotypes from early childhood
Caption: 'Develop the virtue of children doing work'

Even tertiary institutions, especially those concerned with vocational training, sometimes discriminate against enrolling female students because of their future domestic responsibilities. This is particularly true if their chosen occupation involves a lot of travelling. 'You can't expect a woman to travel once she's got a family to care for,' stated an administrator at the Shanghai Metallurgical College.

This sentiment seems to be common throughout China. The overwhelming majority of people one meets 'travelling on business' – the major reason for travel in China – are men. One passenger on the Harbin–Peking train seemed surprised that I even asked why there were so few women on board.

'They don't want to leave their families,' he replied.

'What about men?' I asked.

'Oh, they don't mind so much.'

The combination of women's domestic burden and the current employment problem has created further threats to female job opportunities, at least in the long term. The most radical proposal is the familiar argument that married women should 'return home' to devote their time to domestic responsibilities, thereby making way for unemployed young people. Although this proposal is completely heretical in terms of the socialist argument that women can be liberated only through economic independence, it has been the subject of widespread popular debate in China. Particular support comes from traditionalist male circles.

'When we are freed of domestic chores,' the argument goes, 'we can do better at our jobs.' As few Chinese families would be able to survive on one wage, some men have made the rather extraordinary suggestion that *they* be subsidized with the equivalent of their wives' wages.

A second and more reasonable proposal is that women should not work full time once they marry and have a child. This was publicized nationally when a survey in the north-east province of Heilongjiang revealed that a sample of urban women and men together spent almost twice as much time each day on domestic chores – over nine hours – than men and women in the United States, France and even the Soviet Union. While Chinese men did more work in the house than most men in the other countries, the women's contribution was on average 1½ hours a day greater. The researchers, one male and one female, suggested that women with family responsibilities should be assigned part-time work to take account of their extra burden and to help relieve men's domestic load.[13]

Although the Chinese authorities have come out against the complete withdrawal of women from the workforce, their recent pronouncements have only intensified the popular emphasis on women's domestic role. In the early 1970s, and especially during the anti-Confucius campaign, they urged men to participate equally in domestic labour to lighten women's 'double burden'. But since the late 1970s they have put the major responsibility for domestic chores squarely on women. 'Women workers, commune members, and scientists and technicians need to work hard and study,' stated the Communist Party's theoretical journal *Red Flag*. 'But they have to spend a considerable portion of their time and energies looking after children and doing housework.'[14] No mention was made of similar calls on men's time and energies.

Indeed the authorities have even suggested that women's productive role should be secondary and supportive. Instead of the 'anything men can do, women can do too' focus of the Cultural Revolution period, official spokesmen have recently stressed women's participation in traditional female occupations. Many of these activities are not in the forefront of modernization and are increasingly being carried out by the low-status collective and private sectors. 'Major areas likely to offer employment prospects for young women include child care, knitting and other handicrafts, and making and washing clothes,' declared a recent book on youth employment written by members of the Youth Research Institute.[15]

The government's changed attitudes towards women's roles reflects a general retreat from policies of male–female equality. This retreat has been characteristic of less ideologically motivated phases of China's recent history and particularly of periods of unemployment.

'It's the 1960s all over again,' commented one perceptive professional woman in Harbin. 'Women were mobilized to participate wholeheartedly in the workforce in the Great Leap Forward of the late 1950s. Then in the early 1960s, when their labour wasn't so much in demand, they were told to concentrate on being good wives and mothers.'

Not surprisingly, the renewed stress on women's domestic role at the expense of their working role is only increasing young women's awareness of their future double burden and undermining their socio-economic aspirations. 'What's the use of being too ambitious?' asked one Peking high school leaver. 'We know we'll have to spend a lot of time on housework and child-rearing.'

Even female university students are affected. In a survey of ten higher educational institutions in Peking, 76.5 per cent of women students said they saw a contradiction between being successful in their future work and being able to fulfil a satisfactory domestic role.[16] The researchers did not apparently even consider that it was necessary to ask the same question of young men.

The one-child policy and the increasing availability of labour-saving devices will undoubtedly help relieve women's domestic burden in the long term but Chinese women have a long way to go before they catch up with their Western sisters. Even tiny washing machines are still a luxury. The few people who have refrigerators often find the cost of electricity prohibitive and use them for only part of the year, and then only when absolutely necessary. Shopping has to be done virtually daily, with customers facing lengthy queues and frequent shortages.

As well as devoting more time than men to domestic chores, many Chinese women spend lengthy periods travelling to and from work – maybe an hour or more each way by bicycle or bus – while their husband's workplace is often close by. Despite the official policy on male–female equality, it is normally the man's work unit that assigns housing, just as the woman's unit provides child care.

'I'm only two minutes from the main teaching building and the library,' said Bai Xi, an English language instructor at the Canton Foreign Language Institute. 'My wife works a long way away. It's too far for her to come home at lunch-time – so she prepares my lunch the evening before and I just heat it up the next day.'

There is another issue threatening young women's equal socio-economic role – or at least presenting them with alternatives to male–female equality. This is the resurgence of feminine interests and concerns that has occurred as a result of the general relaxation of official controls and renewed contacts with the West. 'Some young women just aren't interested in studying and in their own professional progress any more,' complained a Women's Federation representative in Harbin. 'They're concerned only with their personal appearance and reading love stories.'

Few people would argue that women should return to the drab days of the Cultural Revolution period when any interest in personal appearance was condemned as bourgeois and individualistic, and when baggy trousers and jackets, pudding-basin haircuts and fresh-scrubbed faces were the order of the day. But there seems to have been something of an over-reaction against the former controls, no doubt caused partly by the sheer novelty of varied clothes and hairstyles. Some young women spend what appears even to a Westerner to be an inordinate amount of time reading fashion magazines, having clothes made, and trying out new hairstyles and jewellery – *diamanté* brooches are a current vogue.

One of the most striking developments in China has been the use of the female face and figure in billboard and magazine advertisements for consumer goods. Attractive young women are shown as users of beauty soap and face creams, as happy mothers with contented talcumed babies, and as happy house-wives with washing machines or electric rice cookers.

Chinese publishers have adopted another capitalist custom: using attractive young women on the covers of magazines. One survey reported that over one-quarter of a sample of 102 popular magazines had what were described as pin-up girls – something of an exaggeration by Western standards – on their covers.[17] Also somewhat innocuous by Western standards, but a dramatic occurrence in China, is the use of photographic posters of Chinese women in calendars. These include not just film stars but a wide range of unidentified attractive women, dressed either as traditional beauties or as 'modern young women' with permed hair, Western clothing and high heels.

The revival of feminine interests, set against the awareness of fewer educational and employment opportunities and the official stress on women's domestic role, has strengthened the traditional female vision of a desirable personal future: not one's own socio-economic advancement but marriage to a man

Baggy trousers and jackets: the drab days of the Cultural Revolution period
(queueing to get into a food store in Peking)

who is on the pathway to success. This attitude is confirmed in the differing male and female concepts of the ideal spouse (see chapter 11). In general, young women tend to look for men with a promising future or a good income; young men look for women who are pretty and good-natured.

Indeed a higher education might be positively detrimental to a young woman's marriage prospects. A 1983 survey of ten higher learning institutions in Peking found that only 28 per cent of male students wanted their future spouses to have a university degree. (In contrast, 79.5 per cent of female students said they would prefer to marry university graduates.)

Even more striking was the fact that approximately 50 per cent of the young men surveyed expressed agreement with the Confucian adage: 'A woman without talent is virtuous.' The survey analysts concluded that the main problem was male students' demands that their future partners should be devoted wives and mothers. 'But by the time she enters college a female student . . . has gradually lost the traditional feminine virtues of gentleness and devotion,' they surmised.[18]

An awareness of such male attitudes no doubt only further undermines young women's own career ambitions.

And for young women without jobs, marriage sometimes presents a means of escape from parental authority. One Shanghai study revealed a strong tendency towards early marriage among unemployed young women. Some of those who were below the recommended minimum age of twenty-three simply set up de facto relationships if officials refused them permission to marry legally.

Women's interests in China are theoretically looked after by an official women's movement: the All-China Women's Federation. In the words of senior Federation official Zheng Renyang: 'The Women's Federation is the representative of Chinese women. It is also a transmission belt between the Communist Party and the masses of women, implementing Party policy on women's matters.' Needless to say, these two functions have not always been compatible. In reality, the Women's Federation is basically a mouthpiece for current Party policy; at the most it attempts to put some pressure on the Party when women's interests are blatantly subordinated to overall national economic development.

The Federation condemns the persistence of traditional patriarchal attitudes towards women, especially any notions of female inferiority. It regularly denounces outright discrimination against young women in education and employment, and argues that women's 'special characteristics' must be catered for, not used as excuses for discrimination.

While the Federation appears to support the concept of part-time work for women, it has reacted strongly against suggestions that married women 'return home' because of the employment problem. 'This would severely weaken the cause of women's emancipation in China and also the drive to modernize the country,' stated Zheng.

The Federation has expressed concern at the revival of traditional feminine concerns to the possible detriment of women's career interests. It urges young women not to become obsessed with their personal appearance at the expense of study and work.

'We are also opposed to the use of women in advertising,' said Zheng. 'It is demeaning to women. The fault lies mainly with greedy manufacturers and publishers keen to boost their sales.'

But the Women's Federation is by and large only echoing current Party policy on women, publicized in a wide range of books dealing with issues affecting young people. The Federation has itself been the main propagandist for the renewed official stress on women's domestic role at the expense of their productive role. This is strikingly illustrated in women's magazines, led by the national magazine *Chinese Women*, which are under Federation control. Closed down at the beginning of the Cultural Revolution because of its stress on love, marriage and the family, *Chinese Women* has featured exactly this emphasis since it resumed publication in late 1978.

Women's magazines have even revived the old debate on whether women are really able to combine marriage, child-bearing and household duties with having a career and/or studying. 'Of course you have to realize that once you're married there are a lot of problems even in studying by yourself,' wrote a woman from Henan province. 'Bearing a child, looking after a child, doing the housework.'[19] Since it is generally accepted in China that all young people will marry and have a child, contributors to the debate tended to take it for granted that it was women's careers, not marriage or a family, that were in question.

The Federation's recent pronouncements and the contents of its magazines reflect the manner in which the official women's movement has always shifted its ground in response to changing government priorities. Once again, it has demonstrated the weakness of its claim to act as the genuine representative of Chinese women.

In theory, there is no place for a Western-style women's movement in China. The Chinese government, like other communist governments, argues that male–female inequalities have a class basis. As class is eliminated through socialist revolution, these inequalities theoretically cease to exist. They disappear altogether as socialist programmes endorsing male–female equality replace capitalist (or in China feudal) concepts. Although revolutions carried out in the name of Marxism–Leninism have not yet brought about complete male–female equality, the Chinese government and the Women's Federation continue to condemn autonomous feminist movements as 'women's rights movements of the bourgeoisie'. 'Chinese women must improve their socio-economic position within the socialist network and under the guidance of the official women's movement,' declared a Women's Federation official in Harbin.

Not all young women in China, in common with their counterparts in Russia and other socialist countries, are satisfied with official progress in bringing about male–female equality in education and employment. Nor are they content to see women's interests being subordinated to overall national priorities. 'The whole political structure is male-dominated and the Women's Federation is just their tool,' declared a rather outspoken young woman at Peking University. 'Send women out to work ... send women back home. Tell women their most important role is to participate in production ... tell women their most important role is to look after children and do the housework. Why are women always the ones to be picked on?'

Although the Women's Federation currently appears to condone the idea of part-time work for married women, some young professional women vehemently oppose the suggestion. They argue that part-time work would be a retrogressive step because their relative lack of experience would inevitably mean losing out to men in job promotion. Some of them criticize one aspect of Engels' argument on the socialization of domestic labour: that the woman retains the basic responsibility for such domestic labour as does exist, even if that labour no longer claims 'anything but an insignificant amount of *her* time'.[20]

'The part-time work proposal starts with the wrong basic premise,' argued a young female researcher at the Chinese Academy of Social Sciences. 'If women currently spend more time on household chores than men do, that's what should be changed. If we have to spend more time on household chores in China than people do in other countries, then both women and men should work shorter hours.'

But the occasional private expression of dissatisfaction with official policies and the Women's Federation has so far stopped short of attempts to establish an autonomous women's movement in China. This is hardly surprising. In spite of the present liberalized climate, any efforts at feminist organization on a public level would undoubtedly meet the same fate as did bids to establish independent political groups in 1978–9.

Little appears to have come of one tentative effort, made at Peking University during local elections in late 1980, just to establish a forum for discussing women's issues. After calling a meeting to debate the role of women, a female election candidate pasted up a wall poster. 'Women are human beings too,' she proclaimed, denouncing the general lack of interest in discussing matters affecting women and spelling out the need to analyse women's particular problems.[21]

A few young women at the university subsequently agreed to meet periodically and even labelled themselves a 'women's research and study society'. But it is unlikely that such nascent efforts at feminist organization will go much beyond the formation of private, even surreptitious, academic study groups. 'We've got our job assignments to think of,' admitted one student. 'Even if we are discriminated against compared with men, we're still among the privileged few in China. No one is keen to step out of line.'

CHAPTER EIGHT

The Misfits

The Guangdong provincial youth prison is situated amid picturesque fertile countryside about an hour's drive from Canton. Inside the compound I talked with 17-year-old Wang Yun.

'I belonged to a street gang in Canton,' said Wang. 'We systematically robbed people and their houses, stealing radios, TV sets and watches, and anything else valuable. One night when we were dividing up our spoils in a dark lane we were interrupted by a policeman. I stabbed him with my dagger.'

The policeman was wounded but survived. Wang, who was sixteen at the time, was sentenced to fifteen years' detention, later commuted to eight years. Because he was under eighteen he was not sent to a regular gaol but to a special prison for juvenile offenders.

Chinese youth's image as the junior version of 'new socialist man', honest and upright in behaviour and helping fellow human beings, has been seriously tarnished since the late 1970s when even the official media began publishing details of juvenile delinquency and youth crime. By 1981 youth crime was being officially cited as 'one of the most outstanding of China's public security problems'.[1] Two years later officials admitted that public security was worse than it had been in the early years of Communist China and that youthful thugs were in some places committing crimes even in broad daylight.[2]

'Hooliganism, rape and robbery have been the most common offences' declared a study of youth crime written by researchers at the Chinese People's University in Peking.[3] At its most moderate, hooliganism includes creating disturbances and fighting in public places such as parks and railway stations. At its more serious, it frequently accompanies the vandalism of public property, despite the broken glass atop the high walls that surround many establishments. Schools have been particularly vulnerable during vacation periods. In mid-1982, for example, the press reported that 10 of the 25 high schools in Xintian county in Hunan province had been wrecked and that nearly 200 of the 481 primary schools had been damaged. One commune school had all its doors and windows smashed during the brief winter vacation and also lost its 200 desks.[4]

Reports of rape and sexual molestation have become so commonplace that many young women are terrified of having to find their way home alone if they work a late shift. 'I always try to go most of the way with other people, and stick to the streets with lighting,' said a Harbin hotel employee, telling me about the case of a young woman committing suicide after being raped on her way home from work, feeling that it would only bring shame on herself and her family.

While the rape reports are the most dramatic, theft and robbery have been the most common crimes. Most vulnerable are the new consumer goods becoming available in China. Also susceptible are construction sites which are simply denuded of building materials – always difficult to come by – if left unpatrolled at night.

The level of robbery with violence has been even more frightening to many people. 'Many young criminals carry weapons,' confirmed the People's University study. 'Air guns, daggers and knives.'[5]

There has also been a substantial amount of personal violence for its own sake. According to one academic article published in the north-eastern province of Liaoning: 'Some delinquents wound people with air guns just for fun. They throw lime in people's faces or put a noose around someone's neck.'[6]

The Chinese authorities' concern about the level of youth crime has been apparent from the attention it has been receiving, not just in the official media but from senior academics and researchers. One of the six sections of the Youth Research Institute is concerned solely with researching youth crime and advising the government on possible solutions. 'We need to know much more about the phenomenon so that we can work out the best remedial action,' the Institute's deputy director, Li Jingxian, told me in Peking.

Research institutes for psychology and law, as well as university sociology departments, are also doing research on the problem. In June 1982 a national congress on youth crime was held in the southern city of Nanning and the National Society for the Study of Youth Crime established. Within seven months of the congress some 200 research papers had been presented to the new society.

Despite the obvious concern about youth crime, officials and researchers argue that China has been a long way behind many Western nations in terms of crime levels. In early 1983 they maintained that, in proportion to the population, the annual number of criminal convictions in China was only about 1.5 per cent of that in the United States. The number of reported crimes was 1.3 per cent of the American figure.[7]

At the same time, researchers have expressed alarm at the growing proportion of total crimes committed by young people. In 1965, on the eve of the Cultural Revolution, people under twenty-five accounted for 38 per cent of total convictions; the official figure for 1977–80 was a high 80 per cent.[8] The youthful criminals themselves have become younger and younger. Between 1980 and 1983 the proportion of all youth offenders who were still at school multiplied three times. According to the analysis undertaken by the People's University: 'Many start their misdeeds at eleven or twelve, carry out illegal acts in society at thirteen or fourteen, and reach the peak of their youth criminal activities at fifteen, sixteen or seventeen.[9]

Commentators have also noted the growing number of girls committing offences. 'They used to be virtually absent from the ranks of youthful criminals,' confirmed one researcher. 'Now we come across them more and more, especially in petty crime.'

Although China's official crime figures might hardly seem to warrant all the hue and cry, comparative statistics are of only limited significance. As in most countries, many crimes in China are either unsolved or unreported. In rural areas, in particular, people still prefer to settle matters for themselves, especially when personal violence or rape are involved. Suspicious of outside authority, they often follow the traditional practice of demanding cash payment as the price for not reporting an offence.

This was illustrated in a complaint to a Peking women's magazine about the rape of a 17-year-old village girl. 'Her father was very angry,' wrote the correspondent. 'He went at once to the home of the young man and demanded 300 yuan, saying it would put an end to the matter.' When his daughter protested, saying she wanted to go to the police, he had replied: 'But if we report it, we won't get the money.'[10]

In dealing with youthful law-breakers, the emphasis is on reform and rehabilitation rather than punishment. Strong efforts are made to get undisciplined high school students back on the right track even before they commit punishable offences. A number of official watchdogs, including the Communist Youth League and local neighbourhood committees, keep their eyes on anyone who seems to be getting out of line. Special supervisory groups have what are described as 'heart to heart' talks with such young people; by 1981 some 40 000 of these groups had been established throughout China.

Stronger action is called for in the case of young people who have committed public misdemeanours and who are acknowledged to have become uncontrollable by parents or teachers. On the recommendation of schools or the local police, or even of their parents, they are sent to reform schools. China now has approximately 120 of these institutions, officially known as 'work-study schools'. In the major cities most individual districts have one work-study school; there are seven in Peking and twelve in Shanghai.

The Zhabei District reform school in Shanghai, located in a basically workers' district of some 800 000 people in the northern suburbs of the city, draws young people mainly from the district's high schools. In 1983 it had just over 200 inmates, a quarter of whom were girls.

The young people at the reform school, ranging in age from fourteen to eighteen, outwardly appear to be what every Chinese official would like youth to be: well-behaved and obedient with fresh-scrubbed faces and short neat hair or pigtails. Their appearance somewhat belies the stories they tell of their former delinquent behaviour, which invariably began with absence from school and refusal to study.

'I started off playing truant a couple of days a week. Eventually I managed to avoid going to school for a whole six months,' said Li Hua, an attractive and demure-looking sixteen-year-old. 'When I did go to school I was always in trouble,' she went on. 'I thought school was boring. So I talked in class and disrupted the lessons. And I used to fight and beat up other girls in the playground.'

What had she fought over? 'Sometimes over boys. One girl tried to steal my boyfriend. Other times just because I was bored.'

Most of the students had managed to hide their truancy from their parents, at least until teachers reported their absence, often extremely tardily as they were probably relieved not to have to face the trouble-makers every day.

'It was much more fun not going to school,' said another sixteen-year-old, Xi Bilei. 'I used to go skating with a friend, or go and see films, or just wander around. A lot of other kids were doing the same and I got into bad company – a sort of gang, I suppose.'

Because the young people lacked money they started stealing from markets and shops. 'It wasn't very difficult,' said Xi Bilei. 'They're so crowded, especially on Sunday. We'd work in groups of two or three.'

How had she got caught? Xi looked a bit embarrassed and replied hesitantly: 'I got pregnant. Then they found out everything.'

Most of the girls at the Zhabei District reform school were there at least partly, if not solely, because of their so-called 'sex offences'.

'Some of the girls we have here were promiscuous,' one of the school's administrators told me solemnly. On further questioning, he admitted that simply being discovered having sexual relations, officially considered unlawful for unmarried people, was sufficient grounds for a period at the reform school. In practice, the discovery had often been made only when the girl became pregnant, a common outcome of youthful sex behaviour in a country where contraceptive measures are available legally only to married couples and where there is a dire lack of sexual knowledge among young people.

'About half the girls here at the present time were pregnant when they came here,' acknowledged the administrator. Following the requisite abortion, they were usually required to spend one to two years at the reform school.

The young men told partially similar stories to the young women: the familiar pattern of disruptive behaviour at school, truancy, fighting and beating up other kids, and stealing in gangs. Instead of the so-called sex offences, which seemed to land young women but not their partners in reform school or prison, the offence most commonly committed by young men was that of gambling, mostly playing cards for money. Although gambling, along with drugs and prostitution, had been officially banned in China since the Communists came to power, it reached such proportions in 1981 that several provinces issued new prohibitory regulations.

'Some of us used to gamble with up to 300 or 400 yuan,' admitted one fifteen-year-old.

Where could a schoolboy get hold of such an amount of money, four or five times the average monthly wage?

'We stole it. Or stole goods and sold them. Then the members of the gang used to gamble with the money to see if they could get some more.'

In contrast to their former erratic lifestyles, the young men and women at the reform school face a strict daily routine: up with the bell at 5.30 a.m., cleaning and tidying the dormitory, breakfast at 7 o'clock, morning school classes, lunch, a rest period and further afternoon classes. In addition to regular school subjects, ranging from mathematics to history, there are heavy doses of ideological education in correct socialist values.

'China's youth are enthusiastically contributing to the establishment of a socialist spiritual civilization,' one student read out loud from a booklet on the latest political campaign.

All students do at least two hours a day manual labour, both ostensibly to fit them for the workforce and to instil a concept of labour discipline. The boys assemble new bicycles for a local factory and repair used cardboard cartons. The girls are taught how to use a sewing machine and put together simple items of clothing, also for a local factory. For their labour they receive a small payment which usually goes towards the 14 yuan a month their parents have to pay the reform school for feeding their offspring.

Dinner at 5 p.m. is followed by a brief free period and then a so-called general discussion with teachers, including more ideological education. Lights-out is at 8.30. On Wednesday evening the inmates are permitted to watch television, providing their behaviour has been satisfactory over the past week. If their home circumstances permit, they are allowed to spend Sunday with their families.

According to administrators at the reform school, the young inmates are not treated as criminals but as teenagers who have temporarily gone astray. 'They must be made to feel as though they're part of society, not alienated from it,' commented one administrator. 'They need firm discipline but they also need friendship and advice.'

Not everyone responded to such methods, he admitted. Some were initially hostile to their new teachers and continued their former errant behaviour, attempting to disrupt classes and even destroying furniture. A few ran away or did not return after their Sunday at home and had to be brought back to the reform school by parents or even the police. But if the threat of being deprived of the right to watch television once a week was not sufficient to restore reasonable behaviour, most young people were persuaded by the prospect of a six-month extension to their usual two-year period at the school.

'There's occasionally an extreme case where a young person doesn't respond at all to discipline,' the administrator told me. 'Then we have to get the police.'

Such young recalcitrants, together with others under eighteen who have already committed more serious offences, with the exception of murder, usually find themselves in the stricter environment of a special youth prison. Prisons in China are not officially called prisons but are described as various types of 'reform institutions'. Youth prisons (or youth reform centres) are the junior version of what is usually called 'reform through education'.

The youth prison for China's southern province of Guangdong has some 400 inmates, under 10 per cent of whom are girls, aged from fourteen to eighteen. Despite its almost idyllic rural setting, the institution has a decidedly prison atmosphere compared with reform schools, with white-uniformed guards patrolling the inside walls and dotted throughout the compound. The prison's clean-cut, soberly dressed inmates might look even less criminal-like than many of the youths wandering the streets of nearby Canton but their

Boys repairing used cardboard cartons at the Zhabei District reform school, Shanghai

Female inmates at the Guangdong provincial youth prison

offences are a catalogue of the more serious youth crimes reported in the Chinese media.

Wang Yun, the seventeen-year-old who had knifed a policeman, was not the only inmate to have committed such a violent act. When I asked a prison officer why another seventeen-year-old had been sent to prison, he replied: 'He took a fancy to his next-door neighbour's new watch. When the man wouldn't give it to him, he stabbed him and took it.'

Recurrent stealing and robbery, usually in gangs, were the most common offences committed by the young men. Administrators described many of them as *liumang*, a rather vague term traditionally meaning a vagrant but currently used to cover a range of hoodlum activity including robbery with violence and sexual molestation or rape.

While the reports of rape convictions in China have been alarming, they have to be viewed with some caution. Some of the young men accused of rape appeared, in fact, to have been guilty only of having sexual relations with a number of young women, not necessarily without their consent. (Sexual relations with one person is not usually called rape but 'anti-social behaviour'.)

The young women in the prison seemed overall to be more cheerful and alert than the rather surly young men. Their misdemeanours were generally more serious versions of those committed by the female inmates of the reform schools; like the young men some were reform school recidivists. The pattern was similar: a background of being uncontrollable and becoming involved, usually in gangs, with stealing and even violence.

Most of the girls had also committed 'sex offences'. On this occasion it usually meant more than simply having a sexual relationship with a boyfriend. Because young men are in the vast majority in youth gangs, the few young women who attach themselves to gangs tend to become sexually active with a number of male gang members. A permissive attitude towards sex is part of the general ethos of fast and loose living that characterizes gang behaviour.

In some cases the young women's behaviour had gone further: to prostitution. While there have been some reports of prostitution in Peking, Shanghai and other major cities, the problem has been rife in the southern city of Canton, just over the border from Hong Kong. Now fresh-faced and neatly dressed in their institutional garb of baggy trousers and loose cotton skirts, the young women looked a world apart from the heavily made-up, high-heeled young women in form-fitting clothes one occasionally sees wandering near the Dongfang and other major Canton hotels.

'It's very tempting for young women in Canton, especially if you're unemployed,' one bright-eyed attractive 17-year-old prison inmate told me. 'Lots of rich men come here from Hong Kong. If you get hold of foreign currency you can buy just about anything you want in Canton nowadays, including the best Hong Kong fashions.'

'It's all right so long as you don't get caught,' added another young woman. 'But I wasn't very smart. Now I'm stuck here for three years.'

Like students in reform schools, the young prison inmates live in a highly structured environment, calculated to train them to accept both studying and labour discipline. Six half-days of labour – from growing crops to assembling radio parts for a nearby factory – are combined with heavy doses of political and ethical studies, as well as regular school work. The fairly low educational level of the young inmates, reflecting not necessarily their basic intelligence but their former lengthy absences from school, is indicated by the standard of the subjects taught: from mid-primary school to first year junior high school (normally the province of about nine- to thirteen-year-olds).

The inmates are divided into groups of twelve or so, sharing a dormitory furnished with little more than two-storey bunks and having a permanent supervisor. The sexes are kept strictly segregated in different sections of the prison.

Was this really advisable? I asked one of the administrators, considering that some people spend three or four years in the prison and are expected to adapt to normal society when they are released.

'We tried letting some of the better behaved young men and women watch television together for a while,' he replied. 'But the boys kept writing dirty notes to the girls or attempted to evade the guards to get together with them. So we had to put a stop to it.'

What are the reasons for youth crime in a socialist society which has long maintained that crime and other social aberrations are basically products of capitalism and bourgeois culture? Essentially, China's present leadership puts the onus on their immediate political predecessors and the influences coming in from the outside world.

Young people, say the authorities, spent their impressionable years in the aftermath of the Cultural Revolution when anarchy and disorder reigned supreme and there was almost a complete breakdown of discipline and public order in the community. As a result, some young people have grown up without a clear idea of right and wrong.

This so-called muddle-headedness is only being aggravated by China's open door policy, argue officials. According to a representative of the Communist Youth League: 'Young people are being influenced by decadent capitalist ideas and lifestyles which are contributing to the rise in crime and other social evils.' In particular, officials put the blame on foreign films – which are largely restricted to those of the pre-sexual revolution and pre-violent movie era – and the illegal importation of what is described as pornographic material. There are numerous stories of crimes allegedly occurring as a result of exposure to material from the West. For example, an official of the Anhui Provincial Law Association told me that one young man in Hefei had gone out and raped a woman after his next-door neighbour had shown him a Western pin-up calendar.

The continuing effects of the breakdown of public order during the Cultural Revolution cannot be denied. Nor can the influence of the open door policy, which is discussed in detail in the next chapter. But they are not the whole story, as many researchers in China now acknowledge. Like their colleagues in the West, they are beginning to explain youth crime in a broader social and domestic context.

As in many countries, a major cause of youth crime in China is the gap between young people's aspirations and their opportunities. For those young people who have already left school, crime is often linked with unemployment. Almost a quarter of all convicted criminals in Peking in 1982 were unemployed.[11] When one district of the city of Suzhou solved its youth employment problem, youth crime fell by 64.3 per cent; a figure of over 90 per cent is claimed for a district of Wuhan in central China.[12]

But unemployment is only the final link in the long chain of personal failures. For many young people disillusionment comes when they fail the university entrance examination and decide they have no real future, regardless of whether or not they get jobs. 'This is a group we have to be particularly careful about,' said a youth researcher in Shanghai. 'They know they're fairly smart, even if they can't get into university. Rather than settle for a boring routine job, some of them think they may as well use their brains to try to outsmart the law.'

Other young people are disillusioned even earlier, when they find themselves in a 'slow class' in high school instead of in a 'fast class' being trained for the university entrance examination. The resulting lack of discipline that teachers and headmasters complain about is only the tip of the iceberg; some of these young people resort to delinquent or criminal behaviour. In an eighteen-month period in 1981–2 in Hunan province alone, over 1000 incidents of abusing and beating teachers were reported to the police. A school in Peking was closed down for over a month after students pelted their teachers' living quarters with stones and rocks, causing three teachers to be hospitalized.[13]

'We know that many young people are very frustrated,' said another Peking high school teacher. 'But it's not very enjoyable having to bear the brunt of their frustrations.'

A further cause of delinquent behaviour is sheer boredom. At a time of youthful exuberance and a surfeit of physical energy, teenagers are confronted not just with a stereotyped, routine way of life but with little to do in their spare time. Like youth living in the poorer, often new suburbs of many cities in the West, some Chinese youth find an outlet for their energies in unruly and even criminal behaviour. 'Many young people start thieving or hooligan activities simply because they have nothing better to do,' admitted a Communist Youth League official. 'We must try to provide more facilities – both sporting and social – so they won't be tempted into crime.'

Young people who are unemployed or playing truant from school have even more time on their hands. According to one book on youth crime, they sometimes turn their households into virtual dens of debauchery when parents go to work during the day. 'They take the opportunity to smoke, drink and read pornographic books, while planning their next burst of criminal activity with their fellow gang members.'[14]

Like Western psychologists, Chinese researchers now put some emphasis on young people's domestic background as a further factor in delinquency and crime, especially when thirteen- or fourteen-year-olds are involved. 'Some of our young people come from a broken or violent family environment,' stated an administrator at the Zhabei District reform school. 'They've sometimes been beaten – even raped – by relatives. That's why it's important for us to show them kindness and affection.'

'There are also those from disrupted family backgrounds,' he added. 'They grow up without any firm discipline.' Although divorce in China is still very limited, a considerable number of children live only with their mother, and maybe one or more grandparents, because of the separation of married couples. Some children see their father only during his two-week annual visit. A few are virtually brought up by grandparents – sometimes in another part of the country – because of the heavy work burden endured by both men and women.

'I simply haven't got time to look after them both properly,' said one of my Chinese-language teachers in Peking of her two young daughters in 1977. 'So I've sent the three-year-old to my mother in Shandong province.'

The family financial situation is also acknowledged to be a significant factor. While the dramatic income differentials of Western society are not immediately visible in China, with most people appearing to live at a fairly basic economic level, some people live at a far more basic level than others. The former relative lack of temptation has been replaced by a virtual abundance of consumer goods and young Chinese, like their counterparts in the West, face a growing onslaught from billboard and TV advertisements.

But not a few youthful criminals come from the families of well-paid professional people and even quite high officials. These are the 'gilded youth', the Chinese equivalent of the Soviet Union's privileged but sometimes delinquent youth who spend much of their time on gambling, 'loose living' and even indulging in hooligan activities. According to an administrator of the Guangdong youth prison: 'Some parents give their children far too much money, even money for gambling. They spoil and indulge their children, then they can't discipline them when they get out of hand.'

Parental indulgence is hardly new in China; in affluent and poor families alike parents find it difficult to deny their children whatever they want. The phenomenon is only worsening with the advent of the one-child family, now virtually compulsory under China's rigid population control policy. Unless parents take the advice offered in a growing range of books on 'how to bring up your only child,' there could well be a whole generation of indulged only-child teenagers in less than twenty years' time.

The predominance of young people from working-class families in reform schools and youth prisons is not necessarily an accurate reflection of their comparative role in criminal activities. Children of people holding prominent positions are more likely to evade detention than their less privileged brothers and sisters. Even Party officials are not exempt from using their connections and influence, as well as bribery and payoffs, to protect their delinquent offspring.

One striking example of parental interference came to light in late 1983. In August a twenty-year-old named Cai Jianzhong had been arrested in Hebei province and charged with raping a fourteen-year-old. Regardless of whether or not it was a genuine rape case in the Western sense, having sexual relations with a minor (anyone under sixteen) is an extremely serious offence in China. Cai's father, the Party Secretary of Linzhang county, rushed to his son's aid. He produced false documentation indicating that the girl was much older and publicly alleged that she was, in fact, an adult prostitute.[15] On this occasion justice prevailed. The provincial judicial department exposed the Party Secretary who was subsequently dismissed from his post. The young man was rearrested.

Official claims of reasonable success in reforming delinquent youth are borne out by the low proportion of crimes committed by people beyond their teens. As in most countries, petty crime is little more than a passing phase for many young people. At the same time, researchers are concerned about the number of offenders in their early twenties who've had an early record of crime and periods in reform schools or youth prisons.

'Despite all our efforts at reform, there's a certain amount of recidivism,' stated one youth researcher. 'And the fault lies as much with social attitudes as it does with the individual.'

Former offenders face a tough road back to conventional society, like their counterparts in most countries. Lacking education because of their pattern of truancy, they confront an already difficult employment situation, whether they attempt to enter the workforce immediately or first return to school. Many leave reform institutions only to find themselves at the bottom of China's 'awaiting employment' pile.

One reform school administrator told me that many factories and other enterprises will not take on young people who have been in trouble with the authorities. 'In addition they try to get rid of any workers committing the most minor offences. There are plenty more young people wanting jobs.' According to a survey of a number of urban districts, between 30 per cent and 50 per cent of former youth offenders who were unemployed committed fresh crimes. Of those who obtained jobs, only 2 per cent were recidivists.[16]

Not surprisingly, young people who have a reform school or prison record also find themselves in a particularly adverse position when it comes to participating in any activity that has good moral conduct as one of its criteria. The majority of the 400 former inmates of the Zhabei District reform school had applied to join the Communist Youth League but, while almost 25 per cent of all young people in China between fourteen and twenty-five are members, only four of them had been accepted. Similarly, the moral criteria for university entrance would make it doubly difficult for even the brightest ex-offender to obtain admission, as university administrators readily acknowledge.

Former offenders also have to bear the weight of general social stigma. They are looked down on by many people, including even family and relatives. 'Some people think that once a criminal, always a criminal,' said an administrator at Shanghai's Zhabei District reform school. 'Even some schoolmates have this attitude.'

The problem of leaving behind one's past is particularly difficult in China because of the relative immobility of the population and the impossibility of simply moving to another part of the country.

According to Chinese researchers, young women face special difficulties in being accepted back into society, particularly in establishing personal relationships and finding a future marriage partner. In the words of one researcher: 'Many people will tolerate a certain amount of unruly behaviour from young men. But not from young women, especially not anything to do with sex.' His comment was endorsed by a young Peking factory worker. 'No young man will have anything to do with that sort of girl – at least not as a marriage prospect,' he said. 'They're branded for life.'

Caught up in the familiar cycle of poor education, unemployment and social ostracism, many former offenders cling to the company of others in the same situation. For some there is a gradual progression up the criminal hierarchy, graduating from being youthful gang members to heading their own gangs. According to one report, many gang leaders have a lengthy youth or adult prison record; some are escapees from these institutions and have no option but to stay outside the law.[17]

At each stage along the criminal track, it becomes increasingly difficult to re-enter conventional society. A record at a youth prison or even a work-study school is bad enough. A record of adult prison sentences – euphemistically described as 'reform through education' and 'reform through labour' – is even more difficult to cope with. And despite the official emphasis on reform, rather than punishment, there are few support services for offenders once they've been released.

The People's University report on youth crime cites the case of a young man who, having apparently been successfully reformed during his sentence, left prison only to discover he had absolutely nowhere to go. His father had died, his mother had remarried, and his former workplace would not take him back. In desperation he returned to the police authorities and asked them to find him a place to live and work.

'We only organize your reform, we don't organize work for you,' replied the police official.

'You've reformed me, but I've got nowhere to go,' said the young man. 'If you don't do something, I'll only have to go and steal again.'

'If you commit another crime, we'll arrest you,' was the official response.[18]

In August 1983 the Chinese government implicitly acknowledged that its efforts to solve the crime problem had been unsuccessful and that more drastic action was necessary. The inauguration of a national crime clean-up was signalled by a mass rally of some 80 000 people in Peking at which over thirty criminals were sentenced to death. Throughout the month the media reported the round-up of criminal gangs all over the country, revealing a level of crime that surprised even many Chinese people.

'Public security organizations in Tangshan [the centre of the disastrous 1976 earthquake] took decisive measures at the end of July to capture 105 criminals in six gangs, all in a single dragnet,' reported the *People's Daily*.[19]

According to the *Sichuan Daily*, nine gangs of hoodlums, robbers and thieves had been destroyed in the provincial capital, Chengdu.[20] Inner Mongolia Radio reported the destruction of a further two criminal gangs and the arrest of fifty criminals. 'These criminals all had an eagle tattooed on their left arms as a symbol and were known as the Bridgehead Squad.'[21]

On 2 September the government issued regulations designed to combat what it described as the growing menace to the social order. Sentences ranging up to death were prescribed for murder, inflicting grave injury, rape, leading gangs and carrying lethal weapons, and embezzlement. Although the campaign was not aimed solely at youth offenders, the authorities both acknowledged that crime was most prevalent among this group and that the campaign itself was designed partly as a deterrent to young people becoming involved in criminal activities.[22]

Over the next few months there were media reports of executions throughout China, with some individual cases receiving substantial coverage in Chinese newspapers and magazines. There was the twenty-six-year-old who had raped and then strangled three women, hiding their bodies under his bed, in a chest and in a closet. There was Xiao Shiduo, a young man who could well be described as the 'Shenyang ripper'. According to a feature story in a women's magazine, Xiao's criminal activities had started in earnest when, angry at being rejected by a young woman, he had raped her at knife point in a local park. He had subsequently gone on a rampage, raping and knifing – or knifing and then raping – a number of women.[23]

Probably the most notorious criminals of all were the Wang

brothers who were not executed but were killed in a shootout with police on 19 September. With a price on their head of 2000 yuan, the brothers had reportedly murdered over thirty people during a seven-month nation-wide rampage.

Even young criminals with high level connections were not immune as the anti-crime campaign gathered intensity. Those executed included a grandson of the late Army chief Zhu De and his wife Kang Keqing, currently President of the All-China Women's Federation, and also a grandson of the late Dong Biwu, one of the original members of the Chinese Communist Party. The two young men were accused of privateering and embezzlement, using part of their profits to import porno-graphic video cassettes which they allegedly screened at nude parties which included group sex. Zhu's grandson was con-victed of 'raping' thirty young women at wild parties in Peking and Tianjin.

The authorities did not release overall statistics of the number of people executed or details of their ages and crimes. Private sources indicate that, by early 1984, there had probably been over 6000 executions. From even a casual glance at news-paper reports, police posters and billboards, it was apparent that the overwhelming majority were young: some only nine-teen or twenty, many others in their early and mid-twenties. A female face on the billboards was a rarity, but did appear occasionally. The most frequently mentioned crimes were murder, robbery and rape (including gang rape).

The execution of serious offenders was not new in China. Thirty-one people had been executed, mostly for murder and robbery, within a short period in 1982 in the north-eastern province of Jilin. In the same year a 25-year-old female taxi driver named Yao Yinyun was executed in Peking after she had driven her taxi into a crowd near Tiananmen Square, killing five people and injuring nineteen others. And a young man was executed for running amok and pushing an innocent bystander in front of an approaching train at Peking Railway Station.

What was novel about the anti-crime campaign of late 1983 was its intensity and breadth, as well as the amount of pub-licity it received, confirming the authorities' intention to make examples of individual criminals as a deterrent to others. The early mass rallies, at which criminals were paraded and railed against, were reminiscent of the early 1950s and the Cultural

Revolution when the accused were mostly alleged counter-revolutionaries. Billboards on the main streets of cities all over the country featured photographs of local people sentenced to death together with descriptions of their crimes. Large crowds of passersby stared at the expressionless faces on the photographs and silently read the graphic details of their misdemeanours.

Outside police stations posters were also pasted up boldly announcing the latest group of people sentenced to death. One of the most macabre sights during the campaign was the appearance of a police official to put a huge red tick on an individual poster: confirmation that the death sentence had been carried out. The execution itself normally took place at the local prison; the convicted person was ordered to kneel and a single shot was fired through the back of his or her neck.

The vehemence of the anti-crime campaign alarmed international human rights activists, disturbed at the speed with which the convictions were being put into effect with sometimes no more than three days between arrest and execution. In response to a formal protest from Amnesty International, the Chinese authorities maintained that severe measures were necessary, like 'a knife to cut out the dregs of society before they disrupt China's social order'.[24]

The actual executions were only the extreme face of the campaign. Over the period there were also an estimated 100 000 arrests or detentions, mostly of young offenders, who were reportedly sent off to work camps in border provinces such as Qinghai. Those rounded up allegedly included some of the young unemployed who were making nuisances of themselves.

For all its ferocity, the anti-crime campaign seemed to have had the desired deterrent effect. Peking's crime rate for October was 50 per cent below that for July, the month before the campaign got under way.[25] In January 1984 the government announced that the national crime rate for September–November 1983 had been a staggering 42.5 per cent below that for the same three months in the previous year.[26]

Not surprisingly, the campaign had created a general atmosphere of fear, bringing back memories of other round-up campaigns. 'We thought the days of such ferocious campaigns were over,' commented a Peking school-teacher. 'But it got to the stage where some young people wouldn't even venture onto the streets at night in case they were arrested.'

Despite the unease, the government's actions were welcomed by people who had become afraid for their personal safety. 'A few months ago you would have been scared to walk around many parts of the city,' a Xiamen resident told me in January 1984. 'The situation has improved a lot already. Even ordinary young people who used to be a bit unruly are now well-behaved. But of course we all wonder how long it will last.'

CHAPTER NINE

Temptations from the West

The young man looked like many a Chinese visitor from Hong Kong as he chatted to me in poor English in the spacious art deco style lounge of Shanghai's Jinjiang Hotel, a reminder of former colonial days in China. With longish hair and wearing jeans, a bright T-shirt and Adidas-type shoes, he fiddled with one of Hong Kong's current gimmicks: a ballpoint pen with an inbuilt digital watch.

'It seems to have stopped working,' he complained.

I asked him how long he was spending in Shanghai and whether he was travelling with a group of young people.

He grinned. 'Oh no, I live here in Shanghai. I've lived in Shanghai all my life. Call me David, that's my name in English.'

David, it turned out, was a 16-year-old Shanghai schoolboy. He liked talking to foreigners, he said, so he spent a lot of time wandering along the Bund or doing the rounds of the tourist hotels. 'The guards on the door don't usually let local Chinese into a hotel like this unless they have a specific reason for being here,' he told me. 'But I don't usually have any problems. They think I'm a visitor from Hong Kong.' He went on. 'It would be wonderful to go overseas, especially to America. China's so backward and boring. I listen to Western music all the time, on the Voice of America. My favourite is Dolly Parton. I like reading Agatha Christie and Arthur Hailey. We can't get most other modern novels here; I don't suppose you've got any with you that you don't want?'

David had come to the Jinjiang Hotel this evening, he told me, to say good-bye to a French mime actor he'd met a few days earlier and who had given him the T-shirt he was wearing and some music cassettes. In return he had bought him some Chinese paper-cuts as a good-bye present.

'I hope one day I'll meet someone who'll sponsor me as a private student overseas, preferably in America,' David said optimistically. 'That happened to one of my friends a while back.'

While David is rather more adventurous than most, he typifies those young Chinese who have completely fallen for the Western way of life, from clothing to music and gadgetry. They are by no means in the majority, but they represent the most extreme outcome of China's open door policy, one of the most dramatic developments undertaken by the country's post-Mao leadership.

China had largely isolated itself from the West soon after the Communist victory in 1949, asserting both its strong nationalism and new socialist image. Most Western popular culture was denounced as bourgeois and imperialist; Western businessmen and missionaries were squeezed out of the country. China's isolation intensified when the government took similar measures against Russians and their culture following the Sino–Soviet split of the late 1950s. The process was brought to completion during the Cultural Revolution when the few surviving remnants of Western culture, including classical music and literature, were suppressed and when several of the remaining Westerners in China were denounced and imprisoned.

Although there was some slight easing of this exclusionist policy during the early 1970s, at the time of Mao's death in 1976 there was virtually a complete absence of information on, and culture from, the West. Along with everything Western, the few individual Western students and teachers in China were regarded as representatives of the bourgeois, capitalist, imperialist world and every effort was made to keep them segregated from Chinese society. The few young Chinese who had any contact with Westerners were both guarded in that contact and revealed their almost complete ignorance of life outside China.

'Who's he?' my 23-year-old roommate at Peking University had asked, pointing to the photo of US President Jimmy Carter on the cover of my freshly arrived *Newsweek* magazine.

'Is Australia far from Canton then?' another student had inquired when I mentioned the plane trip to China. Like many Chinese, she seemed to have the idea that Canton was about as far as one could go and that all foreign countries were somewhere just over the border.

All this changed in 1978–9 when Mao's pragmatic successors, led by Deng Xiaoping, launched China's dramatic drive to modernize the nation. In the early 1950s they had turned to Russia; now they turned to the West and Japan for modern expertise, technology and industrial equipment. As official spokesmen readily admitted: 'Our main purpose in adopting our open door policy is to introduce advanced science, technology and management techniques into China and to attract useful capital.'[1] Even the development of foreign tourism, which in 1982 brought China $US780 million in foreign exchange, had confessed money-making objectives, despite continuing obligatory references to 'international friendship'.

There was also a lifting of the more extreme controls placed on Western culture and contact during the Cultural Revolution. In theory this marked a return to the basic policy, established in the early years of the People's Republic, of selectively learning from foreign culture and art forms. In practice, the open door police has given Chinese people far greater access to Westerners and the Western way of life than at any time since 1949.

It seems doubtful that China's new leadership, who themselves have had painfully little previous experience of the Western world, quite realized the Pandora's box they were opening when they embarked on their open door policy. In the long term China's reopening to the West might well have as far-reaching, if not more far-reaching, effects than any of its other new policies, especially on the youth generation. Compared with other sections of the community, young people overall have both the greatest level of exposure to the outside world and, as Chinese officials themselves complain, are proving to be the most susceptible to Western influences.

Nowadays foreign visitors to China stand almost shoulder to shoulder on the Great Wall of China and special tourist launches sail down the Yangzi. French computer experts install equipment in the far north-east; British companies drill for oil off the China coast. Billboards feature advertisements for Sony cassette recorders and Seiko digital watches. Popular magazines feature the latest Paris fashions and Arthur Miller's *Death of a Salesman* has been performed in Peking.

Despite the individual outward signs of a renewed Western presence in China, readily seized on by journalists as evidence of China's budding Westernization, the level of exposure to Western influences should not be exaggerated. China's door is still only slightly ajar, not fully open. So far as it is able, the Chinese government puts all information and culture coming from the West through an official 'filter' before they reach the population at large.

The most open access is that to Western science, technology and other factual material, the kind of information that will help China achieve its modernization goals. This ranges from translations of Western scientific texts to articles in popular science magazines, such as *Knowledge is Power*, which explain the principles behind everything from refrigerators to computers.

Next in order of relatively free access is general information about overseas countries. Western history, geography, famous personages and sport are favourite subjects. Magazines like *Globe* and *World Knowledge Pictorial* feature articles on topics such as World War I, American architecture, the fast foods industry and Margaret Thatcher. The evening television news bulletin, which frequently includes satellite transmissions from abroad, covers international sports events ranging from water-skiing and car-racing to the Sydney–Hobart yacht race.

Compared with scientific and general information, Western culture is subject to a high level of censorship. As in the 1950s, the more classical elements of Western culture receive official approval: translations of Shakespeare, Tolstoy and the Brontës; performances of Beethoven and *Swan Lake*. Contemporary Western culture is more suspect, with a virtual veto on anything reflecting the sexual revolution and the permissive society. The most widely screened 'contemporary' Western film over the past few years has been *The Sound of Music*; so-called popular songs currently played widely on radio include 'Jingle Bells' and 'Que Sera, Sera: Whatever will be will be.'

There is, though, an occasional and somewhat idiosyncratic offering of contemporary Western culture. Films ranging from *Guess Who's Coming to Dinner* to Australia's *Caddie* and *Breaker Morant* have been screened, sometimes at limited attendance film festivals. While acceptable literature is still essentially limited to the classics, it does extend occasionally to the contemporary scene: not just Agatha Christie and Arthur Hailey but translations of short stories by American writers including Truman Capote, John Updike and Philip Roth. And if the stress is still on classical music, the occasional jazz ensemble and pop group have been permitted to perform in China, although not always with the desired results. A Peking performance in March 1982 by Spyz and Morning Sun, from the United States and Australia respectively, was halted by Chinese officials when hundreds of fans rushed to the edge of the stage and started singing and dancing.

For all the official efforts at censorship, it is impossible to 'filter' all information and culture coming from the outside world. As more and more young people buy radios with short-wave bands, overseas broadcasting services including the Voice of America, the BBC and Radio Australia become important sources of Western material. 'I like VOA for music but I listen to the BBC for news about what's happening in the world,' a Peking student told me. 'It's more objective than VOA – and than Radio Peking.'

There is also the quasi-legal or illegal importation of cassette tapes, books and magazines. At its mildest, this covers the more contemporary and decadent features of Western culture: from *Playboy* magazine to cassette tapes of the latest Western hits and Hong Kong and Taiwanese love songs. At its strongest, it includes the smuggling into China, and often their repro-duction and sale on the black market, of soft and not-so-soft porn magazines and video tapes. In mid-1982 a group of young men – all the sons of high officials – were arrested in Canton for screening and circulating Linda Lovelace's *Deep Throat*.

A growing number of young Chinese also have direct contact with Western visitors and residents in China. Contact with tourists and other short-term visitors (over 1.1 million in 1984) is fairly superficial, even in major tourist centres, leading to the occasional exchange of a few halting words of English. Closer contact, at least for university students, comes with foreign students – in 1983 alone over 5000 arrived in China to study at sixty different tertiary institutions – and teachers and other experts in China, many of whom speak Chinese and travel fairly freely round the country.

But the most significant personal contact for your people is with the huge number of Chinese visitors, reaching almost 11 million in 1984, coming from Hong Kong, Southeast Asia and the United States. These visitors, often the relatives of people in China, usually speak Chinese, make frequent visits and bring with them both officially approved and other products from the outside world.

Although the bulk of overseas Chinese have family connections in the southern provinces of Guangdong and Fujian, few areas of China completely lack overseas contacts. After a luncheon for representatives of the Youth Research Institute, hosted by the Australian Embassy at Peking's luxurious Jianguo Hotel, a young official said to me: 'I'll wait around here for a while if you don't mind. My aunt's visiting from Malaysia and I want to see whether she's checked in yet.'

The overall exposure of young Chinese to the outside world is subject to huge variations. People in big cities such as Peking and Shanghai, and more especially those in Canton, have become fairly blasé about the presence of foreign visitors and even residents, as well as the occasional foreign film and television programme. But much of rural youth, like the rest of the rural population, is still largely ignorant of the outside world. No doubt this will change as the expanding television service and popular magazine market reach the depths of the countryside. At present, though, the sight of a foreigner can still bring wide-eyed gasps and questions such as: 'Why are your hair and skin a different colour from ours?'

In cities and towns, young people still undergoing formal education probably have the greatest access to the West: not just through television and magazines but also through their educational curricula. Most schools now teach some Western history, geography and literature; English is a compulsory high school subject.

At the tertiary level, the study of English is the pathway to a wide range of knowledge not always accessible to the population at large. Language classes during the Cultural Revolution period used little more than Mao's writings and the highly politicized *Peking Review*, producing graduates unable to do much more than regurgitate communist jargon in English – or Chinglish as some foreigners called it. In the interests of competent language learning, students are now generally permitted to read American, British and other newspapers and magazines. 'I like *Time* and *Newsweek*,' commented a student at the Canton Foreign Language Institute. 'They've got short interesting articles which aren't too difficult to read.'

Although some language institutes concentrate almost solely on practical language skills, others also familiarize their students with Western literature, history and social sciences. The ideological emphasis is still strongly evident but students at least read a comprehensive range of Western material. The 1982 final examination paper at the Foreign Language Institute in Peking, set and answered in English for the first time since 1957, included such questions as 'Why did the British Empire decline?', 'How did Hemingway view women?' and 'How did F. Scott Fitzgerald view the rich?' A student at the Institute wrote a final year thesis on the plays of Oscar Wilde, normally considered far too decadent for the general reading public.

Their ability to communicate in English also enables these young people to have a far wider range of foreign contacts than other people, young and old alike. And it eventually places many of them in jobs dealing with foreigners: in diplomatic relations, trade and tourism. In contrast to some of their fellow-youth – and even to a lot of senior Party officials and bureaucrats – many English-language graduates reveal a high level of sophistication about the outside world.

'It's the sheer affluence of people in many foreign countries that's really striking,' commented a young Peking worker. 'Whether it's the huge supermarkets or private cars or people's individual houses. And the furniture and the size of washing machines and refrigerators and colour television sets. It's just a different world from China.'

This picture of economic affluence is probably the major image that most young people have of the West. After years of official rhetoric about the dramatic progress made in China since liberation, they have become only too aware of their country's relative backwardness. Despite the increasing availability of consumer goods, there is an immense contrast between China's overcrowded living conditions and almost subsistence level living standards, and the idea they have of everyday life in the West.

The prosperous images coming via magazines and television only seem to be confirmed by the new international-style hotels springing up in major Chinese cities to cater for foreign businessmen and to lure the tourist dollar. Often built as joint enterprises with American or Hong Kong companies, the giant multi-storey edifices present almost as great a contrast to the surrounding urban scene as do the Hiltons and Sheratons in other developing countries from India to the Philippines.

The Jianguo, modelled on a Californian Holiday Inn and one of the first of Peking's new international hotels, has already been replaced in the luxury stakes by hotels such as the Great Wall with its nine restaurants, roof-top tennis courts, health club and indoor swimming pool, night-club and twenty-four-hour room service. Even the outside of the twenty-two storey edifice is an awe-inspiring sight to people living in Peking's remaining *hutong*, the narrow dusty lanes with their tiny, often dilapidated, grey-walled and grey-roofed houses devoid of running water and sewerage.

In Canton, the White Swan (jokingly called the White Elephant by some foreigners) presents an equal spectacle of wealth and luxury as it towers over the Pearl River from the islet of Shamian, once a major foreign concession in China. The hotel's gargantuan garden-filled lobby outdoes even the crystal chandeliers and red and gold tinsel of the revamped Dongfang Hotel, now almost unrecognizable to long-time China travellers and businessmen.

With the exception of a few members of the 'in set' – the privileged offspring of high officials – the closest most young Chinese ever get to these buildings is to have their photographs taken outside them. Most know about their opulent interiors only by hearsay; lucky friends who work as tourist guides or waitresses tell stories of the carpeted luxury and the amount of money that foreigners pay for a room, a meal or even a cocktail. 'Does it really cost 140 yuan a day to stay here?' a taxi driver asked me as we drove up to the Jianguo Hotel in Peking. 'That's over two months' wages. Foreigners must be terribly rich.'

The other basic image presented by the West is that of political and social diversity, contrasting strongly to China's single 'correct' political line and single set of acceptable social mores. Exposure to the Western way of life is both exhilarating and confusing.

'Is it true that people in your country are allowed to disagree openly with the government – and don't get into trouble?' asked a Peking student.

'Is it difficult to get permission to leave your country?' inquired another student, confessing that he had always been puzzled at how so many foreigners simply visited China just to travel around. 'In China you have to have a particular reason for going anywhere, especially overseas.'

Contact with foreign university students and other young travellers invariably provokes comparisons with the lives of young people in other countries. The questions asked by young Chinese often say as much about their own attitudes and problems as do their spontaneous comments. 'Are young people allowed to choose their own jobs in your country?' 'Is it true that university students are allowed to get married?' 'Can young people wear whatever they want?' And the inevitable: 'Are they allowed to go to discos?'

For some young Chinese, the diversity of Western lifestyles and ideas seems positively bewildering. 'You seem to have to make so many decisions for yourselves,' commented one Peking University student. 'In China most decisions are made for us. We don't really have to work out very much for ourselves – except that it's a good idea to get a good education and a good job.'

A similar comment had been made by a bewildered young Shanghai graduate who defected to the United States after he was sent abroad to a Chinese embassy in the mid-1960s. The hardest thing about living in the United States, he said later, was that no one told him what to do. 'Everyone keeps asking me what I *want* to do. I do not *know* what I want to do because I have never before been expected to consider the matter.'[2]

Of all the foreign images in China, the American one has probably been the most dominant since the normalization of Sino–American relations in January 1979. Continuing differences over Taiwan and 'incidents' such as the defection of Chinese tennis player Hu Na and the explusion of an American teacher from China have dampened the early euphoria, and the welter of publicity about the United States has declined somewhat. But it is still America that most young people look to as the source of the best and most advanced of everything in the outside world.

'Where would you like to study?' I asked a class of thirty or so

English language students at the Canton Foreign Language Institute when they said they all wanted to continue their studies overseas.

'The United States,' they responded in unison.

At the same time, many Chinese people are even more struck by the comparison of China with its nearest Asian neighbour, Japan. In the words of a Peking factory worker: 'Japan was backward, now it's an industrial giant.'

'And it does *not* have a communist government,' added his friend meaningfully.

But the place that most readily springs to young people's minds is Hong Kong. In fact, the picture they have of the West is often its ultra-capitalistic, ultra-materialistic, Hong Kong version. Hong Kong seems to represent the absolute ultimate: cheap and abundant consumer goods of every description, disco music blaring out of every doorway, and everyone having plenty of money to spend.

This view is only reinforced by visiting Chinese relatives who flaunt expensive cameras, the latest multi-functional digital watches and even huge stereo cassette recorders. In an effort to impress their less fortunate relatives with their own success and the superiority of capitalism, they tell inflated stories about their own lifestyles.

'My cousin in Hong Kong earns more than six times what I earn,' a process worker in nearby Canton told me wide-eyed. Protests about high accommodation and other living costs fail to convince many young people that all overseas Chinese and foreigners are not immensely rich. To most people in China, as in other developing countries, people who can afford to buy all the food they fancy, let alone cars and houses, are rich.

The renewed exposure to the outside world is already having a substantial impact in China. It is most visible in the enthusiasm of some young people, like David at the Jinjiang Hotel in Shanghai, for Western clothing, products and music. Compared with the Cultural Revolution period, when young people criticized foreign students for wearing non-Chinese clothing or even using foreign toothpaste or face cream, some young men and women are now completely infatuated with foreign things.

Virtually anything from abroad is considered a status symbol.

Some Chinese youth, like their Russian counterparts, wander around carrying bags with foreign words on them – even plastic carry-bags. As in Russia too, foreign brand jeans, mostly sporting not Levi but Hong Kong labels, have become fashionable despite the traditional contempt for denim (literally called 'workers cloth') as being suitable only for factory overalls. In coastal cities such as Canton and Xiamen, some small clothing stalls in the private markets sell nothing but jeans, usually a combination of Hong Kong imports and local reproductions.

Foreign consumer goods have replaced Shanghai products at the top of the status list: from Sanyo TV sets to Canon cameras. 'I've got a large cassette recorder,' one young man told me in the north-eastern city of Harbin. 'But it was made in China. What I really want is a Sony. Of course they're a lot more expensive. That's one of the reasons why everyone wants one.'

At the extreme, the foreign enthusiasts, of whom young men appear to be in the majority, seem almost like a reincarnation of the Westernized Chinese of pre-revolutionary Shanghai, but updated to the 1950s or 1960s. They wear narrow-legged trousers (bell-bottoms have become rather passé), bright see-through nylon shirts or motor-bike jackets, and have longish hair, sideburns and maybe a moustache. Their female counterparts deck themselves out in tight pants or mini-skirts (still much closer to the knee than the Western variety of the 1960s), sleeveless fitted tops which are daring by Chinese standards, and high heels. A bouffant hairstyle, lipstick and perhaps eye make-up complete the picture. Symbols of Westernization for both sexes are huge sunglasses with a foreign label emblazoned on the outside and perhaps even a Sony Walkman.

China's Westernized youth are at their most numerous in Shanghai, which has never quite shaken off its Western bourgeois influences, and in Canton, just over the border from Hong Kong. The Canton scene is beginning to resemble that of Hong Kong rather than cities in north China: young men and women dressed in the latest Hong Kong gear, casual behaviour between the sexes and, in the evening, necking couples all along the Pearl River embankment.

Party and government officials in Canton are loud and vocal about what they describe as 'the ill wind blowing in from the south'. Canton is the centre not just of the legal importation of consumer goods but of smuggling and black marketing. In 1981

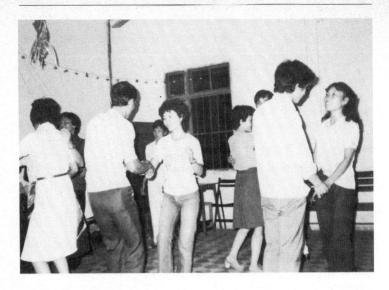

Canton: jeans, T-shirts and casual behaviour between the sexes

alone some 11 000 items were confiscated by customs officials at the Hong Kong border.[3] The authorities had been so worried about the problem that they had installed a 'hot line' telephone on the border at the beginning of the year. In return for information on projected attempts to smuggle luxury goods into China, callers were promised a reward of 15 per cent of the value of any goods confiscated.

Prostitution and gambling are also acknowledged to be greater problems in the Canton area than elsewhere in China. Indeed Canton's reputation as something of a 'sin city' is well known throughout the country. 'We haven't had too many problems yet with the open door policy,' a Communist Youth League official told me in far-off Harbin. 'We certainly don't want the sort of foreign influences they've got down south in Canton.'

If the most visible impact of the open door is the new breed of Westernized urban youth, the most dramatic impact is the desire of some young people to leave China, maybe for good. The authorities originally hoped that images of affluence from the West would encourage young Chinese to work hard for modernization so that China would also be prosperous. Some young people consider that the gap is too wide ever to bridge. 'We'll never catch up,' one youthful Shanghai taxi driver told me, 'At least not in my lifetime. And that's what I'm interested in.'

The easiest personal solution is not to make one's own small contribution to China's modernization but to abandon China for greener pastures abroad. Such action might seem rather dramatic but it has a long history in China; since the nineteenth century and earlier thousands of Chinese have sought a better livelihood in Southeast Asia, America and Australia. Nor is the movement novel in the People's Republic. Both legal and illegal refugees into Hong Kong from neighbouring Guangdong province have been a feature of the colony's existence ever since the Communists came to power.

What is striking at the present time is the number of young people who express a desire to leave China. In the words of one Peking teacher: 'Before, we lacked the opportunity to leave China, and we didn't really have the information about the West, or even Hong Kong, to make us want to leave. Now many young people have the desire and will seize almost any opportunity presenting itself.'

With harsh controls on emigration from China and immigration into Hong Kong and many other countries, probably the easiest way to leave China permanently is to marry an overseas Chinese or a foreigner. Marriage to a Chinese from Hong Kong, in particular, is sometimes actively encouraged by families that lack a direct Hong Kong connection.

Chinese officials acknowledge that a large number of such marriages, which have become particularly rife in the Canton area, are 'not always for the right reason'. 'We're concerned at the number of young people, especially women, who are prepared to marry someone from Hong Kong even after knowing them for only a few days,' said a Communist Youth League official in Canton. 'They mistakenly think that once they get to Hong Kong life will be wonderful and they'll be rich.'

Marriage to a foreigner ostensibly appears more drastic and is sometimes actively opposed by the Chinese person's relatives. But such marriages have sometimes been undertaken with the sole purpose of going abroad. One Australian student in Shanghai, for example, told me that she was regularly approached by male fellow-students suggesting a marriage of convenience to permit them to leave China. 'A few foreign students have agreed to such marriages,' she acknowledged. 'But I think they're a bit irresponsible. Many young Chinese simply don't realize the problems they'll have adjusting to a completely different way of life and even getting a job, especially if they don't already speak English.'

Some Chinese are not so open about their intentions, creating problems for foreign students trying to pursue genuine relationships. As one Canadian student said of her Chinese boyfriend: 'I really don't know whether he's truly interested in me or whether he just wants to leave China.'

The more usual wish is not to leave China indefinitely, but to spend a few years studying or working in the West. Overseas study, which is also extremely conducive to future career advancement, is the dream of most university students. Only about 3000 currently achieve that dream each year.

Like the best assignments, the overseas study programme has been riddled with privileges and abuse. The sons and daughters of prominent officials – as high as Deng Xiaoping himself – have been in the forefront of students receiving scholarships both for government-sponsored exchange pro-grammes and for exchanges between individual universities. In a country where getting things done through personal contacts is all-important, foreign academics visiting China often find themselves being approached by young Chinese seeking scholarships in Western countries.

The great majority of Chinese students who go overseas return to China, assured of a secure prestigious job (which they would not necessarily obtain in the West) and a privileged position in Chinese society. But some students, regardless of their original intentions, decide not to return at the end of their studies. When students started going to the United States, Deng Xiaoping privately estimated that perhaps 10 per cent would not come back. Neither Chinese nor American officials have released any statistics – this is a sensitive issue in relations between the two countries – but private reports indicate that Deng's estimate has proved to be a fairly accurate one.

Initially the Chinese authorities attempted to restrict over-seas sojourns as far as possible to people with spouses and even children who remained in China, thus providing an incentive to return. This practice has to some extent broken down because of the declared need to expose the brightest new graduates to the best possible higher education. For example, the seventy-two graduates of the Chinese University of Science and Technology who were sent to the United States for graduate study at the end of 1982 were all in their early twenties and all unmarried.

The authorities now appeal to students' moral and patriotic sense in the effort to minimize the level of desertion. At receptions held by Chinese diplomatic missions in Washington and New York to mark the 1984 New Year, Chinese students attending universities in the two cities were reminded that their government had made a large investment in their educa-tion, whether they were studying on exchange scholarships or were privately sponsored. The purpose of overseas study was to enable them to contribute to their country's modernization.

'We're faced with something of a conflict,' admitted Zhu Shanqing, Vice-Chairman of the All-China Youth Federation. 'The open door is essential for China's modernization. We need

Western technology and expertise. But it's proving difficult to keep out undesirable Western influences.'

Already officials are partially blaming China's new openness to the West for the nation's youth problems, everything from growing acquisitiveness and personal ambition to unruly behaviour and crime, sexual licence and political disaffection. In official rhetoric: 'The open door with its capitalist influences is having a corrupting effect on the minds, and even on the bodies, of some young Chinese.'[4]

Indeed the authorities are tending to use the open door as a general explanation, and sometimes as a scapegoat, for all that is considered undesirable in China – from individualism and excessive romance in films and literature to a lack of interest in 'serving the people'. These non-socialist attitudes are declared to be a product of 'bourgeois liberalization' and very conveniently blamed on Western influences.

Although officials distort the impact of the open door, it cannot be denied that access to Western images of affluence has intensified the general gap between young people's aspirations and opportunities, just as images of general diversity are contributing to their questioning of China's rigid socio-political system and its values. No longer can the Chinese government convince young people that China has a satisfactory standard of living compared with other countries or that their restrictive way of life is the only possible lifestyle. As one Shanghai teenager put it: 'The open door has really opened our eyes.'

Alarmed by the apparent monster they have created in their midst, the Chinese authorities have since the beginning of the 1980s been attempting to dampen down the tantalizing Western images that they themselves helped to create. Their basic argument is that life is neither as affluent nor as exciting in the West, and especially in the United States, as it might appear to be on the surface.

Not everyone has their own house and car, write Chinese reporters and students who have visited the United States. There is also widespread poverty and destitution: dejected people in rags frequent soup kitchens and homeless vagrants wander the streets. Unemployment is rife in the West – and not just of school-leavers. 'Even many people with PhD degrees are not hired full time,' declared one writer, having in mind the possibility of an intellectual brain drain.[5]

Far from being exciting and diverse, state other writers, most Western societies are 'cultural and spiritual wastelands' where money controls everything and where people are interested only in their own material advancement and do not give a damn about their fellow human beings. 'The life of the impoverished old is most tragic. Many people are simply discarded by their families and left to fend for themselves or placed in old people's homes.'[6]

The basic message is that Chinese people should not equate modernization with Westernization. China must be careful to accept only those aspects of Western society that will be beneficial to modernization, not those that will inhibit it. In the words of Party Secretary Hu Yaobang: 'We should absorb good things from others, but resolutely resist those decadent and backward things.'[7] This formula – distinguishing between the desirable and the undesirable, the useful and the harmful, or the beautiful and the ugly – is repeated *ad nauseum* by high officials, bureaucrats and compliant writers and social scientists.

"——你不去夜校学点现代化的技术？"
—— "我从头到脚已经够'现代化'了卟。"
徐克仁画

Modernization should not be equated with Westernization
Caption: 'Aren't you going to night-school to learn a few modernized techniques?'
'I'm modernized enough from head to toe.'
(*Jiefang Ribao (Liberation Daily)*, 11 April 1979)

The formula of selective borrowing from the West is, of course, based on a fundamental fallacy: that any Western contact can be value-free and that even Western education and technology, considered vital for modernization, can be isolated from their socio-political context. The present concept bears striking similarities to that put forward by Chinese self-strengtheners in the late nineteenth century when it proved a dramatic failure.

Despite the fallacy, the Chinese authorities make earnest attempts to eradicate from China those foreign influences that they consider most undesirable. Youth's susceptibility to Western fashions and music have been particular targets. Newspapers and youth magazines urge young people to shun what are described as 'weird hairstyles and dress'. One of the *China Daily*'s officially sponsored letter-writers complained: 'Some young men have such long hair that if you see them from behind you can't tell whether they're male or female.'[8]

Mini-skirts and bell-bottom trousers, somewhat out of date by Western standards, came in for particular censure in the early 1980s. 'What sort of skirts are the most becoming?' asked an article in a women's magazine, telling its readers that they should not wear skirts that were too tight or too far above the knee.[9]

The sustained attack on bell-bottom trousers eventually gave way to a controversy – taken up even by the national press – on whether or not jeans were suitable attire. After lengthy debate it was decided that they were acceptable, provided they were neither too wide nor too tight-fitting. But they are still regarded with some suspicion, along with other allegedly Western bourgeois affectations. 'He wore jeans, reflective sunglasses, and had a gold-plated ring on his finger,' stated the media report on the young rapist/murderer in Shenyang.[10]

On the subject of selectivity in popular music, even the Party's theoretical journal *Red Flag* entered the discussion. Western songs were acceptable so long as they were 'melodious and sung in a friendly pleasant environment', it maintained. 'Quite another matter are singing performances in night-clubs, dance halls and bars. We must resolutely reject this decadent, rotten, vulgar and corrupt trash.'[11]

Taiwanese singer Deng Lijun (known in Hong Kong as Teresa

Teng) came in for particular criticism. Even more popular than most contemporary Western pop music which sounds fairly strange to Chinese ears, Teresa's love songs had become a fad throughout the country. 'Two Dengs rule China,' the saying went. 'During the day it's Deng Xiaoping; at night it's Deng Lijun.'

I asked a Communist Youth League official why the singer had been subjected to such a welter of denunciation. 'Her songs are vulgar,' he replied. 'Far too soft and sexy. They give young people bad ideas.'

The amount of attention given to these seemingly superficial issues amounts at times almost to an official obsession. This obsession is not, of course, concerned with Western clothing and music as such but with what they represent: the individual freedom and independence of Western and even Hong Kong youth, as well as the whole ambit of the sexual revolution and the permissive society. For all the stilted rhetoric, the concern is not simply a contemporary Chinese phenomenon. Many other socialist and non-socialist countries – from Russia to Singapore and India – are doing all they can to prevent their youth becoming involved in the same problems as youth in the West, at least as they see them.

'What are the faults of Western youth?' one article in a Chinese youth magazine asked rhetorically and went on to picture the youth generation in the United States and Western Europe wallowing in a trough of rebelliousness, spiritual emptiness, homelessness, drunken debauchery, drugs and violence.[12]

But the official denunciations of much of contemporary Western culture fall largely on deaf ears, only provoking scorn and laughter from many young people. Despite all the torrid warnings about bourgeois decadence and moral corruption, they continue to listen to foreign or Hong Kong popular music on shortwave radio and regularly complain about the paucity of foreign films. Even one young tertiary-educated Party official appeared embarrassed by the simplistic rhetoric trotted out by his elderly superior during an interview in Peking. 'I think the officials responsible for the open door policy should read more about Western countries and maybe visit them for themselves,' he confessed to me later.

His point was well made. The majority of officials dealing with youth policy, including virtually all members of the Youth Research Institute, have never been to the West.

A potentially more effective weapon in moderating youth's enthusiasm for the West is the appeal to Chinese patriotism. Officials from Deng Xiaoping downwards warn that the worship of 'undesirable foreign influences' – from popular songs to weird dress and even moustaches – is a threat to China's national dignity.

'If we accept everything from the West wholesale without discrimination, it shows that we have lost our national dignity,' declared senior Party spokesman Zhou Yang. 'We must develop our national culture and cherish our socialist motherland.'[13] And according to the *People's Daily*: 'Some people believe that anything foreign is good, making no distinctions whatsoever. They worship foreign goods, scramble for imported goods and go crazy at the sight of foreign goods. To get hold of foreign goods, they would sacrifice national and personal dignity.'[14]

The Communists' utilization of patriotism or nationalism in a bid to obtain support for their socialist policies is as old as the Party itself. It was a particularly potent force in the early years of communist rule when the country's century-long humiliation at the hands of Western imperialism was still a vivid memory. But while these sentiments do have some significance to the older generation, they have less impact on young people to whom contact with the West is an intriguing novelty.

Even so, patriotism has a certain appeal even to Chinese youth and already there have been a few signs of a backlash against Western influences. Some young people express resentment at the special privileges and facilities enjoyed by foreigners in China. These include not just a network of hotels, restaurants and the so-called friendship stores which sell both imported and export quality Chinese goods, but segregated sections of stores which sometimes have a sign at the entrance, 'foreign guests only'. 'They tell us about the time before liberation when Chinese people were banned from many places in our own country,' remarked a young man in Peking. 'But it seems to be getting that way again.'

Some young people, especially the well-educated, also criticize those of their fellow-youth whose interest in foreign people and culture amounts almost to an obsession. 'They spend all their time hanging out on the Bund and talking to foreigners about foreign music and films,' a recent Shanghai university graduate commented. 'Some even want to pretend they're foreigners. They forget that they're Chinese.'

But even this young man was an avid reader of whatever modern foreign literature he could get his hands on. The contradiction is an old one: a virtual love–hate attitude towards the West. Ever since Chinese people came into contact with the West in the nineteenth century, they have exhibited both an enthusiasm for Western culture and lifestyles, and a deep desire to prove the equality – if not the superiority – of things Chinese.

The government's ideological and patriotic exhortations have been accompanied by practical restrictions on young people's contacts with Western influences, especially those escaping the official 'filter'. In early 1982, when foreign video and music cassettes were flooding the country, the authorities imposed a formal ban on what they described as 'reactionary, pornographic and obscene' music and video recordings. The undesirable category included not just most contemporary Western popular music but many of the romantic songs performed by Hong Kong and Taiwanese singers: songs with titles such as 'A Taste of First Love' and 'Unforgettable Young Love'.[15]

In Canton the authorities also banned the watching of television programmes from Hong Kong – a combination of American and British features and local Cantonese programmes – which could be picked up with special 'fishbone' aerials. An 'anti-pornography day' was set aside to dismantle the aerials under official supervision.

In practice, the formal bans were of only limited effectiveness. There were continuing reports, not just from the vulnerable Canton area but even from the far-flung provinces of Ningxia and Liaoning, of the widespread playing of decadent music (available on shortwave radio and personal cassette recorders) and the sale of pornographic literature. Even the ban on fishbone aerials was not completely successful. According to one local resident, the authorities had to resort to jamming Hong Kong television by using the same frequencies for their own broadcasts. 'Now some people stay up late – after 11 or midnight – so they can watch Hong Kong television after the local channels close down for the night,' he told me.

More effective is the government's effort to restrict young people's contacts with foreigners themselves. After a short-lived period of near normal relations between Chinese and Westerners at the end of the 1970s, when informal visits to Chinese homes and eating out with Chinese people became almost commonplace, people who associate unofficially with foreigners now lay themselves open to official interrogation. Sustained contact can lead to detention and the charge of 'selling state secrets', a charge that was levelled against dissidents who talked with foreign journalists during the Democracy Movement in 1978–9 and led to a five-year prison sentence for a prominent journalist in 1982. With even basic information about everyday life being classified as 'state secrets', it's little wonder that many Chinese have become somewhat guarded in their contacts with foreigners.

The opposite charge, 'stealing state secrets', has been levelled against a few foreigners who have gained access to material that is considered *neibu*, for internal eyes only. In March 1982 American teacher and graduate student Lisa Wischer was expelled from China on this charge. A young Australian visitor was also expelled in early 1984 after he took as a souvenir a poster announcing criminal executions in Xi'an and reportedly attempted to view an execution.

The current line between general interest or academic research and what Chinese officials brand as 'spying' is a very fine one, bringing back memories of accusations levelled against foreigners (mostly missionaries) of being intelligence agents by both the Communist government and its pre-decessors. In the early 1950s and the Cultural Revolution period some foreigners were gaoled as spies for little more than being the citizens of bourgeois capitalist countries or perhaps after being seen chatting to a foreign diplomat based in Peking. According to a former Chinese student now living abroad: 'Foreigners are still politically suspect in China. Officials tend to regard them all as potential, if not actual, spies. Especially if they live there and speak Chinese.'

When it comes to personal relationships with the opposite sex, young Chinese face tremendous hurdles even in having a relationship with a foreign student at the same university. 'I went out with a Chinese girl a couple of times,' one foreign student in Shanghai told me. 'But then the authorities put pressure on her not to have anything more to do with me. They told her that Western men go out with girls for only one reason.'

Young Chinese men dating foreign female students are sometimes warned that foreign women have a very casual attitude towards men, either being uninterested in establishing long-term relationships or marrying and divorcing at random.

The restrictive atmosphere has not deterred a few young Chinese from having personal relationships with, and even marrying, foreign students – whatever their motives. Times have changed dramatically since the mid-1970s when a French student and an Australian teacher, both female, had drawn-out battles with the authorities before being permitted to marry Chinese men; they received permission only after Mao died and the matter was reconsidered by the new leadership at the highest levels.

Although there are no longer official barriers to such marriages, only the most determined couples ever reach this stage. First, they have to survive constant surveillance. 'You can't put a foot wrong – or any other part of your anatomy for that matter,' an English student said half-jokingly. 'Officials tend to be even more strict about Chinese men or women having a physical relationship with a foreigner than they are about two Chinese. Any Chinese person who's caught having a so-called unlawful relationship is likely to be sent off to the countryside for reform.'

Second, the Chinese person has to survive repeated diatribes on the inadvisability of marrying a foreigner. The media features articles on the sad fate awaiting those young people, especially women, who marry foreigners or overseas Chinese and subsequently leave China. One twenty three-year-old, for example, wrote to a Canton newspaper complaining that her husband had expected her to go nightly to winebars and discos where she'd had to face being propositioned by his friends; she also eventually had to face his infidelities with other women. Realizing her terrible mistake and the superiority of the socialist system, she decided to return to China to 'start a new life'.[16]

Another young woman who married an English student and

subsequently left China had no such misgivings, 'The official attitude towards Chinese marrying foreigners is basically racist,' she told me. 'Many Chinese still can't accept the idea of marrying a foreign "barbarian", far less having children of mixed race. Foreigners and half-foreign children have never really been accepted in China. Under a socialist government there's a political aspect too that also affects overseas Chinese. During the Cultural Revolution, for example, anyone with foreign relatives or even contacts overseas was likely to be put in gaol for being contaminated by bourgeois capitalist ideology.'

Concerned at the limited success of its media exhortations and practical measures, the government has also launched the occasional intense onslaught against undesirable Western influences. Such attacks have undoubtedly been encouraged, and possibly even provoked, by those high officials who are critical of the level of China's contacts with the West and who even have serious doubts about the 'open door' policy itself.

The most vehement assault to date occurred in late 1983 when the government conducted its 'campaign against spiritual pollution', directly linking everything anti-socialist and hence undesirable to the bourgeois decadent influences coming in from the outside world. On 28 October propaganda chief Deng Liqun told foreign press representatives that spiritual pollution included 'obscene, barbarous or reactionary materials, vulgar taste in artistic performances, and indulgence in individualism.'[17] The media subsequently outdid its early anti-Western rhetoric, writing about the latest 'exercise in cleaning up cultural contamination' and alleging that obscene music and video tapes were a kind of 'spiritual opium ... undermining morals, polluting the atmosphere, and poisoning the minds of the young.'[18]

The welter of media rhetoric was accompanied by fresh practical restrictions. As well as imposing new bans on the importation or recording of allegedly pornographic video and music tapes, the authorities called on young people (including Party officials) to hand over any such tapes in their possession and to indulge in self-examination and self-criticism.

With Premier Zhao Ziyang forsaking his Western suits for Mao jackets, the stage was also set for a further assault on Western-style clothing and affectations. Individual institutions banned female office workers from wearing tight-fitting skirts and universities outlawed high heels and make up. Peking's municipal government ordered its male employees to shave off their moustaches.

The overall assault seemed to have some effect, not least because it was running concurrently with the anti-crime campaign. Young people were terrified of being seen doing anything wrong and some temporarily reverted to their baggy clothing and clean-cut appearance. As one young woman in Shanghai later put it: 'Why risk being denounced or even arrested for the sake of a fancy hairstyle or a well-fitting skirt?'

But the onslaught also threatened to undermine China's modernization programme. Chinese people involved in private enterprise feared denunciation as individualists and bourgeois profiteers; many foreign businessmen and experts in China began getting cold feet about their continued presence in the country. In the words of a British businessman in Shanghai: 'Some of us became scared of a return to the anti-foreign hostility of the Cultural Revolution period. The reassurances we received from officials didn't really help. They virtually told us that they liked our money and our technical expertise but they didn't like anything else about us.'

Realizing that the attack had been misplaced, the government scaled down the campaign after barely a month, retreating to the weary formula that Chinese people must learn to distinguish between the beneficial and harmful effects of the West but not being explicit about the dividing line. The retreat only illustrated the government's underlying dilemma: the impossibility of encouraging private enterprise and opening China to outside influences while at the same time maintaining what it considers to be desirable socialist ideals and behaviour.

CHAPTER TEN

An Alienated Generation?

In February 1981 the *People's Daily* published a lengthy article on the youth generation. The article began with an anecdote. '"Do you believe in Marxism?" "No, I do not." This is the reply of a young person to a question in a survey. Though the number of people who gave this reply is not large it is still quite shocking.'[1] Such a reply comes as no shock to anyone who has had the opportunity to discuss the question with young people in China, whether in 1981 or 1984. As a young factory worker in Peking put it: 'Of course we've been told, again and again, that socialism is a superior political system. But who really believes it any more?'

Quantifiable opinions are still difficult to come by in China. There are no public opinion polls and the results of official surveys are released only when it suits the government's interests. One survey that did receive widespread publicity was undertaken in 1981 among 2000 young people (in factories, a department store, two universities and a high school) in Fujian and Anhui provinces. Approximately 65 per cent of those questioned stated that they thought that socialism was indeed a superior socio-political system, a result utilized by the Chinese media to demonstrate that 'the majority' of young people in China believed in socialism.[2]

The fact that the results were published at all was probably an indication that they were considered favourable. Rather more significant was the fact that 35 per cent of respondents were prepared to admit, in the face of constant political rhetoric and pressure, that they did *not* believe socialism to be superior. And as a sociological researcher in Hefei told me: 'Even when we use anonymous questionnaires many young people tend to say what they think we want them to say.'

In another official survey at Peking University in mid-1982, 77 per cent of students reportedly listed 'Marxism–Leninism', 'socialism' or 'the Communist Party' under the heading 'Your belief'.[3] But only 30 per cent had given such responses in a private unpublished survey undertaken by students at Fudan University.[4]

Admittedly the terms used in these surveys are extremely vague. Even survey respondents sometimes attempt to clarify the issue, making such comments as 'the genuine socialist system is superior' and 'the socialist system is good, but not its implementation.' (The term 'socialist' is normally used in China to describe the political system; China had a socialist revolution but has not yet achieved communism. The term 'communist' is used basically with reference to the single political party: the Chinese Communist Party.)

Recent survey findings, vague though they are, tend to be backed up by the government's own pronouncements. Over the past few years officials have spoken at length about a wavering of faith, and even a crisis of confidence, in the socialist system. While these feelings are by no means limited to the youth generation, it is this sector of the community that is causing the authorities the greatest level of concern.

The lack of faith in the socialist system includes a lack of confidence in the Chinese Communist Party and its ability to modernize China. In the official survey of youth attitudes undertaken in Anhui and Fujian, only half the respondents said they were confident that the government's goal of modernizing China by the end of the century would be achieved. In one Shanghai survey, only 38 per cent of young people questioned – tertiary level liberal arts students – expressed such confidence.[5]

In personal conversations, young people generally show little enthusiasm for suggestions that China's backwardness will be overcome as the government pursues its modernization drive. 'Not in my lifetime it won't,' was the cynical response of the young taxi driver in Shanghai. 'Not with the Party the way it is at the moment,' commented a female student in Harbin.

'There's not just a lack of belief in socialism and the Communist Party,' a young hairdresser in Peking told me. 'Many young people these days are generally apathetic and indifferent towards politics altogether.'

In most countries, a lack of interest in politics is of limited significance. But in China life itself is political. Socialism is not just an ideology or a form of government but an all-embracing social and cultural system, providing the ground rules for everything from literature to love and everyday behaviour. The rejection of socialism places some young people in what is officially described as a 'spiritual void'. 'Some young people have no far-reaching ideals, no belief in their own future, and even serious doubts about the meaning of life itself,' admitted a Party official in Peking.

In the private survey undertaken at Shanghai's Fudan University, students were asked the rather simplistic question: 'What do you believe in?' Approximately one-third replied 'socialism', a quarter responded 'fate' and another quarter 'nothing at all'.[6]

One of the major topics covered in the youth press since the early 1980s has been the so-called 'meaning of life' issue. The debate began in January 1980 when two Shanghai newspapers published an anonymous letter from a local high school student. Her mounting confusion about the significance of life had left her dull and listless, she complained. 'I feel so downhearted and bewildered that my studies have been seriously affected ... The people I meet always seem to put their own interests above those of the state and others ... As time goes by, my ideals, like a cloud of smoke, vanish into the air.'[7]

Within a few months, most youth magazines and newspapers had taken up the meaning of life issue, none more actively than the national monthly *Chinese Youth*. This time it was ostensibly a 23-year-old Peking factory worker named Pan Xiao who confessed her loss of faith in communist ideals. 'Why is life's road getting narrower and narrower?' she asked. 'I should say that I am just beginning life, but already all of life's mystery and charm are gone for me. I feel as if I have reached the end.'

Her earlier positive illusions about life, she confessed, had been shattered by political disruption, family quarrels, public denunciation by a friend, and a broken romance. 'People are selfish,' she concluded. 'There is no such thing as a selfless, noble person. The propaganda of the past was exaggeration or fiction.'[8]

In reality, Pan Xiao's letter was the combined work of two

people: a young woman worker and a male university student. Written at the magazine's instigation following a panel discussion on young people's views of life, it summed up their personal attitudes and experiences. The motives of *Chinese Youth* and other officially controlled publications in giving youth alienation a public airing were unclear but it seems likely that the authorities wanted to assess the seriousness of the problem and then hopefully do something about it.

Whatever the motives, Pan Xiao's expression of disillusionment struck a raw nerve among young Chinese. Over the next few months, some 40 000 letters were received by *Chinese Youth* alone. Other magazines and newspapers were also inundated with correspondence as they took up the issue. 'We were surprised at the response,' acknowledged Wang Cuizhen, deputy editor of the national newspaper *Chinese Youth News*. 'Even though *Chinese Youth* was the main focus of the debate, we received over 20 000 letters ourselves.'

No statistical analyses of correspondence were ever released. While newspapers and magazines published some letters agreeing with Pan Xiao and like-minded young people, they predictably also published many letters expressing supreme faith in socialist ideals. Senior Party officials and compliant intellectuals joined in the emerging media campaign, assuring 'troubled youth' of the significance of life in a socialist society.

Just as predictably, the Shanghai high school student who had set off the debate soon had second thoughts about her disillusionment, at least for public consumption. Six weeks after her first letter, she wrote: 'I have received many letters from various parts of the country. People expressed enthusiasm and encouragement from the bottom of their hearts, making me realize that this society really is concerned about the younger generation. I have seen where the superiority of the socialist system lies.'[9]

Despite her turnaround, the officially sponsored debate had largely misfired. In the words of a young Shanghai clerk: 'It only aroused young people's awareness and set them talking about their feelings to others.'

While some young people wallow in disillusionment, others admit they are positively searching for something to replace their shattered socialist ideals. 'There's no point just being negative about life,' commented one young man in Canton. 'One must look for something – anything – to believe in.'

The heartfelt need to discover an all-embracing meaning to life partly reflects young people's experience within a single belief system that claims to provide all the answers. To someone from the West, the questions asked by young Chinese can be rather perplexing. 'But what *do* young people in your country believe in?' they ask again and again. 'Democracy? Capitalism? Religion?'

The response that most young people's beliefs are not that straightforward – but rather a diverse amalgam of ideas – does not satisfy most Chinese. 'Well, they must be just as confused about life as we are,' one university student commented.

The search for a meaning to life has led some young Chinese to investigate a range of ideas and philosophies, mostly emanating from the West. Those who still see political systems at the root of everything have flirted with ideas of Western liberalism and democracy; others have merely promoted the concept of true 'socialist democracy' for China. While the expression of such beliefs was severely dampened down in early 1979 when the short-lived Democracy Movement was brought to an abrupt halt, it did not die away immediately. At the 1980 local elections in Peking's Haidian district, for example, some of the Peking University candidates harked back to the eighteenth-century Enlightenment philosophers, expounding basic human rights and democratic ideals, and quoting J. S. Mill *On Freedom*.

'They are trying to introduce bourgeois democracy and ideas of bourgeois rights,' declare media commentators in response to the mention of such ideas, accusing their proponents of 'failing to be on their guard against the corruption of capitalist ideology.'[10]

If official censure does not always quieten questioning students, the threat of harsh assignments following graduation usually does. 'Most outspoken students learnt their lesson in 1979 and 1980,' a Peking student told me in 1982. 'Nowadays only the bravest – or the most foolhardy – are prepared to risk their future careers. But just because we don't speak out doesn't mean we don't talk about these things in private.'

My suggestion that students were being bought off by a

system they did not really believe in only brought nods all round. 'It's the only sensible thing to do. Protest doesn't get you anywhere in China. Except to Tibet – or gaol.'

Other young people in search of a meaning to life have been looking beyond political systems.

'Do Western students believe in existentialism?' I have been asked again and again in recent years by Chinese university students. 'Or in other philosophies? Do they read Sartre? Kafka?'

Along with such writers as Camus and Joyce, Sartre and Kafka have a wide following among university students – when they can get hold of the books. While the authorities generally concede that access to these Western writers is essential for humanities students, they periodically bundle most Western thinkers together under the label of 'bourgeois liberalization' or 'spiritual pollution' and warn of their corrupting influence on socialist ideas.

But profound Western thinkers are basically for those of an intellectual bent. More widespread has been Chinese youth's flirtation with religious ideas. Although religion is officially denounced in China as a remnant of feudal superstition which is incompatible with socialist materialism, the post-Mao leadership has adopted a slightly more liberal attitude than its immediate predecessors. Indeed there has been something of a revival of religious activity in China.

'Religion is often the first thing that comes to young people's minds when they feel disillusioned with life,' remarked a Shanghai youth.

In her famous letter to *Chinese Youth*, Pan Xiao had written: 'My heart is so confused, so contradictory . . . I confess, I have gone secretly to watch services in the Catholic church, I have thought of becoming a nun.'[11]

The bulk of worshippers at religious services are elderly but there is invariably a substantial sprinkling of young people. At the 1983 Christmas morning service at Shanghai's main Protestant church, for example, around one-third of the congregation of over 3000 were in their teens or twenties. 'We've noticed an increase in youthful worshippers since our church reopened in 1980,' the pastor told me.

Even so, Christians, who are attracted partly by the novelty of a religion that has always been identified with the West, are probably in the minority of young religious believers. For all the efforts of former Catholic and Protestant missionaries, Christianity has never had more than a limited following in China.

Young people are more likely to hark back to Chinese tradition: Buddhism, Taoism and popular folk religion. Some go little further than lighting incense sticks and praying at the recently renovated temples. Others are more serious. The son of one prominent Chinese official has taken up the contemplative life of a Taoist, at least in his spare time, refusing to go overseas to further his technological studies.

The level of religious belief among young Chinese is impossible to estimate but it has already aroused the alarm of officialdom. 'A religious fever has emerged in some places,' complained a Chinese youth newspaper in March 1982. 'Even cases of female Communist Youth League members having their heads shaved to become Buddhist nuns have occurred.' Young people should be warned that religion is an illusory flower, stated the article. 'Who has ever seen the divine power and the realization of the kingdom of love?'[12]

'Yes, we're faced with a problem of youth alienation,' admitted top youth official Zhu Shanqing. 'First we need to understand why some people are losing their faith in socialism and looking for something else to believe in.'

The Chinese authorities publicly attribute the problem mainly to the two great scapegoats – the Cultural Revolution and the open door policy to the West – conveniently shifting the blame from themselves. Few people would deny the significance of these factors, but they are only part of the story.

As officials point out, many young Chinese did go through their impressionable childhood and even early teens during a period of political disruption. They also perceived the effects on their family and relatives, including imprisonment and suicide, and continue to hear horror stories of that period. 'I was six years old when it all started,' said one young man approaching his mid-twenties. 'The Red Guards came and threw our family out of our house – they said we were too bourgeois and we should just live in one room. My grandfather was a professor and he was sent off to the countryside to work like a peasant. It was all too much for him. He drowned himself in the river.'

But disaffection with the political system does not stop with its past performance. The Communist Party has continued to lack credibility in the eyes of many young people, not least because of its frequent ideological somersaults. In the words of a young woman in Peking: 'We were told this – in the name of the Communist Party. Then were told that – in the name of the Communist Party. What are we supposed to believe? No one even takes the *People's Daily* seriously any more.'

The Party's image is not improved by the poor reputation of the middle-ranking officials and bureaucrats with whom young people have the most contact. 'These are the people who are supposed to be guiding our nation towards modernization,' remarked a young teacher. 'But look at them. They're old, bureaucratic, poorly educated, inefficient and corrupt. Many of them are more interested in obtaining special privileges for themselves and leading comfortable lives than they are in improving the lives of the Chinese people.'

The open door must also be held partly responsible for youth's political alienation. China's reopening to the West has exposed young people to a wide diversity of alternative political and social ideas, as well as to societies far more affluent than their own, and the Chinese government can no longer convince young people that Chinese communism is the only possible way forward.

'If socialist institutions are superior, why haven't our productive powers developed as quickly as those of capitalism's?' asks a young female factory worker in Jiang Zilong's 1979 short story 'The Foundation'. 'When I listen to technical reports and read magazines on technology, it is clear that capitalism is more advanced than socialism. How can this be explained?'[13]

There is also a more fundamental personal reason for youth alienation which partly incorporates the two official explanations. This is the wide gap that currently exists between young people's rising expectations and their limited opportunities, a product of both a rigidly controlled society and a continuing low level of economic development. As another factory worker expressed it: 'The standard of living is low. Housing problems are horrendous. Many young people have unsatisfying jobs and don't think they have any future. Others don't have jobs at all. When the Communist Party solves these problems, then maybe they'll get my support. In the meantime I'll be looking for something else to believe in.'

When it comes to taking measures to overcome youth alienation, the government faces severe problems. 'Unfortunately
there's a limited amount we can do in practice to combat
disaffection,' admitted a Communist Party official in Peking.
'For example, little can be done about the continuing legacy of
the Cultural Revolution.'

The authorities are taking some steps to improve the Party's
present image and instil confidence in its modernization
potential. In particular, they are attacking some of the major
complaints about officials. But their assault on privilege and
corruption has only made people aware of just how rampant
the abuses have been.

'They give lots of publicity to the big cases,' a young
school-teacher told me. 'Like the bureaucrat who converted the
top floor of a building into luxury apartments for himself and
his friends – all with public funds. And the officials in Canton
who ran a smuggling and tax evasion racket. They illegally
imported over 100 000 television sets and almost that number
of cassette recorders. Over 5000 officials have already been
expelled from the Communist Party for corruption. But of
course most of us know individually of many cases that have
not been exposed – and often at fairly high levels.'

Official efforts to persuade elderly officials to retire, and to
promote younger better-educated men and women in their
place, have predictably met strong resistance from those
holding entrenched positions. 'No one wants to give up their
own privileges,' said the same young school-teacher. 'Not just
good jobs but the whole paraphernalia – access to official cars,
superior housing, the best restaurants, and so on.'

Nor does the Chinese government have a magic solution to
the wide gap between youth's rising expectations and limited
opportunities: a gap that is keenly felt by young people in most
developing countries. 'China is still a relatively backward
country,' stressed a Party official in Harbin. 'Young people's
expectations are going to be greater than their opportunities for
a long time to come, especially as they learn more about the
outside world.'

With little scope for remedial action, the Chinese government has had to fall back on its customary strategy of ideological persuasion. In the early years following Mao's death,
there was a welcome respite from political meetings and

ideological diatribes about revolution, class struggle and adhering to the socialist line. People were urged to put their energies to practical use and work hard for modernization. But since the early 1980s there has been a renewed stress on maintaining socialist values. As many a Party official expresses it: 'China must be modernized. But it must also be socialist.'

China's entire youth propaganda network has been mobilized in the attempt to combat political alienation. The attack has been spearheaded by the Communist Youth League which has expanded its activities in schools, universities and factories alike. Youth newspapers and magazines, controlled by the League, spread the socialist message. A special youth publishing house churns out booklets on subjects ranging from 'the correct outlook on life' to detailed expositions on 'individualism and co-operation' and 'work and pleasure'.

These youth publications, as well as the general media, also publicize the latest mass political campaigns. The mass campaign, the conventional means of implementing communist policies at the everyday level, utilizes radio, television, loudspeaker broadcasts, newspapers and magazines to propagate a single-minded message over a period of weeks or even months. Much of the media's attention since 1981 has been focused on variations of the 'campaign for a socialist spiritual civilization'. This has conducted a broad assault on the undermining of socialist values by 'bourgeois liberalization' and 'capitalist ideologies'.

One of the campaign's more concrete forms, directed particularly at the youth generation, has been the socialist ethics movement which aims to restore desirable socialist behaviour. Individual months are designated 'socialist ethics month' and 'anti-slovenliness month' with young people being urged to behave in a civilized manner in public places, help their neighbours and be polite to one another.

The familiar strategy of holding up individual young people for emulation has also been utilized. In 1980, the model young soldier Lei Feng – the selfless hero who worked only for the common good – was resurrected yet again. This time Lei Feng was praised not so much for his spirit of self-sacrifice as for being 'prepared to do whatever the Party told him to do'.[14]

1982 saw the emergence of a new youth model. In July, a 24-year-old medical student named Zhang Hua entered the

新一代优秀大学生

张华

战士出版社

Cover of booklet entitled *Zhang Hua: An Outstanding University Student of the New Generation*

annals of communist martyrdom when he tried to rescue an elderly peasant from a pit of nightsoil. Zhang was overcome by fumes and died in the attempt. 'Zhang Hua's personal sacrifice set a fine example to the youth of today,' declared a booklet devoted to the young man's short life.[15]

For all their intensity, the recent mass campaigns seem to have had little impact. As one Party official admitted, it is becoming more and more difficult to mobilize the population. 'Young people just don't respond the way they did in the 1950s,' he complained.

This is hardly surprising. Youth's political cynicism is directed largely against the very people who are trying to mobilize them.

The Lei Feng campaign was greeted with apathy. 'Not him again,' was the most common response. 'Can't they think of something new?' The campaign had a further twist. Some young people dared to suggest that Lei Feng was not really a good communist at all. Like the Gang of Four and their supporters, he was an 'ultra-leftist' – a dirty word in China – because he ignored the value of the individual.

China's new candidate for moral honours, Zhang Hua, fared little better. Instead of arousing admiration, he provoked jokes and a stream of sarcastic correspondence to newspapers and magazines. One university student's letter encapsulated the feelings of many young people. 'Can this be the real meaning of life?' he asked. 'To die in a pit of nightsoil?'[16]

The government has been paying particular attention to two groups of alienated youth. The first, fairly predictably, is the unemployed. 'What's so great about socialism? It didn't give me a job,' is a comment heard over and over again in China.

Political alienation among the unemployed is not, of course, a phenomenon limited to socialist countries. Seeing themselves outside mainstream society, unemployed youth are equally alienated in Western democracies where they often fail to exercise their voting rights. Governments of whichever political persuasion tend to get the blame for the unemployment problem.

Official attempts to instil socialist values in unemployed youth are inhibited by their lack of identification with a 'unit' – whether university or factory – through which mobilization normally takes place. Some neighbourhood committees make efforts to organize political and ethical study sessions as an adjunct to their other activities, but usually to no avail. As one young man in Shanghai put it: 'We want jobs, not political education.'

The second group whose political attitudes cause particular concern are university students. One of the first projects undertaken by the Youth Research Institute was a three-month survey, during 1981, of students in six major cities. The researchers found that some students were dissatisfied with the Party's unhealthy tendencies and were breaking away from Party leadership. Some could not distinguish between capitalist and socialist democracy, and tended towards liberalism. 'Compared with students in the 1950s, students nowadays have many weaknesses,' the researchers concluded. 'Some lack a firm belief in socialism, discipline and collectivism, and in public moral concepts.'[17]

The alienation of university students ostensibly seems rather surprising. China's new elite, they are virtually guaranteed a leading role in the nation's modernization and are the one sector of youth that seems to have some chance of fulfilling their aspirations. But even university students see barriers to their personal advancement – in the form of bureaucrats and Party officials trained during the Cultural Revolution. 'They know, and we know, that we're better trained than they are,' said one final year student. 'But they're going to do all in their power to protect their positions and prevent us being promoted.'

Nor is the alienation of university students so unexpected when one considers their social background. Many come from intellectual families. With some exceptions in the late 1940s and early 1950s, this social group has always viewed the Communist Party with extreme suspicion. Their fears were only reinforced by the attacks on individual freedom and ideas during the anti-rightist campaign of the late 1950s, and again in the Cultural Revolution, when many intellectuals were denounced and imprisoned.

The alienation of university students whose parents are high Party or Army officials seems more puzzling. But this group probably has the clearest insights into the reality, as distinct from the public image, of the Communist Party and the functioning of the political system. Like their counterparts in the Soviet Union, the sons and daughters of the privileged are cynical about politics but are usually only too keen to share the perks of their parents' offices.

Compared with unemployed youth, university students are readily accessible to Party pressure. Most tertiary institutions have restored political study classes, with students spending at least two hours a week studying subjects including dialectical materialism, Marxism–Leninism and the history of the Chinese Communist Party. But there is little enthusiasm. Compulsory attendance merely means that students tend to spend the time, just as they did in the early 1970s, writing letters, reading novels and doing other university work. Many teachers resent what they see as interference in the real work of the university and only aid and abet their students.

When examinations were introduced in the effort to get students and teachers to take political study seriously, there were threatened boycotts in several universities. And there has been widespread cheating in exams. 'Everyone takes their notebooks,' one Peking student told me. 'The teachers simply turn a blind eye.'

The Chinese government claims to be achieving some success in restoring young people's socialist beliefs. As evidence, it points to their increasing political participation. 'There are now 48 million Communist Youth League members throughout the country, of whom 26 million have been recruited during the past four years,' declared Youth League Secretary Wang Zhaoguo at the League's national congress in December 1982.[18]

An article published in May 1983 maintained that, after some backsliding, Peking University students were exhibiting increased conviction in Marxism–Leninism. Nearly 50 per cent of recent graduates of the Chinese and Physics departments had applied for Party membership, as had every Youth League member in the Law and International Politics departments.[19]

But political participation is a doubtful measure of political commitment. So far as many young people are concerned, it is merely one of the necessary criteria for getting into university or obtaining a good job. As a young technologist put it bluntly: 'Many young people who apply to join the Party don't do so because of idealism. They think it's the best way to get ahead.'

A cynical attitude towards the Party is not, of course, limited to youthful Party members. One recent official campaign was directed at restoring political commitment among all Party members, the 4 per cent of the population who are theoretically the guardians of socialist ideals. Nor is the phenomenon unique to China. In the Soviet Union, the acquisition of a Party ticket is commonly acknowledged to be the surest pathway to promotion, perks and being considered 'safe' for the much-sought trips abroad.

When called on, young Party members and Youth League activists are able to recite fluently the current 'correct line' on any subject, sometimes to the obvious disdain of their fellow-youth. 'We are happy to go wherever the country needs us, whether to cities or to rural areas,' responded the most vocal, clean-cut and obviously politicized student in a group of English language students when I asked them, in the presence of two university administrators, where they would like to be assigned following graduation. Some of the other students could hardly stifle their giggles.

No doubt there are still some young political activists firmly committed to communist ideals. 'Sometimes you can't really tell whether they're genuine or whether they're just doing it for personal gain,' admitted one student. 'Either way, they're a bit suspect. Most university students belong to the Youth League as a matter of course – but the Party's a different matter. We tend to keep quiet when there's a Party member around.'

'Of course Party membership can be a bit risky if you're not really committed,' another student told me. 'Party members are usually expected to set a good example to others, even volunteering to go off to Tibet or other out-of-the-way places. So political activism for the wrong reasons sometimes misfires.'

Despite their official pronouncements, sometimes designed for foreign consumption, Chinese spokesmen occasionally acknowledge their continuing problems in restoring socialist ideals among young people. In the words of one Youth League official: 'We've tried just about everything. But we're still facing quite a battle.'

The authorities constantly stress the need for improved methods in conducting ideological education among the youth generation. Rather than simply instructing young people, they say, they must present facts and reason things out. But the propaganda aim of so-called political education is readily acknowledged. As an academic journal expressed it: 'Students with negative and wrong ideas must be guided to do their own thinking – *until* they can come up with correct conclusions.'[20]

Teaching methods reflect not only the rigid political framework within which officialdom is acting but also the wide generation gap that currently exists in China. The nation's geriatric rulers – the average age of the six members of the Politburo's Standing Committee is over seventy-five – are simply out of touch with the youth generation. So too are many senior officials in their fifties, sixties or seventies. These power-holders share with others in their age group the attitudes of a generation that has its roots in pre-1949 China.

'Many officials seem to think we're all still peasants with little education, like their early supporters,' commented a sophisticated physics student. 'Imagine trying to mobilize today's university students – or even factory workers – by telling them to emulate someone who jumped into a pit of shit to save an old peasant.'

While the authorities stress the need to involve younger officials in decision making, they still take and publicize such actions as appointing 'four old generals' – People's Liberation Army veterans – as advisers on youth affairs.[21] When all else fails, these and other youth mobilizers invariably fall back on stories of the bad old days in China. 'They're worse than our parents and grandparents,' remarked one eighteen-year-old. 'They keep telling us about how terrible life was before liberation, and how good it is now in comparison. They might be right. But we're not interested in the past. We're concerned with the present and the future. The old people running the country don't seem to understand this.'

For many young Chinese, socialism and even political systems have become merely a fact of life. The less they have to do with them the better. 'Most of us don't even talk about politics any more,' ventured a young hotel worker in Shanghai. 'Except when it affects us personally, and that's too often. We're more interested in getting on with our own lives – finding jobs, falling in love, getting married, and all that.'

CHAPTER ELEVEN

Falling in Love with Love

'I have this feeling, here in my heart. I've never had it before. Is it love?' The earnest inquirer was 22-year-old Cao Wenyuan, a good-looking bright-eyed young man working in Harbin's International Hotel.

Cao explained his predicament. Six months earlier he had met Wang Xilei, a 21-year-old Hong Kong girl who was visiting relatives in China and had spent ten days in Harbin. Cao had shown her round the city when he wasn't working and they had been to the cinema. The evening before she left Harbin he had kissed her at the door of the hotel.

'I realized then she was something special,' Cao said blushing. 'We promised to write to each other.' They had been exchanging letters ever since, he added, producing a colour photo she had enclosed with her last letter. A pretty girl in white fitted trousers and a reasonably low-cut pink cotton shirt, she was perched on a bed in her family's small Hong Kong apartment.

'This must be very significant,' the young man pontificated. 'Sitting on a bed? I think she's trying to tell me something.'

It sounds like the naive romantic stuff of which many a Hong Kong or Taiwanese film is made. But Cao, who had spent his entire life under the rigid socialist moral code, was deadly serious.

Could there be any future in their relationship, he wondered. After all, she lived in Hong Kong and, even as an office worker, earned about six times what he did. Surely she would not be prepared to live in China, especially not married to an ordinary hotel employee. Even though Cao was a senior high school graduate and studied English conscientiously, he had little chance of improving his job. And he had heard about Hong Kong's strict immigration laws. He might not be able to go there even if he received official approval to leave China.

Like most young people in love, Cao was not particularly impressed by the obvious solution: that he forget Wang Xilei and meet a nice local girl. 'But I don't want a local girl. I want Wang Xilei.'

Cao's feeling in his heart, as he called it, reflects the new infatuation with romantic love in contemporary China. As an elderly man in Harbin put it: 'Falling in love is the thing for young people to do these days – for the first time in the People's Republic.'

When the Communists came to power in 1949, they attempted to define 'love' in socialist terms, denouncing what they described as bourgeois love as individualistic and self-centred. Socialist love, they said, must not be based on strange feelings in one's heart or flights of passion but on common political attitudes and interests. And personal feelings must always be subordinated to the development of socialist new China, even if this meant separation from the man or woman one loved.

Still, love was allowed to exist and even to be written about, albeit in the socialist realist boy-loves-girl-loves-tractor style characteristic of the Soviet Union. It was only during the Cultural Revolution that all mention of love disappeared from the face of China, condemned as an undesirable manifestation of bourgeois decadent thought: vulgar, cheap and even obscene.

'We're not supposed to talk or even think about love,' my roommate at Peking University had responded when I queried her on the subject in 1976. 'We're only supposed to think about class struggle and continuing the revolution.'

Soon after Mao's death love began making a tentative reappearance, initiated by the more adventurous writers and poets and flourishing in the short-lived new realism literature of 1979–80. There was Zhang Jie's moving short story 'Love Must Not Be Forgotten', a tale of romantic but chasté love between two officials who were married to other people. Zhang Xian's story 'The Corner Forsaken by Love' took love beyond the romantic into the realms of passion. And Shu Ting's love poem

'Longing' dealt with inner feelings in a more direct manner than almost any poetry had done in the history of Communist China: 'O in the vistas of the heart, in the depths of the soul.'[1]

The revival of traditional Chinese culture, with its human emotions and love intrigues, placed the new attitudes firmly in a historical framework. In late 1978 the famous traditional Peking opera *The Tale of the White Snake* was featured on stage and television. It was all there: the beautiful maiden falling in love, her victimization and her imprisonment by a wicked abbot, her eventual rescue by her lover and his army. New films, such as the production of Lao She's novel *Rickshaw Boy*, temporarily brought audiences into contact with flesh-and-blood individuals instead of bland class stereotypes.

By the early 1980s love had gained a secure foothold in China. Indeed writers and magazine publishers soon realized their readers were no different from people elsewhere in the world in enjoying the titillation of personal love stories and romantic dramas. One tabloid entitled *Story*, filled with traditional fables about concubines and libertines, attracted some 2 million readers across the country. Regular subscribers reportedly included 700 of the 800 students at one Shanghai high school.

Young people's selective access to Western culture only heightened their interest in romantic love as they came into contact, not with the sexual revolution and the permissive society but with the Brontës and the Hollywood era of the 1930s and 1940s. For the most part, it was an image of handsome men and beautiful women falling in love, tender but chaste embraces in the moonlight, and couples living happily ever after.

The new atmosphere was soon reflected in young people's attitudes towards one another. Of course, love and romance – even illicit sex – had never been completely eradicated from China. A wander through the more deserted spots of a public park in the mid-1970s was bound to bring glimpses of young men and women holding hands and even having a quick embrace in the bushes, completely oblivious to passers-by.

But it was furtive and even guilt-ridden.

'A few years ago love seemed to me something vulgar, a petty-bourgeois sentiment,' one young man told a Chinese magazine in 1979. 'And once when I did love someone, I didn't dare acknowledge it even to myself.'[2]

漫步在婚姻介绍所内外（之二）

陈晓轩　刘朱婴　杨泉福

The new romantic image: a short story illustration showing a young man and woman, moonlit sky – and a cassette recorder

Nowadays, young couples who a few years ago would have met secretly at the back of Peking's Summer Palace – if they had been brave enough to meet at all – wander along the main streets hand in hand. The quick hug or kiss in public is still considered rather brazen, just as it is in Hong Kong or Taiwan, and used to be in the West. Still, there is a new naturalness in male–female relations that was entirely absent ten years ago.

But love and romance are not always clear sailing for young Chinese. Newspapers and magazines now have special advice columns, such as *Chinese Women*'s 'Window on Love', to deal with their anxieties. The columns are headed with romantic line drawings: a young man and woman silhouetted against a moonlit sky; a young woman staring wistfully at a sky filled with hearts and flowers.

'I'm madly in love with a young man in the same workshop,' wrote one female factory worker. 'I don't know how to express my feelings to him. I'm afraid he'll reject me. I'd be so embarrassed. What should I do?[3]

'I think I'm in love with two men at the same time,' wrote another young woman. 'I've been going out with both of them and they both say they love me. I can't decide between them and I'm worried that, if I do choose one of them, the other one will be very upset. I'm hopelessly confused. Can you help me?'[4]

The replies are invariably models of commonsense, similar to those in traditional women's magazines in the West. The young factory worker was advised to strike up a conversation with the young man, maybe at lunch-time or when they left work, and perhaps even suggest that they go skating or see a film. The young woman in love with the two men was sternly told that it was unfair to lead them both on. She had to make up her mind and tell the young man who had missed out, even if he was upset at the time.

Like other letter-writers, these young people were also told that they should not become obsessed with their personal problems and allow their work or studies to suffer. 'Love must be kept in its proper place,' declares many an editorial article, reflecting the government's alarm at the somewhat over-enthusiastic public response to its slightly liberalized attitudes towards personal relations. Cartoons in newspapers and magazines ridicule the alleged surfeit of love being fed to young people on television and in novels and films. In one cartoon, a disappointed 9-year-old girl and her grandfather stand in front of a theatre marquee advertising nothing but plays about love.

Official commentators warn writers and film and television producers not to refer to love excessively. 'Love is only part of real life,' declared the national newspaper *Guangming Daily*, accusing some writers of 'seeking love themes like a swarm of bees alighting on one flower.' When love is portrayed, it should not 'emphasize wooing, embracing and kissing. Rather it should conform with reality, national customs, communist morality and the socialist legal system – especially the Marriage Law.'[5]

Love, then, is directly related to marriage, at least as the Chinese Communists see it. This connection is emphasized in the huge number of advice books bearing such titles as *Love and Marriage, Young People and Falling in Love* and *Correspondence on Love*. Even ostensibly academic books treat the two subjects as one. 'The outcome of young people falling in love is marriage,' the book *Youth Psychology* declared categorically.[6]

With the Chinese authorities encouraging young people not to marry until around their mid-twenties, the teenage years are considered too early to be thinking about love. Magazine editors offer little sympathy to love-sick high school students.

'I'm a 16-year-old male student,' wrote one correspondent to a women's magazine. 'Recently I've had strong feelings about a classmate. Sometimes our eyes meet and we gaze at each other. When I get home I think of her all the time.'

'One day I admired my male classmate's bookmark,' said a female student. 'That evening when I arrived home I found he'd put it in my schoolbag. I can't really give it back to him. Nor can I keep it. All my friends would know. What will I do?'

These and similar letters, published under the heading 'The Secrets of My Heart', provoked a stern response from the editor of the column. 'Separating off and pairing up is not right,' she stated. 'Nor is talking and thinking about love. How can you establish genuine friendships if you behave in this way?'[7]

But the admonitions have little effect. A recent academic work on youth issues complained that Chinese boys and girls, influenced by films and television, are thinking about love at a younger and younger age. 'Even third and fourth year primary school pupils talk about falling in love', it revealed.[8]

For all the obsession with love and romance in present-day China, there is still little idea of Western-style dating and going out with a variety of members of the opposite sex before deciding on a marriage partner. The traditional segregation of the sexes is still strong, especially in rural areas. Most young men and women in their teens and even early twenties spend their spare time with members of their own sex, whether going to the cinema, shopping or strolling in the park.

Even on university campuses there is little of the 'coed' atmosphere characteristic of most Western universities. While male and female students attend the same classes, they usually sit in separate groups. In a discussion with thirty or so English-language students at the Canton Foreign Language Institute, for example, the girls sat on chairs lining the left side of the room, the boys on the right side. In between was a no man's land of empty seats.

'It's the custom,' is the invariable response to queries about the high degree of sexual segregation. 'If a young man sat with the women, or a young woman with the men, they would be considered very forward and rather strange. We're more used to being with the members of our own sex.'

To a Westerner, the sight of young Chinese women – and sometimes young men – wandering around arm in arm, even hand in hand, can be somewhat disarming. 'What a great place to be a homosexual,' commented an Australian friend. 'No one would even look at you.'

Some Westerners interpret physical contact between members of the same sex in China as a sign of latent homosexuality, or perhaps as a sublimation of heterosexual drives. But this behaviour is also common in many countries in Asia and elsewhere in the world where it is customary for young men and women to socialize mainly with members of their own sex.

Living in a virtually single-sex sub-culture does, though, reinforce sex-stereotyped characteristics: men tend to talk about football, women about clothes and knitting. It also makes some young people rather awkward, even tongue-tied, in their limited contacts with the opposite sex. 'I always blush when a young man comes up and talks to me,' confessed one twenty-year-old. 'I know it's silly, but I can't help it. And everyone looks at you.'

Once young men and women are seen spending any time together they are normally assumed to have entered the stage of 'going steady'. Some people working or studying together complain that they are unable to have a casual friendship with a member of the opposite sex without being teased and labelled as boyfriend and girlfriend. 'Xiao Wang and I work in the same section of the factory,' said a young woman in Shanghai. 'We share a number of interests and enjoy talking to each other. People assume there is something personal between us. But there isn't. Can't young men and women just be friends?'

The countryside is even more tradition-bound, as many a young rural dweller grumbles. One twenty-year-old told a youth advice column that after a village film show he had merely walked home with a young woman who was his neighbour and former classmate. The gossip spread round the village that the two young people were now 'in love'. 'This is the 1980s,' protested the young man. 'Do we really still adhere to the old ideas? I'm too young to think about such things.'[9]

What things? Marriage. Once a young man and woman are assumed to be boyfriend and girlfriend, they are also assumed to have embarked on the road towards matrimony. 'Not everyone marries their first boyfriend or girlfriend,' commented a teacher in Peking. 'But many do. Young people get a bad reputation if they take up with different people and then discard them.'

If love has its proper place in China, so has sex: not mentioned publicly and confined within marriage. The Chinese Communists have never had any time for the early Soviet ideas on free love expounded by feminists including Aleksandra Kollontai who argued that the sexual act was no more significant than drinking a glass of water. Rather they took up Lenin's puritanical idea that 'dissoluteness in sexual life is bourgeois ... Self-control, self-discipline is not slavery, not even in love.'[10] Although the private behaviour of some members of the Chinese Communist leadership has not always been exemplary – Mao himself discarded a sick wife to take up with young actress Jiang Qing – the Party has imposed a rigid code of moral behaviour on the Chinese people.

'Before they marry, young people in love must protect their bodies like jade and not rashly lose their virtue,' declared the book *Youth Psychology*. 'Premarital sex is contrary to the principles of social ethics. It can produce psychological conflict and affect physical and mental health.'[11]

Letters of anguish involving sexual matters receive rather less sympathy from magazine editors than those about romantic love. One villager said her boyfriend had visited her house one evening with the present of a woollen sweater, a conventional symbol of intended matrimony. He told her they would be together forever.

'I had faith in him – and I gave myself to him,' she confessed. 'Who was to know that three months later he would go off to the city to work and that our relationship would cool? I've heard he's already got a new girlfriend at the factory. I'm a girl who's lost her virtue. What am I worth now? I feel desperate. Please help me.'

Instead of receiving understanding, the young woman was subjected to a stern lecture. 'Sexual relations are lawful only after marriage. You have therefore indulged in unlawful behaviour.'[12]

Nor does the Chinese government have any time for the argument put forward by Western feminists that sexual freedom is vital to male–female equality. Another young woman who had forsaken her chastity wondered whether it was really so important. 'Losing one's chastity is no great thing in the West,' she declared. 'Isn't our attitude rather feudal?' 'No, it is not a feudal attitude,' was the solemn response. 'It is a socialist attitude. Dissolute behaviour between the sexes is a phenomenon of capitalist society.'[13]

If official admonitions do not always deter young people from engaging in sexual relations, sheer logistics often do. Finding a place to be alone in Chinese cities and towns can be a formidable challenge. The cramped housing conditions are hardly conducive to intimacy for married couples, let alone for young people wanting to indulge in what is considered unlawful behaviour. 'We can't wait to get our own flat,' one recently married young woman told me in Peking, blushing as she did so. 'It's very difficult for couples when they have to share tiny flats with relatives – often just one room with a partition.'

Young people living away from home, whether in a university or factory dormitory, are often faced with six or more room-mates. And the buildings are usually sex-segregated. 'You can't get much privacy when you go out either,' complained a university student. Broad daylight is a deterrent to all but the most adventurous and park gates are usually securely locked at sunset. Bicycles are no substitute for the West's cars and panel vans.

But China is not the puritanical wonderland some officials would have one believe. Despite the greater conservatism of the countryside, the opportunities for privacy probably result in a higher level of sexual activity among young rural dwellers than their urban brothers and sisters. Even young urban couples manage, in the words of a favourite communist expression, to 'overcome difficulties'. A symposium held in Peking in mid-1982 by the Society for Marriage and the Family expressed concern that cases of pregnancy before marriage were on the increase.[14] And a survey of abortions carried out at one hospital revealed that over half involved unmarried women.[15] 'Some young people these days are adopting a rather casual attitude towards sex,' a women's magazine complained in mid-1983.[16]

Although the Communist authorities and even social scientists vehemently denounce pre-marital sex, they do not deny the existence of youthful sex instincts and passions. The basic responsibility for keeping these instincts under control until marriage is laid squarely on young women, just as it was in traditional China. 'It is a small matter to die of starvation, but a grave matter to lose one's chastity,' was one of many common sayings firmly imprinted on young women's minds over the centuries.

Recent comments in the Chinese media sound familiar not just to women who grew up in pre-revolutionary China but also to anyone who was a teenager in the West in the 1950s or earlier. 'One must make girls understand that they should hold fast to their morals,' declared one article in *Chinese Women*.[17] 'If your boyfriend makes excessive demands, you must calmly and graciously decline,' urged another.[18]

This might not always be easy, the magazine acknowledged when it cited the case of one Xiao Dan and her persuasive boyfriend. 'If you refuse me, it shows you don't really love me, and we might as well break up,' her boyfriend had told her.

Afraid of losing him, Xiao Dan had succumbed to his advances –
several times. To her dismay, the young man did not marry her,
as he had promised, but moved on to another young woman to
whom he made similar promises and advances.

'Sexual desire and love are not the same thing,' concluded
the article. 'Young people must be careful to distinguish
between the two.'[19]

When the inevitable does happen, the traditional Holly-
wood-style scenario is also rather familiar: the young man
stirred by the sight of a female body and the young woman,
against all her better judgement and sense of morality,
succumbing to sheer physical passion. Such a scenario takes
place in the short story 'The Corner Forsaken by Love' which
describes a relationship – not in traditional China but in the late
1970s – between two young peasants. Fairly astounding even in
China's new realism literature, it is probably the closest to a sex
scene that has yet appeared in contemporary Chinese literature.

That instant Xiao Baozi froze as if electrified. He stared blankly, his
breath stopped – and a gush of warm blood rushed to his head. It was
because when the young woman took off her sweater, her shirt was
pulled up, exposing half of a pale, full, and bouncing breast.

Like a leopard springing from its cave, Xiao Baozi leaped forward. He
embraced her tightly as if he had completely lost his senses. Startled,
the young woman tried to lift her arm to block him. But when his
burning, quivering lips touched her own moist lips, she was overcome
with a mysterious dizziness. Her eyes closed and her outstretched arms
were paralysed. All her intentions to resist disappeared instantly. A
kind of primitive reflex burned like a fierce flame in the blood of this
pair of materially poor, spiritually barren, but physically robust young
people. Traditional morality, rational dignity, the danger of breaking
the law, the shame in a young woman's heart – all of these, everything,
in a moment were burnt to ashes.[20]

Their punishment was not long in coming. Found out by the
villagers, they were abused and beaten for their illicit
behaviour. The young woman, Shen Cunni, was so completely
overcome by the shame and disgrace she had brought on herself
and her family that she took the traditional Chinese way out,
drowning herself in the village pond.

The theme in this and similar stories is that of the universal 'fallen woman', irretrievably soiled and spoiled for any other man. Losing one's chastity might no longer be a graver matter than dying of starvation, but it is very serious – if one is female. For all the official assertions of male–female equality, the double standard is still alive and well in contemporary China. And it is only reinforced by the expounders of so-called socialist morality.

In a discussion of youth issues at the Chinese Academy of Social Sciences, I mentioned that some young people in the West live together without being married. Although the idea initially met with puzzlement, some of the researchers seemed reasonably responsive.

'It's quite a good idea in the West considering the high divorce rate,' one ventured.

'What about in China?'

'Oh, it wouldn't work in China. If the couple broke up, the woman would have great difficulty finding another man to marry her. Chinese women are expected to be virgins when they marry.'

'What about men?'

'That's not so important.'

The young woman who succumbs to her boyfriend's advances finds herself in a highly vulnerable position, especially if he decides not to marry her. Unless she can hide her past misdemeanours, which can be difficult in a society with little physical mobility, she has placed her marriage prospects in serious jeopardy. 'I'm feeling desperate,' a young woman in Heilongjiang province wrote to an advice column. 'My boyfriend and I had been planning to get married for some time. Suddenly he told me that we were breaking up. Why? When I saw his cold expression, I knew he'd found out that I had had sexual relations with a former boyfriend.'[21]

No mention was made in her letter, or in the predictably unsympathetic reply, of whether or not her husband-to-be had also had a previous sexual relationship.

The lack of formal sex education for young people until they are about to get married, together with the difficulty of obtaining contraceptives, means that quite a few young women face an even more traumatic situation: the discovery that they are pregnant. The stereotyped raging father in the West is a mild character compared with his Chinese counterpart, especially in the countryside. Threatened with family shame and disgrace, he may well beat his daughter and then, accompanied by other male family members, go and beat up the young man and even his family.

'It can cause complete uproar in a village when a girl gets pregnant,' confirmed one former rural resident. 'It's bad enough when a young couple are caught having a sexual relationship – or even assumed to be having one.'

But even in China raging fathers are quick to face reality. 'What usually happens in the case of pregnancy is that a speedy marriage takes place,' a Women's Federation official told me in Harbin. 'If the couple are not old enough to get married officially, then the young woman will probably have an abortion at the local clinic. In the countryside, the young couple might just have a traditional marriage ceremony and live together. They'll probably register the marriage when they reach the official minimum marriage age – twenty-two for men and twenty for women.'

In 1981, almost 400 000 babies – one in every fifty newborns in China – were born to women nineteen years old or under.

'Can a woman have and keep a baby if she's not living in an official or traditional marriage relationship?' I asked.

'I've heard that quite a few women become single mothers in the West,' the Women's Federation official replied. 'But in China it's against both traditional morality and socialist ethics – as well as the present policy of one child per *couple*. It happens occasionally, of course, and illegitimate children have the same formal rights as other children. But the woman would be regarded as something of a social outcast, as well as bringing disgrace to her family. And she would probably be resigning herself to a life without a husband. No man is likely to want to marry a woman who already has a child, not just because of her reputation but because of the one-child policy. He'd want to have his own child, not bring up someone else's.'

The single mother would also face severe practical difficulties unless she had her family's close support and financial backing. Without formal marriage registration, a woman is not entitled to paid maternity leave or subsidized hospital costs and child care. And while the father is legally responsible for part of the cost of the child's upbringing and education, he is no more likely to acknowledge paternity than many men in similar circumstances in the West.

If possible rejection by a boyfriend, pregnancy, parental rage and abortion are not sufficiently traumatic, the young woman discovered having a sexual relationship also has to face official censure. If she is still at high school, she might well find herself spending a year or two in reform school to ponder the error of her ways. If she is lucky, she will only be subjected to criticism and a substantial burst of ideological education about correct socialist morality.

'We classify sexual relations in the category of behaviour liable to expulsion,' one university administrator told me. 'It depends to some extent on the attitude and behaviour of the person concerned. If she is repentant and promises to behave in future, we'll usually give her a second chance. But repeated behaviour of this sort cannot be tolerated. It has a corrupting influence on others.'

In one recent case, he told me, a young woman who became pregnant was suspended from the university for one year as punishment.

What about the young man? I asked.

'We criticized him.'

CHAPTER TWELVE

'Marriage is a Serious Business'

'Once you put the chains of a loveless marriage around your neck, you will suffer for it for the rest of your life,' concludes Zhang Jie in her story 'Love Must Not Be Forgotten'. 'Even waiting in vain is better than willy-nilly marriage. To live single is not such a fearful disaster.'[1]

These sentiments would hardly raise an eyebrow in the West. But Zhang's suggestion that some people might prefer not to marry at all has created widespread controversy in China.

'Just about everyone gets married these days,' a middle-aged woman told me in Peking. 'It's natural for people to get married.'

'What if they don't fall in love with anyone?' I asked.

'Well, it's nice if people are in love when they get married. But marriage is a serious business.'

Despite the virtual obsession with love and romance in present-day China, love is not always the major consideration when it comes to marriage. Traditionally, marriage had nothing at all to do with love. The perpetuation of the Confucian family system was considered far too important for marriage to be left to the whims and emotions of young people. Marriages were arranged by their families, normally through a matchmaker, and the young man and woman sometimes did not even see each other until their wedding day. The arrangement was sealed with the payment of a 'bride price' by the man's family to compensate the woman's family for her upbringing and the loss of her labour. Teenage marriages tended to be the rule rather than the exception.

Early twentieth century Chinese literature is filled with the sad tales of young women, sometimes in love with another man, being dragged screaming into the red bridal sedan chair to be handed over to the new husband and his family. One of Mao Zedong's early articles was the story of Miss Zhao, who slit her throat in protest as she was lifted aloft in the chair. Other young women, like Mingfeng in Ba Jin's novel *Family*, drowned themselves in ponds, lakes or rivers rather than face life with a man they did not love. (In Mingfeng's case it was to be as a concubine, not even as a legal wife.) Young men were not usually so dramatically inclined. While women were expected to be faithful and virtuous, men had social sanction to bring concubines into the house or to visit the euphemistically named 'flower streets and willow lanes' for extramarital sensual pleasures.

In theory, marriage without the consent of the people involved was outlawed by the Nationalist Government in 1931. But their new Civil Code had little impact beyond the urban educated elite. When sociologist Olga Lang did a survey in the countryside in 1936–7, she found that scarcely anyone had even heard of modern marriage.

It was only after the Communists came to power that sustained efforts were made to abolish arranged marriages throughout the country. 'Marriage must be based upon the complete willingness of the two parties,' declared the 1950 Marriage Law, one of the first pieces of major legislation enacted by the new government. 'Neither party shall use compulsion and no third party is allowed to interfere.'[2]

But despite constant exhortations to people to adhere to the Marriage Law, old customs die hard, especially in the countryside. In 1981 the Chinese media released details of a survey undertaken in two counties in Anhui province in central China. Of almost 15 000 recent marriages, only 15 per cent had been by free choice. Some 10 per cent had actually been arranged by parents while the vast majority, 75 per cent, were classified as having been 'agreed upon,' meaning that the people involved had not actively opposed their parents' choice. In official parlance: 'Marriage is first agreed upon, and then the two young people try to develop compatibility.'[3]

Individual reports confirm that young people are still sometimes forced to marry against their will, often for mercenary reasons. In late 1983 an 18-year-old girl told *Chinese*

Youth that her father had made her marry a man she did not even like. The young man's father had helped her father build a new house and then, when it was burnt down, helped them rebuild it. The girl's father had subsequently accepted the young man's request to marry his daughter. In response to her protests, both before and even on the day of the wedding, he had merely replied: 'We received their kindness, so we must repay it. There's no point objecting.'[4]

It is only a short step from using a daughter as a method of repaying kind deeds to selling her for a cash payment. Young women are themselves sometimes unwitting volunteers in the transaction, lured by false promises of good jobs or better living conditions. A senior high school graduate named Xiao Ling complained to a Shanghai youth magazine in 1983 that she had been promised a good job close to Hangzhou. Bored with rural life, she jumped at the offer. But when she arrived at her destination, she found that she was far from the city and that the living conditions were no better than they had been at home in the western province of Sichuan. Soon a man was produced for her to marry. 'I later discovered that he had paid 400 yuan to my family . . . I'm just like goods, belonging to someone. Now his family watch my every move, because they're afraid I'll run away. I know it's my fault . . . but please save me.'[5]

For some young people, the only way out of an arranged marriage – or parental interference in a desired marriage – still seems to be suicide. In early 1981 a young couple in the north-west province of Gansu committed suicide rather than marry others. A year earlier the bodies of a young couple had been found, their arms wrapped around each other, in a pump house near Peking airport. Forbidden by their families to see each other after they had been caught having a physical relationship, they had hanged themselves with a single piece of rope.

While urban residents normally adhere more closely than their rural counterparts to the concept of marriage by free choice, it is still often parents who arrange introductions and initiate meetings. On a Sunday afternoon one sees many a nervous looking young man or woman waiting at the gates of a public park to meet a prospective spouse.

Even if the young man and woman meet each other independently, they are usually subject to considerable parental influence when it comes to the question of marriage. For all their ideas of youthful independence, few people marry in the face of strong parental defiance.

'I wouldn't want my parents to pick my wife for me, but I don't think I'd marry without their approval,' commented one fairly worldly university-educated young man in his mid-twenties. As he pointed out, such an attitude was only practical as he and his wife, like countless other young couples, would initially have to live with his family in fairly cramped surroundings. 'There are still enough problems between young married women and their mothers-in-law without starting off in an atmosphere of hostility,' he rationalized.

The authorities have been slightly more successful in persuading people to conform to the so-called late marriage policy than they have been in enforcing free choice of marriage. Although the official minimum marriage age is twenty-two for men and twenty for women, there is strong pressure on young people not to marry until around their mid-twenties. Incentives for late marriage include up to two weeks extra honeymoon leave.

But admonitions, incentives and even basic laws are sometimes to no avail. According to the 1982 census, some 30 per cent of all young people twenty and over – but below the recommended ages of twenty-five for men and twenty-three for women – were in fact married. Over 4 million young people listing themselves as married were below the minimum legal marriage age.

When revising the Marriage Law in 1980, the Chinese government had considered putting the legal age for marriage even higher; it was already being raised two years from twenty for men and eighteen for women. But the proposal was rejected on the grounds that it would only increase 'the number of instances of couples living together before marriage, illegitimate children, and abortions by unmarried mothers.'[6]

As the authorities complained, this situation had become rife in the countryside even with the lower official marriage age. When local authorities refused to register marriages below the legal age, or attempted to postpone marriages in accordance with the late marriage policy, young couples simply bypassed officialdom and set up house together. A survey in Guizhou province in 1977 revealed that unions without legal registration made up a staggering 40 per cent of all marriages. The traditional marriage procedure of paying a bride price and holding a banquet continued, and still continues, to be regarded as the 'real' marriage, regardless of whether or not the union had been registered with the authorities.[7]

Although young Chinese generally favour marriage by free choice and often resist parental involvement or interference, it is not always easy to find a marriage partner. The countryside presents particular problems, with the persistence of the traditional custom of marrying someone from a different village and little contact between villages. Chinese officials acknowledge that the continuing high level of arranged or semi-arranged marriages is probably as much a product of young people's limited opportunities to meet members of the opposite sex as it is of parental wishes.

Even finding a spouse in urban areas is not always a simple matter, especially within the limited time period that seems to be available. 'You're not supposed to get married until your mid-twenties, and you're not really encouraged to have a relationship much before then,' a young woman told me in Peking. 'At twenty-three or twenty-four there's suddenly strong pressure on you to find a husband. And if you're not married by the time you're twenty-seven or twenty-eight, people think you've missed out – especially if you're female.'

With few organized social activities, the only real opportunity to meet members of the opposite sex is at one's place of work. If the comments of many factory workers, teachers and others are anything to go by, this is where a lot of marriages originate. But the strong sexual division of labour creates problems. While women represent some 80 per cent of commercial and textile workers, heavy industries such as iron and steel employ mainly male workers.

Some individual organizations make efforts to remedy the situation. In Canton, for example, I attended a dance arranged by two factories, one with predominantly male workers and one with predominantly females, to enable their employees to get together. When I arrived at 8.30 p.m. though, the plan did not seem to be going too well. Many of the young men sat chatting on one side of the room. The young women sat on the other side, anxiously waiting to be asked to dance and looking for all the world like the wall-flowers of the 1950s.

'But I don't know how to dance,' protested one young man when I asked why he wasn't on the dance floor.

'No, we can't ask the men to dance. It's not the custom,' was the reply of an attractive young woman, decked out in a full-skirted dress, knee-high nylon stockings and high-heeled shoes.

Some of the young men who knew how to dance rather defeated the purpose of the function by dancing with each other. 'I like dancing so my friend and I often practise together,' said one good-looking young man as they tangoed quite professionally to the tune of 'Jealousy'. 'Anyway, I'm too embarrassed to ask a girl. Which one would I pick?'

Some of the young women, growing tired of waiting to be asked, also danced together.

Of the mixed-sex pairs, a few appeared to be established couples, taking the opportunity to be together and sitting with each other in groups between dances. Other pairs were rather different, holding each other gingerly in the formal dance position and looking intense as they concentrated on the steps of the waltz or foxtrot, rarely uttering a word. When the music stopped, they scuttled back to their own side of the room.

'Well, we thought it was a good idea,' one of the organizers told me. 'But the sexes are not really used to being together in this sort of situation. I think it will take time.'

More direct measures have also been initiated to find spouses for urban men and women. Over the past few years the Women's Federation and the Communist Youth League have partially stepped into the role formerly occupied by parents and private matchmakers. A number of official matchmaking agencies, called marriage introduction bureaux, have been set up in cities and towns all over the country. Peking alone has six.

The Chaoyang District marriage bureau is splendidly located in Ritan Park in eastern Peking. The city's busiest marriage bureau, it was established in October 1980. 'At the present time we have about fifteen new registrations each day,' said the bureau's director Shi Guijun, a kindly grey-haired woman in her early fifties.

On registration, the applicant fills in a card providing

Director Shi Guijun and a colleague sort through registration cards at the Chaoyang District marriage bureau in Peking

information on age, height, educational level, occupation and family background (official, intellectual, worker, etc.), together with details of the type of person being sought. The card, with the applicant's photograph in the top right-hand corner, is matched up with the cards of those persons of the opposite sex whom bureau officials think might make a suitable match. The applicant then selects a 'possibility' and the chosen person is shown the applicant's card to decide whether he or she wishes to go ahead with a meeting.

'There is a 1 yuan registration fee, covering up to three meetings,' said Mrs Shi.

What if the applicant is still dissatisfied?

'Most tend to give up then. But one young woman finished up re-registering three times.'

The marriage bureau was alive with activity on this Tuesday morning, with young men and women registering, reporting on their progress, and chatting with the staff. The atmosphere was relaxed and the five matchmakers seemed friendly and co-operative.

'Isn't there a stigma attached to having to go to a marriage bureau?' I asked Mrs Shi, thinking of similar services in the West.

'There was initially,' she admitted. 'But we've had a lot of good publicity lately in the press. Some parents still aren't too keen, even though they keep telling their children it's time they got married. Some young people don't tell their parents when they first come here.'

The registrants I talked to said they thought the bureau was quite a sensible solution to the problem of finding a spouse. 'At least you have some choice of your own this way,' remarked Li Bihua, an attractive young woman wearing a pale blue pants suit. 'The two men my family have introduced me to so far have been awful. I didn't even want to go out with them, let alone marry one of them.'

A 24-year-old textile worker, Li said her parents and friends were beginning to put pressure on her to find a husband. But she rarely had the opportunity to meet anyone outside work, where there were very few men anyway. 'I'm not really in any great hurry to get married myself,' Li admitted. 'But it does seem to be the thing to do in China.'

Other registrants told similar stories about parental urgings and sometimes their own growing fears that maybe they would miss out. 'My mother says I should find a husband before I lose my youthful appearance,' said a pretty, vivacious twenty-five-year-old. 'She thinks it will be more difficult if I wait much longer.'

One young man registering at the marriage bureau had a rather unusual story. On the surface Tang Pu seemed the ideal future husband. Tall, good-looking and twenty-six-years-old, he was a recent science graduate of Sichuan University. He had not met anyone while he was still at university, he said, because he had been concentrating on his studies. Now he wanted to find a wife – and to find her fairly quickly.

Why?

'In eight months I'm going to Berkeley to do a PhD in physics,' he replied in reasonable English. 'I'll be in America for five years or more. That means I'll be over thirty when I come back to China. All the best girls will have got married by then and it will be hard for me to find someone suitable.'

Was such a marriage plan really feasible? In accordance with government policy, Tang would not be permitted to take his wife with him to America. Could she be expected to wait for him for over five years? And might not he meet someone else while he was away?

'I suspect that's one reason why my parents are urging me to get married before I go,' he confessed. 'They think I'm more likely to come back if I leave a wife behind.'

Mrs Shi admitted the case was an unusual one and there might be problems finding him a spouse. But five years' absence had to be weighed against the prospect of having a husband with a prestigious overseas degree and no doubt a top research job.

My own suggestion that maybe such a marriage was not a very sensible idea, bearing in mind the likely changes in Tang's attitudes while he was overseas, did not particularly impress Mrs Shi. 'Being married should help him resist bourgeois capitalist influences,' she declared somewhat unrealistically.

The requirements listed by the applicants on their registration cards gave a fair indication of male and female attitudes towards marriage in contemporary China, strongly influenced by tradition, including strong sex stereotyping, and the new consumerism. Young men ostensibly seemed the easiest to please. A similar background was considered important, though not essential. But men invariably said they would like a spouse who was good-looking, if not beautiful. The frequency of this requirement reminded me of a passage in Liu Xinwu's novel *Overpass*: 'When someone from a high cadre's family goes looking for a wife, if he's not after someone of his own class, then he's after a great beauty.'[8]

The next most frequently listed requirement was the young woman's personality: good-natured and congenial. Educational level, like background, was sometimes mentioned but was not considered of major importance, so long as the woman did not have a higher level of education.

'No man wants to marry a woman who seems cleverer than he is,' said Mrs Shi. This attitude was confirmed in the 1983 survey, already referred to, which revealed that only 28 per cent of a sample of male university students in Peking wanted to marry a woman with a tertiary education and that 50 per cent of them agreed with the Confucian adage: 'A woman without talent is virtuous.'[9]

Mrs Shi's general comments only reinforced the other male attitudes revealed in that survey. 'I suppose you could say that overall young men want to marry someone who is nice-looking, with a pleasant personality – not a bossy dominant one – and who conforms to the ideal of a good wife and mother.'

Young women had rather different requirements of their spouses, reflecting the continuing perception of the male as the dominant figure in the marriage relationship and the practical reality that the woman normally enters her husband's family. Social status basically derives from the man's position and family background, not the woman's. 'A man with a good job'; 'good income and prospects'; 'a man from a good family – but no dependent relatives'. These were the most frequently listed requirements on the registration cards I looked through.

'There's a fairly precise ranking of favoured occupations,' Mrs Shi told me. 'First come professionals, such as engineers and technologists, and bureaucrats. Then ordinary school-teachers. Then skilled workers.'

But a state job, any state job, was usually considered desirable over employment in a collective or private enterprise. One young man complained he had been frustrated three times because he worked in a neighbourhood collective. Each time he and a young woman had been paired up by the marriage bureau they had got on well together, until she found out he worked in a collective or he was taken home to be introduced to her parents who vetoed the relationship. 'I've simply lost confidence that I'll ever find anyone who'll want to marry me,' he grumbled.

Even considerations of occupation and status were sometimes outweighed by a young woman's desire to marry someone with access to housing. As one registrant expressed it: 'a reasonably sized room in his parents' flat or preferably access to his own accommodation through his work unit.'

This requirement is reflected in any number of cartoons in popular magazines. One in *Culture and Life*, for example, featured a young woman being wooed by four young men. The first was wealthy, the second good-looking and the third well educated. But the young woman chose the fourth man. Although he was deformed and sinister looking, he had the ultimate offer: housing.[10]

挑女婿　　　　　　　　　　庄敏瑄

The choice of husband
Translation: 'large bank account, good appearance, good education, has housing'
(from left)
(*Wenhua yu Shenghuo* (*Culture and Life*), no. 1, 1982)

For anyone with experience of China's overcrowded housing conditions, this concern is hardly surprising. Even people in show-piece cities like Peking and Shanghai regularly list housing as China's major urban problem; the average floor space per person in the capital is only 5.7 square metres (about 7 square yards). Indeed the general battle for adequate living accommodation is so great that even marriage itself is sometimes only a secondary consideration. A symposium in Shanghai in mid-1982 revealed that the need to produce a marriage certificate to get housing was spurring marriages and that 'hasty marriages' were becoming more and more common.[11]

Good housing is, of course, often inseparable from job and status. In dire contrast to the ramshackle dwellings in the centre of many large cities are the relatively spacious apartments of prominent Party and Army officials: three or four main rooms, a private kitchen, bathroom and flush toilet. When Hou Yong married the daughter of an Army officer in the novel *Overpass*, his mother was occasionally invited to the family home. How different it was from her own family's single partitioned room! How luxurious it seemed when 'the maid polished the bathtub, filled it with warm water, then asked her to bathe.'[12]

If young women at the Chaoyang District marriage bureau tended to seek a husband with the accoutrements of the 'good life' and young men wanted an attractive congenial wife, some requirements were common to both sexes. An age difference of two to three years – with the man being older – was commonly prescribed. Both sexes were also fairly definite about the height of the desired spouse: the man should be a few centimetres (maybe 2 inches) taller than the woman. 'People are fairly adamant about this,' said Mrs Shi. 'And it can present problems.

Later the same morning, two striking young women came into the marriage bureau. Slim, attractive and smartly dressed, they were both around 175 cm (5'9"), extremely tall for people even in north China. 'We're having a lot of difficulty finding them husbands,' smiled Mrs Shi. 'They're really nice girls: lively with bright personalities. But most men won't consider marrying anyone taller than themselves.'

It was evening when I visited another marriage bureau, this time in the Hongye neighbourhood in the southern city of

Canton. The preliminary selection procedure had already been completed and nine couples were meeting for the first time. They sat facing each other at small tables in two rather bare rooms, completely devoid of atmosphere. Some of the young women had brought along a friend, or even their mother, for moral support and no doubt for a second opinion on their potential spouse.

While most of the couples were around their mid-twenties, some looked rather older. They comprised the second category of people seeking partners: the former educated youth sent to rural areas during the Cultural Revolution. Most had not married in the countryside and now, back in the cities and in their early thirties, they were having difficulty finding spouses.

One of the younger couples, both primary school teachers, seemed to be getting on quite well together. I chatted with them about why they had come to the marriage bureau and the general problem of meeting members of the opposite sex in China.

The young man, Li Wangxin, left first.

'Well, what do you think? Are you going to see him again?' I asked the young woman, Wang Bi.

'No, I didn't like him at all,' she replied. 'He fidgeted all the time and his hair was too long. Although he's a teacher he must come from a workers' background. His language was a bit rough.'

Later I asked the bureau director what the young man had said about Wang Bi. 'He wasn't too keen,' she replied. 'He thought she was a bit stuck-up. We're having quite a problem finding her a husband. She's very attractive but she has a slight limp, from a childhood illness. It's difficult to find spouses for people with physical problems.'

Although the eighteen young people meeting each other that evening had been sufficiently anxious about their single status to register at the bureau, they had no intention of leaping into marriage. Of the nine couples, only two decided to meet again – to see a film or go for a stroll in the park.

The wariness was reflected in the bureau's limited success rate. Only fifty-two marriages had so far resulted from over 2000 registrations. 'One problem is the discrepancy between the numbers of male and female applicants,' said an official.

'Young women tend to be much shyer than men about coming here. So far we've had almost four times as many male applicants as females.'

But she was reasonably satisfied with the bureau's record. 'We've only been operating for two years. As well as the marriages, well over a hundred couples are seeing each other regularly. We don't aim to push people into marriage. After all, men and women in China are expected to stay married. The national divorce rate is still only around 3 per cent which is very low compared with most countries in the West.'

While marriage in China is often seen in a fairly practical light, most young people also hope to fall in love. And there are, of course, some marriages prompted purely by personal feelings, regardless of a partner's family background or income. This is when parents, urban and rural, often step in with their own ideas about what makes a suitable spouse. In 1982 the Shanghai Women's Federation complained about the extent to which parents were still meddling in their children's marriages with regard to their prospective partners' economic status, occupation, age and even appearance.[13]

Continuing family interference is confirmed in the huge number of complaints from young people which appear in popular magazines and youth booklets. 'My parents are dead against my marriage. My boyfriend's mother is sick and his family has a lot of economic difficulties.'[14] 'My boyfriend is in the army. When he's demobilized it will be difficult for him to get a job. My mother is opposed to our marriage. She says she will kill herself rather than see me marry him.'[15] 'My girlfriend has a job in a state factory, but I work in a collective enterprise. Her father says I have no future and is resolutely opposed to our marriage.'[16] 'I am a young official. My girlfriend is not much to look at but she has a pleasant personality. My friends say "You're an official. You could find someone beautiful." My mother says "She's all right but she's only a hairdresser".'[17]

The idea of a slightly unconventional marriage can provoke not just parental opposition but public controversy. Large age gaps are frowned on, even when the man is older than the woman. A play called *The Bright Moon Begins to Shine* aroused widespread debate when it was performed in Peking in 1981. The young woman in the play wants to marry her professor who is some twenty years her senior. Her mother, a Women's Federation official, initially opposed the match but eventually lends her support in the face of general social opposition.

An even greater controversy occurred when a woman of twenty-five wrote to *Chinese Women* complaining that her mother vehemently opposed her intended marriage. Not only was the man thirteen years her senior; he had a chronic illness and might not live more than another five years or so. The young woman declared that love was all-important and that she wanted to be married to the man, even if it was only for a short time.[10]

Her mother's reply was printed in a subsquent issue of the magazine. 'What happens when he dies?' she asked. 'My daughter will be a widow and over thirty. It's unlikely that she will be able to find another husband. She should not throw away her life.'[19]

The magazine was deluged with letters from readers expressing their opinions. Some agreed with the mother that the young woman was being emotional and foolhardy. Others expressed admiration for her, maintaining that she should be allowed to exercise her free choice in choosing a marriage partner. And the occasional reader used the opportunity to express her own heartfelt feelings about meddling parents. 'Years ago my family interfered when I wanted to get married,' wrote one woman. 'I accepted their decision and I've regretted it ever since. I've never fallen in love again. Don't listen to anyone. Go ahead and marry him.'[20]

In publishing approximately equal numbers of letters on each side on this and similar issues, the authorities have indicated that their own views are somewhat ambivalent. They insist that love should be the basic motivation for marriage and strongly criticize marriage based on selfish materialistic interests. But socialist love is not, of course, the same as 'bourgeois love'.

Love is all very well, officials suggest, so long as it is sensible and likely to lead to a harmonious and preferably long-lasting marriage. 'We urge young people to avoid rash and hasty marriages,' a Women's Federation official told me in Peking. 'They should get to know each other fairly well and make sure they are personally compatible.' According to a 1982 symposium held by the Research Society for Marriage and the

Family, almost half of all recent divorce applications in several districts of Shanghai had resulted from 'hasty marriages'.[21]

In practice, the limited experimentation with personal relationships, together with an official ban on pre-marital sex, means that most people have very little experience of the opposite sex, and even of their prospective spouse, before they get married. This lack of previous contact may be partly responsible for the disillusionment that some people, especially women, express with their spouses within only a few months of getting married.

And although the Chinese authorities stress the importance of love and free choice in marriage, the strong hand of officialdom can create as many impediments to a proposed marriage as parental interference and traditional social attitudes. Tight control over personal mobility, for example, sometimes has heart-rending results. 'I fell in love with a young man and we were planning to get married,' one young woman wrote to a correspondence column. 'But he was transferred to another town. I didn't think I'd ever see him again and eventually I married someone else. But within a few weeks of the marriage he returned to the town. I realize I still love him – and he still loves me. What can we do?'[22]

Others have their hearts broken when calculating young men and women use marriage to break through official controls to obtain housing or the precious urban residence permit. One of many such cases was publicized in *Chinese Women* as a warning to others. When studying at Jinzhou Teachers' College in the north-east province of Liaoning, a young woman had been courted by a male fellow-student who told her he loved her. Perhaps she should have been suspicious, the article implied, as she was two years his senior and slightly taller than him! When they graduated, she was assigned a job teaching music in Jinzhou but the young man, who was from a rural commune, was sent back to the countryside. The young couple married anyway.

'Don't worry, I love you and I'll manage to be with you somehow,' he had assured her.

After pulling a lot of strings, he finally managed to obtain a job transfer to be with his wife in Jinzhou. Eventually he also received his own urban residence permit.

Thereupon he demanded a divorce.

'Don't you love her any more?' one of his colleagues asked.

'It's not a case of not loving her any more,' he replied. 'I never loved her.'

'Then why did you get married?'

'If I hadn't married her, would I have been able to come to Jinzhou?'[23]

Having decided to marry, for whatever reason, the couple still have a few hurdles to overcome. First they are advised to undergo a thorough medical examination. 'There is a close relationship between the physical condition of both partners and their future conjugal happiness,' one magazine article declared somewhat euphemistically.[24]

Young men and women living in a major town or city can go to one of the special pre-marital clinics set up within many hospitals. If one of them is found to have an illness such as TB, acute hepatitis or kidney disease – all common medical problems in China – they are usually advised to postpone marriage until the person has been cured. Similar advice is given in the case of minor problems with the reproductive organs.

More traumatic, especially for young women, is the diagnosis of gynaecological defects that cannot be remedied. The same applies to heart disease which often results in the doctor's advice not to have children. With many men being unwilling to forego parenthood, such disorders can lead to the cancellation of a planned marriage. But the media argues it is only fair that young couples should be fully aware of their partner's state of health before taking on a life-long commitment. Indeed, it promotes the idea of a medical examination as a form of insurance against one partner not being able to fulfil his or her expected marital role.

One magazine article, for example, cited the case of a young woman who discovered only after getting married that she had rheumatic heart disease and should not become pregnant. Instead of offering sympathy, 'her husband accused her of dishonesty and of cheating him into marriage'.[25]

Young couples given a clean bill of health receive information on sex physiology, family planning and pregnancy. Although some basic material on sex and birth control is becoming available in books and even popular magazines, there is still a high degree of sexual ignorance among people about to get married. According to one report, many men and women visiting pre-marital clinics in major cities know absolutely nothing about family planning methods.[26] This deficiency needs to be quickly remedied in the interests of the country's rigid population control policy.

'Husband and wife are in duty bound to practise family planning,' Article 12 of the 1980 Marriage Law proclaimed, adding contraception to the long list of official controls imposed on the personal lives of Chinese people.[27]

Pregnancies in China often have to be planned in accordance with a birth roster of an organization or factory. 'We know what form of contraception each woman is using and we decide when she's allowed to become pregnant. We don't want too many women away at one time,' the woman in charge of family planning at Peking's No. 2 Machinery Factory told me in 1977 during my brief stint working in the factory. If the woman had not been sterilized or fitted with an IUD, she was a regular recipient of birth control pills or condoms from her workshop's contraceptive cupboard. (In China, as in many countries, the onus for birth control is placed heavily on women and female sterilization is far more common than vasectomy.)

The recent advent of the somewhat Draconian one-child policy, with penalties and fines for people having a second child, has made official controls on pregnancy even tighter – at least in urban areas. For all the regulations and exhortations, the countryside still tends to be a different matter, with people regarding their offspring as future sources of labour power for the household and as insurance for their old age. Although some major cities have approached the one-child ideal, the 1982 national census revealed that less than 50 per cent of babies born throughout China in 1981 had been first babies; 26 per cent were second, 13 per cent third, 7 per cent fourth, and almost 8 per cent fifth or more.

Getting married in contemporary China is theoretically a simple process, uncomplicated by religion or ceremony. The official requirement is that the couple merely register their marriage with the local authorities. Making some allowance for the desire for a celebration, the government suggests that maybe the families have a small tea party after the registration.

The reality is usually rather different. As the media complains, a huge amount of money is still spent, usually by the young man and his family, on the process of getting married. A survey of 180 newly married couples in Peking in 1980 revealed an average expenditure of over 1500 yuan, roughly twice a young person's average annual income.[28] Expenditure in the countryside is sometimes even greater, although the average per capita income is little more than half that of urban areas. Comments from individual villagers tend to confirm the results of a survey undertaken in one village in Hebei province which found that the average amount of money spent on a marriage was approximately 3000 yuan.[29]

Even in cities, wedding banquets are often lavish, with a hundred or more guests being invited to a fashionable restaurant to eat their way through course after course of Chinese delicacies. When I had dinner at Canton's famous Panxi Restaurant, a huge complex of traditional Chinese buildings surrounding a picturesque lake, room upon room was filled with wedding parties. One bride wore the traditional ankle-length red *qipao* (popularized in Hong Kong as the *cheongsam*), another a pink pants suit, yet another a Western-style white wedding gown, complete with tulle bridal veil.

'I hadn't even met a lot of the people at my own wedding,' one young man in our group remarked. 'Many of the guests were my father's colleagues or superiors. Inviting people to weddings is one way of establishing personal connections in China.'

But the wedding banquet accounts for only a portion of total expenditure on the marriage – in the Peking survey about one-fifth. A larger amount is spent on new clothes for the couple and on what would be described in the West as 'setting up house', mainly buying furniture and household appliances. (In the countryside marriage costs often include the purchase of materials for building a separate housing unit for the young couple.)

The total expenditure depends not just on the resources and willingness of the bridegroom and his family, but also on the attitudes of the bride. In the present consumer-oriented environment, some young women are making fairly heavy demands of their future spouses. 'Many of them expect far too much,' complained a Women's Federation official in Peking, putting part of the blame on women's own limited earning capacity and the continuing perception of the man as the main provider.

Young brides-to-be are frequently ridiculed in newspaper

and magazine cartoons. One cartoon entitled 'Modern-day Romeo and Juliet' featured an earnest young man with a bunch of flowers looking aghast as a somewhat flamboyant young woman pointed to a chart filled with sketches: a TV set, camera, radio, wristwatch, motor-bike, sewing machine, electric fan, washing machine, refrigerator and various items of household furniture.[30]

Even the satisfaction of these demands does not always put an end to the matter. In the countryside, at least, the young man's family normally faces the payment of the traditional 'bride price' to the woman's family as compensation for the loss of their daughter. This practice has persisted despite an official prohibition on the 'exaction of money or gifts in connection with marriage' and denunciations of 'mercenary marriages'. The marriage transaction was once conducted primarily in animals and grain. In the words of one traditional saying: 'When a daughter goes out, an ox comes in.' Nowadays it is more likely to involve the latest consumer goods on the market.

Even if the young woman herself makes minimal demands, her parents may impose a heavy price for agreeing to the marriage. 'My family's economic situation is fairly poor so Xiao Li and I decided just to buy a few pieces of furniture and some agricultural implements, and to have a simple wedding,' one young man wrote to *Youth Letterbox*. 'Suddenly Xiao Li's father and mother presented my family with a list of the marriage condtions. These included a furniture suite, a new double bed, sewing machine, bicycle, Shanghai model watch, radio and a variety of clothing.' The young man was beside himself. 'I simply don't know what to do,' he wrote. 'Please help me.'[31]

Many young men and their families go into severe debt, just as they did in traditional China when the marriage of a son was the major expense in many people's lives. Where there is more than one son, the debts can simply accumulate. One report cited the case of a rural family which, still owing 400 yuan of the 1200 yuan borrowed for the first son's wedding six years earlier, had to borrow another 1800 yuan for the second son's marriage. In his effort to pay off the debt, the father resorted to selling his own blood – on over forty occasions.[32]

Some desperate young men turn to crime to raise money, stealing livestock or grain and selling them on the private market. For others the strain simply proves too great. A young villager in Shaanxi province was found hanging from a tree when his friends went searching for him on the day of the wedding. Having borrowed 780 yuan, sold his bicycle and some of the family's grain, the young man could not face the problems that lay ahead. And in one county in Hebei province, marriage debts led forty-five young men to commit suicide in 1980–1 alone.[33]

Alarmed by the persistence of traditional marriage practices, the Chinese government puts strong pressure on young people to break with the old customs. Youth magazines publish declarations by young men and women that they intend having simple weddings. Newspapers feature stories about group weddings involving up to one hundred couples, often organized by the Communist Youth League. Following the marriage registrations, there is usually a simple tea party to which ten or so members of each family are invited.

But it takes a lot of courage to go against tradition, especially in the countryside, as one young couple in Jiangxi province found out. They had decided simply to register their marriage and go off on a honeymoon. 'When we returned we were vehemently criticized, especially by my wife's family,' the young man complained to a Shanghai youth magazine. 'The whole family came and swore at us. They said I was mean and miserly to do such a thing.'[34]

The concern of the young woman's family was not really surprising. As one former rural resident explained: 'A family still often relies on the money or goods obtained for a daughter's marriage to fund their son's marriage.' The marriage cycle is a vicious one. Many families try to marry off a daughter first, sometimes under pressure from a son to make as profitable a 'deal' as possible so that he will be able to make a good match.

'Some people outside China are surprised at the extent of these traditional practices after almost thirty-five years of socialist government,' a Youth League official told me in Canton. 'Believe me, we have done our utmost to introduce simple marriages. But we're up against 2000 years of Chinese feudal tradition. If our regulations are too severe, like the late marriage policy, peasants simply ignore them. All we can do is try to educate people, especially young people, to change their attitudes. But it's not easy.'

One advantage of having a simple wedding is that there may be some money left for a honeymoon, perhaps at a famous historical spot like Hangzhou where honeymooners are only beginning to be outnumbered by foreign tourists. Dressed in their new clothes, the young couples wander hand in hand round the beautiful West Lake, eat the local fish, and maybe buy an imitation diamond ring at a lakeside kiosk. If they have a camera of their own, they might ask someone to take their photo instead of posing for one of the commercial photographers.

One young man actually blushed, and his new wife giggled, when I asked them whether they were on their honeymoon.

'Yes, we got married three days ago,' he replied.

They had no doubt already found out about the physical aspect of their new status – if they had not already done so before the marriage. Both should have had some idea of what to expect, whether they had visited a pre-marital clinic or merely read some of the relevant articles in popular magazines. Assuming a higher level of virginity than probably exists in practice, these articles offer advice to newly-weds on everything from impotence and premature ejaculation to cystitis – also called 'honeymoon disease' in Chinese.

But first the articles usually attempt to put old wives' tales to rest by warning young men not to jump to the conclusion that their wife is not a virgin if what they expect to happen on their wedding night does not eventuate. 'Sometimes a man may even demand a divorce immediately,' one article commented. 'This is because he has been influenced by feudal attitudes.'[35] Another article was more explicit. 'These days women do not get married as young as they used to. They participate in work and every sort of activity – running, hurdling, riding bicycles, and so on.'[36]

Needless to say, the article did not suggest that a man's expectation that his wife be a virgin, regardless of his own previous sex life, was itself a remnant of feudal attitudes.

In the early days of their marriage, warned a further article, young couples could expect to feel tired, perhaps even dizzy, in the fluster and excitement of it all. 'Newly married couples should gradually moderate the initial phenomenon of having repeated sex in the one night,' it cautioned. 'Excessive sexual indulgence is not advisable. Sex is not the one and only interest in an individual's life.'

And after the initial fluster and excitement? 'Having sex no more than once or twice a week is recommended for both partners' health, work and study.'[37]

Following the honeymoon, it is back to everyday life. If they are lucky, the rural couple will at least have their own small house and the urban couple their own tiny flat – if not immediately then at least eventually. A sample survey of rural residents of Guangdong province in the mid-1970s revealed that some 50 per cent of all families were of the nuclear type, consisting of husband, wife and perhaps children – but no grandparents.[38] A high proportion of 80 per cent nuclear families was revealed in a 1982 survey in Tianjin, a city of 4 million people in north China.[39] This change from the traditional lineal family reflects not just an improving housing situation but a desire among married people to live apart from their parents.

'We are trying to exchange one medium-size flat for two small ones so that we can live separately,' one recently married school-teacher told me in Peking. 'Most of our friends feel the same way. They want to be independent.'

A billboard in Xiamen: 'Marry late, have children late, keep your mind on the four modernizations!'

CHAPTER THIRTEEN

The Passage is Complete

And so the passage from childhood to adulthood is complete. Each year another 20 million young Chinese have grown to self-awareness, undergone the transition from education to employment, developed ideas about their own and other countries, and assumed their place in society.

This passage is undertaken by people throughout the world and the Chinese have many experiences in common with youth in other countries. There is teenage self-doubt, the development of distinct leisure and cultural interests, conflict with parental authority, and anxiety about exams, jobs and relationships with the opposite sex. Nor is China immune to the youth problems that plague many societies: unemployment, juvenile delinquency and crime, and socio-political alienation.

But for all the similarities, the lives of young Chinese are very different from those of Western youth. It is during the teens and early twenties that people in China are most subject to the heavy hand of officialdom which allows little scope for personal decision making. The choices that Western youth take for granted – not just where they live and what work they do but even their clothing, sex life and age of marriage – are not considered purely a matter for the individual in China. If some young people in the West complain about family interference in these matters, in China they have to tolerate official direction and even regulations.

At the same time young Chinese are probably also more subject to parental pressure and traditional values than most of their Western contemporaries. The more we find out about present-day Chinese society, especially in rural areas, the less customs seem to have changed since pre-communist days.

Life in the countryside: still plenty of back-breaking labour

Young people feel the weight of 2000 years of Confucian tradition when it comes to family pressure on them to succeed scholastically or to marry a person who is wholeheartedly approved of, if not actually chosen, by their parents.

In addition to greater official and parental pressure, young Chinese bear the burden of living in a much poorer country than their Western brothers and sisters. Admittedly, the youth employment problem in many Western countries means that many people are unable to benefit from the general high standard of living and are even further socially alienated because of the contrast between their own lifestyle and that of more affluent residents. But in China the fact that 80 per cent of the population is still basically engaged in rural labour, together with the lack of diversification of the urban economy, creates both a lower standard of living all round and a general lack of satisfying career opportunities.

Despite the controls, pressures and burdens, China's young people are developing a distinctive lifestyle and are openly expressing their desire to have more control over their own lives. If the nation's youth of the 1950s and 1960s knew little different, the teenagers of the 1980s are becoming increasingly aware of the outside world and more critical of their own society. They might not be part of the Western – or international – youth culture scene, but they can no longer be regarded as an isolated quarter of the world's youth population.

And what of the future? What of the children of today's newly married couples as they themselves enter the youth phase of life early next century? Or, as a recently married young school-teacher in Peking expressed it when talking about bringing up the next generation: 'I wonder whether they will be very different from us.'

They will be different, of course, just as young Chinese in the 1980s are unlike their predecessors. Exactly how different they will be depends basically on the factors that have affected youth since the communist revolution: the extent of government control over individuals' personal lives, the continuing strength of traditional values, and the level of China's economic development.

The relative importance of these factors in the future depends in turn on the general direction of Chinese government policies, in particular on whether the nation maintains its current pragmatic stress on economic development – including its openness to the West – at the expense of communist ideology. If present policies continue with only limited modifications, as many political analysts believe likely, China's young people will grow up in an environment of increasing personal expectations. Whether these will be satisfied hinges partly on the success of the government's modernization programme which includes expanding youth's educational opportunities, developing and diversifying the economy to provide a wider range of satisfying and well-paid jobs, and producing desirable consumer goods. It also hinges on how flexible the government will be in allowing young people some choice in their own careers and lifestyles, thereby lessening its interference in their everyday lives. Although there could be a further resurgence of traditional family and moral values, these are likely to come up against the anti-traditional forces characteristic of a society undergoing industrialization.

Chinese youth in the early twenty-first century will have an additional feature. If the government's drastic steps to control the population are even moderately successful, large numbers of teenagers will come from one-child families. Already Chinese newspapers and magazines are complaining about the 'spoilt only child' syndrome and worrying about its effects as the children turn into teenagers. Indeed there is likely to be an intensification of current trends: excessive material expectations because of the early satisfaction of personal demands, over-anxious parents pushing their only child to pass school and university entrance exams or using 'backdoor' methods to assure them of a good job, pressure to 'marry well' to ensure the family's future socio-economic security.

Tomorrow's generation of Chinese youth, already being hailed as the bearers of the nation's future, will be no less problematical than the present generation. As a sociologist in Peking commented: 'The lives of young people in China are already quite complicated. It could well be that young people's lives in the future will be even more complex.'

Notes

The notes have been kept as brief as possible. Citations are given only for direct quotations from published material and for references to specific reports. Because full Chinese references can be very lengthy, the conventional 'short form' is used for all books and articles. Full citations appear in the bibliography.

Abbreviations

> JPRS   (US) Joint Publications Research Service
> NCNA   New China News Agency
> SWB FE (BBC) Summary of World Broadcasts: Far East

Chapter One *Chinese Youth in the 1980s*

1 Kenneth Keniston, 'Youth: A New Stage of Life', in Erikson, 1963, p. 104.
2 *Quotations*, 1972, p. 288.
3 *China Daily*, 11 November 1982.
4 Garside, 1981, Chapter 5.

Chapter Two *Self and Society*

1 Fan, 1982, passim.
2 ibid., p. 137.
3 ibid., p. 233.
4 ibid., p. 220.
5 *Renmin Ribao*, 24 February 1981.
6 *China Reconstructs*, January 1982, p. 67.
7 *China Daily*, 9 October 1982.

8 *Qingnian Yidai*, no. 1, 1981, p. 39.
9 *Selected Works*, III, p. 86.
10 *Xingfu zhi Lu zai Hefang* (*Where is the Road to Happiness*), 1982, p. 30 [*Qingnian Xinxiang* no. 7].
11 *Rensheng, Xinyang, Qiantu* (*Life, Faith and Future*), 1980, pp. 1–2 [*Qingnian Xinxiang* no. 3].
12 *Beijing Review*, 5 September 1983, p. 7.
13 Ezpeleta, 1972, pp. 185–6.
14 Zhongguo Qingnian, no. 5, 1983, p. 60.

Chapter Three *Between the Generations*

1 Siu and Stern, 1983, pp. 9, 14.
2 Cited in Conger, 1973, pp. 4–5.
3 Pa Chin (Ba Jin), 1972, p. 3.
4 ibid.
5 NCNA, Peking, 26 February 1984, in JPRS (CPS-84-020), 7 March 1984.
6 *China Daily*, 28 December 1983.
7 Siu and Stern, 1983, p. 40.
8 *Beijing Review*, 28 February 1983, p. 28.

Chapter Four *The Rungs of the Ladder*

1 *Zhonguo Qingnian*, no. 1, 1981, p. 68.
2 *China Daily*, 30 December 1983.
3 Zhongguo Qingnian, no. 4, 1980, pp. 14–15.
4 Zhongguo Funü, no. 2, 1983, p. 25.
5 Su, 1983, p. 26.
6 Zhongguo Qingnian, no. 4, 1980, p. 12.
7 ibid.
8 ibid., p. 13.
9 ibid., p. 12.
10 *China Daily*, 18 September 1982.
11 NCNA, 13 May 1981, in SWB FE/6726/B11/4, 17 May 1981.
12 NCNA, 6 July 1983, in *Inside China Mainland*, October 1983, p. 18.
13 *Hebei Ribao*, 13 September 1981.
14 NCNA, 6 July 1983, in *Inside China Mainland*, October 1983, p. 18.

Chapter Five *The New Elite*

1 *Gaojiao Zhanxian*, no. 3, 1982, pp. 9–10.
2 ibid.
3 NCNA, 27 October 1981, in SWB FE/6894/B11/6, 1 December 1981.
4 NCNA, 27 November 1981, in SWB FE/6894/B11/16, 1 December 1981.
5 *Renmin Ribao*, 20 January 1984.
6 Lhasa Radio, 12 January 1982, in JPRS (80020, CR 267), 3 February 1982.
7 NCNA, 25 June 1982, in *Inside China Mainland*, August 1982, p. 15.
8 *Zhongguo Funü*, no. 5, 1983, pp. 25–6.
9 *Renmin Ribao*, 30 June 1983.
10 *Guangming Ribao*, 22 November 1981.
11 *Jingji Ribao*, 1 February 1983.
12 ibid.

Chapter Six *'Waiting for Employment'*

1 *Zhongguo Qingnian*, no. 1, 1982, p. 28.
2 *Liaowang*, 20 March 1982, pp. 18–19.
3 *Renmin Ribao*, 18 September 1981.
4 *Liaowang*, 20 March 1982, pp. 18–19.
5 *Chinese Youth Bulletin*, no. 26, 1982, p. 6.
6 Chen and Zhou, 1983, p. 74.
7 Hu, 1982, pp. 78–9.
8 *Gansu Ribao*, 15 January 1982.
9 *China Reconstructs*, June 1983, p. 33.
10 *Beijing Review*, 27 September 1982, p. 20.
11 *Liaowang*, 20 March 1982, pp. 18–19.
12 ibid.
13 Cited in IIu, 1902, p. 04.
14 Heilongjiang provincial radio, 2 May 1981, in Foreign Broadcast Information Service, *Daily Report: China*, 4 May 1981.
15 *Beijing Review*, 19 September 1983, p. 7.
16 *Beijing Review*, 29 August 1983, p. 15.

Chapter Seven *From Feminism to Femininity?*

1 Quoted in Waley, 1946, p. 84.

2 Pruitt, 1967, p. 29.
3 Smith, 1899, p. 262.
4 Engels, 1975, p. 221.
5 Andors, 1983.
6 *Beijing Review*, 5 September 1983, p. 26.
7 *China Reconstructs*, March 1982, p. 25.
8 *Zhongguo Funü*, no. 6, 1983, p. 15.
9 *Zhongguo Funü*, no. 2, 1983, p. 25.
10 *Zhongguo Funü*, no. 7, 1983, p. 40.
11 Zhongguo Shehui Kexueyuan, *Qingnian Jiuye zhi Lu*, 1983, p. 90.
12 *Zhongguo Funü*, no. 6, 1983, p. 15.
13 Wang and Li, 1982, pp. 177–90.
14 *Hongqi*, no. 3, 1978, p. 90.
15 Zhongguo Shehui Kexueyuan, *Qingnian Jiuye zhi Lu*, 1983, p. 91.
16 *Beijing Review*, 5 September 1983, pp. 26–7.
17 NCNA, 25 March 1982, in SWB FE/6997/B11/7–8, 6 April 1982.
18 *Beijing Review*, 5 September 1983, pp. 26–7.
19 *Zhongguo Funü*, no. 11, 1982, pp. 15–16.
20 Engels, 1975, p. 221.
21 *Guardian*, 16 August 1981.

Chapter Eight   *The Misfits*

1 *Renmin Ribao*, 24 February 1981.
2 *Renmin Ribao*, 3 September 1983.
3 Cheng, Li and Yin, 1982, p. 6.
4 *Guangming Ribao*, 24 July 1982.
5 Cheng, Li and Yin, 1982, p. 7.
6 *Age*, 6 June 1982.
7 *Beijing Review*, 21 March 1983, p. 15.
8 *China Reconstructs*, November 1982, p. 40.
9 Cheng, Li and Yin, 1982, p. 7.
10 *Zhongguo Funü*, no. 10, 1983, p. 37.
11 *Beijing Review*, 12 September 1983.
12 Cheng, Li and Yin, 1982, pp. 186–7.
13 *Guangming Ribao*, 24 July 1982.
14 Cheng, Li and Yin, 1982, p. 93.
15 *China Daily*, 25 December 1983.
16 Cheng, Li and Yin, 1982, p. 126.
17 ibid., p. 7.
18 ibid., p. 27.

19 *Renmin Ribao*, 13 August 1983.
20 *Sichuan Ribao*, 27 August 1983.
21 Cited in *Inside China Mainland*, November 1983, p. 14.
22 *Renmin Ribao*, 3 September 1983.
23 *Funü*, no. 11, 1983, p. 10.
24 *Renmin Ribao*, 10 November 1983.
25 *Renmin Ribao*, 11 December 1983.
26 *Renmin Ribao*, 11 January 1984.

Chapter Nine *Temptations from the West*

1 *Renmin Ribao*, 13 March 1982.
2 Tung and Evans, 1966, pp. 253-4.
3 *Renmin Ribao*, 13 March 1982.
4 ibid.
5 NCNA, 19 March 1982, in SWB FE/6985/B11/2, 23 March 1982.
6 *Renmin Ribao*, 6 January 1982.
7 *Hongqi*, no. 1, 1983, p. 7.
8 *China Daily*, 10 April 1982.
9 *Funü zhi You*, no. 5, 1982, p. 15.
10 *Funü*, no. 11, 1983, p. 10.
11 *Hongqi*, no. 8, 1981, p. 15.
12 *Zhongguo Qingnian*, no. 20, 1981, pp. 22-3.
13 *Renmin Ribao*, 13 March 1982.
14 *Renmin Ribao*, 5 June 1982.
15 NCNA, 19 November 1981, in SWB FE/6887/B11/2, 23 November 1981.
16 *Nanfang Ribao*, 12 October 1982.
17 *China Daily*, 2 November 1983.
18 *Renmin Ribao*, 11, 18, 22 November 1983.

Chapter Ten *An Alienated Generation?*

1 *Renmin Ribao*, 24 February 1981.
2 ibid.
3 *Beijing Review*, 2 May 1983, p. 22.
4 *Time*, 10 November 1980, p. 57.
5 Shanghai Kexuexue Yanjiusuo, 1980, p. 166.
6 *Time*, 10 November 1980, p. 57.
7 *Wenhuibao, Jiefang Ribao*, 20 January 1980.
8 *Zhongguo Qingnian*, no. 5, 1980, p. 14.

9 Printed in Su, 1982, pp. 34–7.
10 *Renmin Ribao*, 24 February 1981.
11 *Zhongguo Qingnian*, no. 5, 1980, p. 14.
12 *Zhongguo Qingnian Bao*, 27 March 1982.
13 Siu and Stern, 1983, p. 132.
14 *Hongqi*, no. 7, 1981, p. 7.
15 Zhanshi Chubanshe (ed.), 1983, Introduction.
16 Cited in *Far Eastern Economic Review*, 10 December 1982, p. 37.
17 Su, 1982, p. 46.
18 *Renmin Ribao*, 25 December 1982.
19 *Beijing Review*, 2 May 1983, p. 23.
20 *Jiaoyu Yanjiu*, no. 12, 1981, p. 4.
21 NCNA, 3 May 1982, in SWB FE/7020/B11/10, 7 May 1982.

Chapter Eleven   *Falling in Love with Love*

1 Siu and Stern, 1983, p. 125.
2 *China Reconstructs*, January 1979, p. 9.
3 *Zhongguo Funü*, no. 3, 1982, p. 60.
4 *Zhongguo Qingnian*, no. 1, 1980, p. 46.
5 *Guangming Ribao*, 26 November 1981.
6 Wang, 1983, p. 182.
7 *Funü*, no. 3, 1982, pp. 17–18.
8 Zhongguo Shehui Kexueyan, *Dangdai Qingnian*, 1983, p. 4.
9 Zhou, Wu and Zhao, 1983, pp. 206–7.
10 Lenin, 1975, p. 84.
11 Wang, 1983, p. 196.
12 Zhang, 1983, pp. 54–8.
13 Zhou, Wu and Zhao, 1983, pp. 108–9.
14 *China Daily*, 16 May 1982.
15 Zhou, Wu and Zhao, 1983, p. 110.
16 *Zhongguo Funü*, no. 6, 1983, pp. 20–1.
17 *Zhongguo Funü*, no. 3, 1981, p. 18.
18 *Zhongguo Funü*, no. 7, 1981, p. 21.
19 *Zhongguo Funü*, no. 7, 1983, pp. 20–1.
20 Siu and Stern, 1983, p. 112.
21 Zhang, 1983, p. 54.

Chapter Twelve   *'Marriage is a Serious Business'*

1 *Seven Contemporary Chinese Women Writers*, 1982, p. 228.

2 Croll, 1974, p. 110.
3 *China Reconstructs*, March 1981, p. 19.
4 *Zhongguo Qingnian*, no. 12, 1983, p. 14.
5 *Qingnian Yidai*, no. 1, 1983, p. 29.
6 *China Reconstructs*, March 1981, p. 20.
7 ibid.
8 Siu and Stern, 1983, p. 53.
9 *Beijing Review*, 5 September 1983, pp. 26-7.
10 *Wenhua yu Shenghuo*, no. 1, 1982, p. 30.
11 *China Daily*, 16 May 1982.
12 Siu and Stern, 1983, p. 343.
13 *China Daily*, 16 May 1982.
14 Zhou, Wu and Zhao, 1983, p. 97.
15 *Zhongguo Qingnian*, no. 12, 1983, p. 14.
16 *Falü Guwen* (*Legal Advice*), 1981, pp. 87-8 [*Qingnian Xinxiang* no. 5].
17 Liao and You, 1983, pp. 333-4.
18 *Zhongguo Funü*, no. 3, 1981, p. 15.
19 *Zhongguo Funü*, no. 4, 1981, p. 17.
20 *Zhongguo Funü*, no. 6, 1981, p. 18.
21 *China Daily*, 16 May 1982.
22 Zhou, Wu and Zhao, 1983, p. 104.
23 *Zhongguo Funü*, no. 10, 1983, pp. 26-7.
24 *Funü Shenghuo*, no. 1, 1983, p. 27.
25 ibid.
26 NCNA, 18 February 1981, in SWB FE/6684/B11/4.
27 *Beijing Review*, 16 March 1981, p. 24.
28 *Beijing Review*, 19 January 1981, p. 11.
29 *China Reconstructs*, March 1981, p. 19.
30 *Beijing Review*, 22 June 1981, p. 26.
31 *Lixiang, Xuexi, Aiqing* (*Ideals, Study and Love*), 1979, pp. 81-2 [*Qingnian Xinxiang* no. 1].
32 Gongqingtuan Zhongyang Gong Nong Qingnian Bu, 1983, p. 100.
33 ibid.
34 *Qingnian Yidai*, no. 6, 1983, p. 27.
35 *Zhongguo Funü*, no. 1, 1983, p. 47.
36 Fan, 1982, p. 238.
37 *Zhongguo Qingnian*, no. 12, 1980, p. 36.
38 Parish and Whyte, 1978, p. 134.

Bibliography

The following published sources provided material to supplement personal interviews and discussions in China during September–October 1982 and December 1983–January 1984, set against my earlier experiences in China in 1975–7 and 1979.

Books and Articles

Andors, Phyllis, *The Unfinished Liberation of Chinese Women, 1949–1980*, Bloomington: Indiana University Press, 1983.

Ayscough, Florence, *Chinese Women Yesterday and Today*, London: Jonathan Cape, 1936.

Ben Shi (ed.), *Qingnian Gongzuo Shouce (Youth Work Handbook)*, Peking: China Youth Publishing House, 1982.

Brodsgaard, Kjeld Erik, 'The democracy movement in China, 1978–79: Opposition movements, wall poster campaigns, and underground journals', *Asian Survey*, vol. 21, no. 8, 1981, pp. 747–74.

Chen Xueliang and Zhou Qing'ao, *Daiye yu Liye (Awaiting Employment and Embarking on a Career)*, Jinan: Shandong People's Publishing House, 1983.

Cheng Rongbin, Li Kantai and Yin Jiabao, *Guanyu Qingshaonian Fanzui de Jige Wenti (Several Questions Concerning Youth Crime)*, Peking: China People's Publishing House, 1982.

Conger, John Janeway, *Adolescence and Youth: Psychological Development in a Changing World*, New York: Harper & Row, 1973.

Croll, Elisabeth, *Feminism and Socialism in China*, London: Routledge & Kegan Paul, 1978.

——, *The Women's Movement in China: A Selection of Readings*, London: Anglo-Chinese Educational Institute, Modern China Series No. 6, 1974.

Engels, Fredrick, *The Origins of the Family, Private Property and the State*, New York: International Publishers, 1975.

Erikson, Erik H. (ed.), *The Challenge of Youth*, New York: Anchor Books, 1963.

Ezpeleta, Mariano, *Red Shadows over Shanghai*, Quezon City: Zita Publishing Corporation, 1972.

Fan Zhengxiang, *Zhu Ni Jianmei (Wishing You Health and Beauty)*, Peking: China Youth Publishing House, 1982.

Feng Lanrui and Zhao Lukuan, 'Urban unemployment in China', *Social Sciences in China*, vol. 3, no. 1, 1982, pp. 123–39.

Garside Roger, *Coming Alive: China after Mao*, London: Andre Deutsch, 1981.

Gongqingtuan Zhongyang Gong Nong Qingnian Bu (Workers and Peasants' Youth Section of the Central Committee of the Communist Youth League), *Nongcun Tuan Ke Shier Jiang (Twelve Lectures for Rural Youth League Cadres)*, Shanghai: Shanghai People's Publishing House, 1983.

Hooper, Beverley, *Inside Peking: A Personal Report*, London: Macdonald and Jane's, 1979.

'Hu Yao-pang's speech on young people awaiting employment (2 March 1982)', *Issues and Studies*, vol. 19, no. 2, 1983, pp. 78–85.

Kassof, Allen, *The Soviet Youth Program: Regimentation and Rebellion*, Cambridge Mass: Harvard University Press, 1965.

Kraemer, Hazel V., *Youth and Culture: A Human-Development Approach*, Monterey: Brooks/Cole Publishing Company, 1974.

Lang, Olga, *Chinese Family and Society*, New Haven: Yale University Press, 1946.

Lenin, V. I., 'Lenin on the woman question', in *The Emancipation of Women: From the Writings of V. I. Lenin*, New York: International Publishers, 1975.

Liao Shihuo and You Lunzhong, *Qingnian yu Lianai (Youth and Being in Love)*, Chengdu: Sichuan People's Publishing House, 1983.

Pa Chin (Ba Jin), *Family*, New York: Anchor Books, 1972.

Parish, William L. and Martin King Whyte, *Village and Family in Contemporary China*, Chicago: University of Chicago Press, 1978.

Pepper, Suzanne, *China's Universities: Post-Mao Enrollment Policies and their Impact on the Structure of Secondary Education: A Research Report*, Ann Arbor: Center for Chinese Studies, University of Michigan (Michigan Monographs in Chinese Studies, no. 46), 1984.

Pruitt, Ida, *A Daughter of Han: The Autobiography of a Chinese*

Working Woman, Stanford: Stanford University Press, 1967.

Quotations from Chairman Mao Tse-tung, Peking: Foreign Languages Press, 1972.

Rosen, Stanley, 'Obstacles to educational reform in China', *Modern China*, vol. 8, no. 1, 1982, pp. 3–40.

Selected Works of Mao Tse-tung, vol. III, Peking: Foreign Languages Press, 1967.

Seven Contemporary Chinese Women Writers, Beijing: Panda Books, 1982.

Shanghai Kexuexue Yanjiusuo (Shanghai Science of Science Research Institute), *Kexuexue Yanjiu Lunwenxuan* (*Selected Articles on Research into the Science of Science*), Shanghai: World Sciences Publishing House, 1980.

Siu, Helen F. and Zelda Stern, *Mao's Harvest: Voices from China's New Generation*, New York: Oxford University Press, 1983.

Smith, Arthur, *Village Life in China*, New York: Felming Revell, 1899.

Su Wenming, *A Nation at School*, Beijing: Beijing Review Publications, 1983.

——, *From Youth to Retirement*, Beijing: Beijing Review Publications, 1982.

Tung Chi-ping and Humphrey Evans, *The Thought Revolution*, New York: Coward-McCann, 1966.

Unger, Jonathan, *Education under Mao: Class and Competition in Canton Schools, 1960–80*, New York: Columbia University Press, 1982.

Waley, Arthur, *Chinese Poems*, London: Allen and Unwin, 1946.

Wang Jicheng, *Qingnian Xinlixue* (*Youth Psychology*), Peking: China Social Sciences Publishing House, 1983.

Wang Yalin and Li Jingrong, 'Chengshi zhigong jiawu laodong yanjiu' ('Research into urban staff and workers' housework'), *Zhongguo Shehui Kexue* (*Chinese Social Sciences*), no. 1, 1982, pp. 177–90.

White, Gordon, 'Urban employment and labour allocation policies in post-Mao China', *World Development*, vol. 10, no. 8, 1982, pp. 613–33.

Wu Lianrong, 'Yao guanxin zhongqingnian nü keji renyuan de chanzheng', ('Take interest in the growth of young and middle-aged women staff in science and technology'), *Shehuixue Zazhi* (*Sociology Journal*), no. 4, 1983, pp. 10–13.

Yang, C.K. *The Chinese Family in the Communist Revolution*, Cambridge, Mass: MIT Press, 1959.

Youth Mobilization for Development in Asian Settings: Asian Regional Youth Meeting, 17–22 September 1978, *Final Report*, Paris: UNESCO, 1979.

Zhang Qingyun, *Nü Qingnian Shujian (Female Youth Correspondence)*, Shenyang: Liaoning People's Publishing House, 1983.

Zhanshi Chubanshe (ed.), *Zhang Hua: Xin Yidai Youxiu Daxuesheng (Zhang Hua: An Outstanding University Student of the New Generation)*, Peking: Soldiers' Publishing House, 1983.

Zhongguo Shehui Kexueyuan Qingshaonian Yanjiusuo, Qingnian Laodong Yanjiushi (Youth Work Research Office of the Research Institute for Youth and Juvenile Affairs of the Chinese Academy of Social Sciences), *Qingnian Jiuye de Tansuo yu Shijian (Investigations and Practice of Youth Employment)*, Peking: China Social Sciences Publishing House, 1983.

Zhongguo Shehui Kexueyuan Qingshaonian Yanjiusuo, 'Qingnian Yanjiu' Bianjibu (Editorial Department of 'Youth Research', Research Institute for Youth and Juvenile Affairs of the Chinese Academy of Social Sciences), *Dangdai Qingnian Tedian yu Gongchanzhuyi Jiaoyu (The Characteristics of Contemporary Youth and Communist Education)*, Shanghai: Shanghai People's Publishing House, 1983.

Zhongguo Shehui Kexueyuan Qingshaonian Yanjiusuo and Sichuan Renmin Guangbo Diantai (Research Institute for Youth and Juvenile Affairs of the Chinese Academy of Social Sciences and Sichuan Broadcasting Station), *Qingnian Jiuye zhi Lu (The Road to Youth Employment)*, Peking: Broadcasting Publishing House, 1983.

Zhou Jinxi, Wu Zhenbiao and Zhao Zhengda, *Tianyuan Tongxin (Letters from the Countryside)*, Harbin: Heilongjiang People's Publishing House, 1983.

Book Series (volumes published 1979–83)

Dangdai Qingnian Congshu (Contemporary Youth Series), Chengdu: Sichuan People's Publishing House.

Qingnian Xinxiang (Youth Letterbox), Shanghai: Shanghai People's Publishing House.

Qingnian Xiuyang Tongxun (Youth Self-cultivation Reports), Peking: China Youth Publishing House.

Qingnian zhi You Congshu (Friend of Youth Series), Shanghai: Shanghai People's Publishing House.

Newspapers and Magazines

		Place of publication
Age		Melbourne
Asiaweek		Hong Kong
Beijing Review		Peking
China Daily		Peking
China Reconstructs		Peking
Chinese Youth Bulletin		Peking
Dazhong Dianshi	(Popular Television)	Peking
Dazhong Dianying	(Popular Cinema)	Peking
Dianying Huabao	(Film Pictorial)	Peking
Far Eastern Economic Review		Hong Kong
Funü	(Women)	Shenyang
Funü Shenghuo	(Women's Life)	Chengdu
Funü zhi You	(Women's Friend)	Harbin
Gansu Ribao	(Gansu Daily)	Lanzhou
Gaojiao Zhanxian	(Higher Education Front)	Peking
Guangming Ribao	(Enlightenment Daily)	Peking
Guardian		Manchester
Hebei Ribao	(Hebei Daily)	Peking
Hongqi	(Red Flag)	Peking
Huangjin Shidai	(Golden Generation)	Canton
Huanqiu	(Globe)	Peking
Inside China Mainland		Taibei
Jiaoyu Yanjiu	(Educational Research)	Peking
Jiefang Ribao	(Liberation Daily)	Peking
Jingji Ribao	(Economic Daily)	Peking
Liaowang	(Outlook)	Peking
Mengya	(Sprouts)	Shanghai
Nanfang Ribao	(Southern Daily)	Canton
Qingnian Wenxue	(Youth Literature)	Peking
Qingnian Yidai	(Youth Generation)	Shanghai
Qishi Niandai	(The Seventies)	Hong Kong
Renmin Jiaoyu	(People's Education)	Peking
Renmin Ribao	(People's Daily)	Peking
Shanghai Huabao	(Shanghai Pictorial)	Shanghai
Shijie Dianying	(World Cinema)	Peking

		Place of publication
Shizhuang	(Fashion)	Shanghai
Sichuan Ribao	(Sichuan Daily)	Chengdu
Time		New York
Waiguo Wenxue	(Foreign Literature)	Peking
Waiguo Xiaoshuo	(Foreign Stories)	Harbin
Wenhua yu Shenghuo	(Culture and Life)	Shanghai
Xin Shiqi	(New Era)	Peking
Zhongguo Funü	(Chinese Women)	Peking
Zhongguo Qingnian	(Chinese Youth)	Peking
Zhongguo Qingnian Bao	(Chinese Youth News)	Peking
Zixue	(Self-study)	Peking

Translation Series

BBC Monitoring Service, *Summary of World Broadcasts: Far East*, Reading, Berkshire.

Foreign Broadcast Information Service, *Daily Report: China*, Washington, DC.

US Joint Publications Research Service, *China Report*, Washington, DC.

Index

MORE ABOUT PENGUINS AND PELICANS

For further information about books available from Penguin please write to Dept EP, Penguin Books Ltd, Harmondsworth, Middlesex UB7 ODA.

In the U.S.A.: For a complete list of books available from Penguin in the United States write to Dept DG, Penguin Books, 299 Murray Hill Parkway, East Rutherford, New Jersey 07073.

In Canada: For a complete list of books available from Penguin in Canada write to Penguin Books Canada Ltd, 2801 John Street, Markham, Ontario L3R 1B4.

In Australia: For a complete list of books available from Penguin in Australia write to the Marketing Department, Penguin Books Australia Ltd, P.O. Box 257, Ringwood, Victoria 3134.

In New Zealand: For a complete list of books available from Penguin in New Zealand write to the Marketing Department, Penguin Books (N.Z.) Ltd, Private Bag, Takapuna, Auckland, 9.

Priests on Trial

Alfred W. McCoy

In 1982 the Philippine Army filed criminal charges of murder and rebellion against an improbable group of Catholic conspirators – a Filipino parish priest, Irish missionary Fr Niall O'Brien, and Australian missionary Fr Brian Gore. Using perjured testimony from paid witnesses, the Army pursued them with prosecution and imprisonment for two years. Pressured by international protests, President Marcos finally ordered the charges dismissed and the priests deported.

Gore and O'Brien were victims of the growing conflict between Church and State in the Philippines. For over a decade, they worked to shatter the subservience of peasants on Negros Island, the poorest of Third World poor. In revenge, the island's wealthy sugar planters persecuted the priests to silence the Church.

Their trial exemplifies the plight of priests in the Third World. Seeking salvation from their degradation, poor peasants have turned to both Catholic priests and Communist guerillas. Throughout the Third World, the Church is now caught in a cross-fire between dictatorship and revolution.